THE
BOY WHO LURKS
IN
SHADOWS

RACHEL RENER

OTHER WORKS BY RACHEL RENER:

AMETHYSTS & ALCHEMY

THE GILDED BLOOD SERIES
I. INKED
II. JINXED
III. LINKED
IV. SYNCED

THE LIGHTNING CONJURER SERIES
I. THE AWAKENING
II. THE ENLIGHTENING
III. THE CHRISTENING
IV. THE RECKONING

THE BONE WHISPERER CHRONICLES
I. THE GIRL WHO TALKS TO ASHES
II. THE BOY WHO LURKS IN SHADOWS

THE LITTLE MORSEL

THE PRECIPICE OF SIN
(AS PART OF THE *FROM THE SHADOWS*
ANTHOLOGY)

AUTOGRAPHED BOOKS AVAILABLE AT
WWW.RACHELRENER.COM

Table of Contents

Note from the Author

. . .

Dear Reader,

If you like creepy, supernatural, and/or dark thematic elements in your fantasy stories, keep reading – this book is definitely for you.

But if you're like me, and you prefer milk chocolate over dark, watch scary movies through the slits of your fingers, and/or require the occasional minor (or major) spoiler to get through difficult chapters, we need to have a little chat before you turn the page.

Look, I'm not going to sugarcoat this: this book has some dark themes. I'm talking "slow-brewed Colombian black coffee without a drop of cream or sugar" dark. Possible triggers include:

- Death
- Depression
- Alleged S.A.
- References to murder / suicide
- Animal death (off-page / zero suffering)
- Elements of horror
- And (worst of all) sexist douchebags

If that's not your typical cup of sweetened tea – especially when you're so used to reading my prior books, most of which have relatively light themes and decidedly happy endings – I totally get it. Set down this book and go snag *The Little Morsel* instead, which is possibly the most light-hearted and darling little tale you'll ever read. My feelings won't be hurt, I promise.

BUT.

If you're feeling brave and adventurous and want to try pushing your own boundaries, I promise you this: there is light at the end of every dark tunnel. And this story, like all of my others, will have a hard-fought happy ending – as well as a payoff that I truly believe will make the difficult scenes worth it.

So if you're still here for this, go flip on all the lights, wrap yourself in a warm, weighted blanket, and settle in for what I promise will be one of the most unique tales you've read in a long, long time. I'll be right there with you in spirit, holding your hand (maybe a little too tightly for comfort) and yelping at the occasional creepy moment.

Happy reading. You've got this.

...

PART
I

...

Chapter 1
Friends in Low Places

Five-year-old Elliot Whitman wasn't like the other children at St. Nicholas of Myra Orphanage for Wayward Youth. He didn't play Jacks or tug on girls' pigtails with the rest of the boys; nor did he hit rocks with sticks and call himself Mickey Mantle. He preferred to wander off on his own, speaking only when spoken to. While the other children made a beeline for the rusted playground choked by overgrown weeds, where they would dream of swing sets with intact chains and smooth slides that didn't leave flakes of peeling paint embedded in their bottoms, Elliot chose to stay inside and play quietly on his own. He didn't daydream about the nice couple with a spotted dog that might one day bring him to their big house with a white picket fence, and a soft bed that was all his own – a stark contrast to the squeaky bunk bed he had to share with Ralph, who often had night terrors and wet himself so frequently the underside of his mattress was permanently stained.

Elliot was lying underneath those very stains now, dressed in his play clothes. He clasped his hands over his growling tummy, impatiently waiting for the lunch bell. Ignoring the honied sunlight streaking through the barred windows, his gray eyes darted to the clock on the far wall. He hadn't yet learned how to tell time, but he knew that when the two hands pointed straight up, it would be lunch time. Unfortunately, the big hand was still pointing at the windows, which meant he had the better part of forever to wait.

Sighing, Elliot pushed himself off his groaning mattress, then plopped down beside Mariela and Kimberly, the only other children in the otherwise vacant dormitory. They were sitting at one of the two wooden play tables, pouring themselves imaginary tea from an imaginary tea set.

"Hello," Mari greeted him as he sat beside her. "Would you like one or two lumps of sugar with your tea?"

"Two," he answered. "And a ham sandwich, if you have one."

"I just so happened to make a plate of peanut butter and banana sandwiches," Mari's big sister Kimmy said with a rather prim tone, handing him an imaginary plate. Nine years old and the oldest of the three, she often took it upon herself to play Mother, though she'd never known her own.

"You don't have any ham sandwiches?"

Kimmy rolled her eyes at Elliot. "You'll eat what I make and like it."

"Fine," he grumbled, taking the invisible sandwich from her. He crinkled his freckled nose as he took the first bite. "You could have at least cut the crusts off."

"I did! See?"

He followed her finger to the pile of imaginary crusts that had been tossed into the imaginary waste bin. "Oh, okay." He took another bite, chewing thoughtfully. "Do you have any Ovaltine? My mommy always made me Ovaltine with—"

"Elliot!" a shrill voice called, making him jump.

He scrambled to his feet, hiding his make-believe sandwich behind his back as a wide-eyed nun appeared in the doorway of the boys' dormitory. "H-Hello, Sister Maggie."

Ignoring him, she gaped at the two girls, who were still casually sipping tea from their imaginary teacups, her wide eyes lingering on their puffed sleeves and the white pinafores they wore over their pressed powder-blue dresses. "Where in the world did you two come from?"

Constance, the sternest and oldest of the nuns by at least a decade, appeared in the doorway beside her. "What's he done this time, Sister Maggie?"

When the young woman didn't answer her, Constance's eyes trailed back to Elliot, narrowing sharply, and her lips pursed together like a wrinkled prune. She planted her fists on her narrow hips. "Mister Whitman, you know better than to bring young ladies into the boys' dormitories. Such transgressions are wholly uncouth in the eyes of the Lord, not to mention…" Her voice trailed off as she, too, took in Kimmy and Mari's strange attire. "What in the world…?"

"I know girls aren't 'sposta be in the boys' dorms." Elliot shrugged one sheepish shoulder. "But Kimmy and Mari can't go anywhere else."

Constance's frown deepened. She leaned over to Maggie and whispered, "When did these two arrive? Father Isaac never mentioned anything about—"

Whatever she was about to say next was derailed by Maggie's ragged gasp.

Constance whirled back around to find the air around the two girls shimmering like a mirage. Their perfectly-pressed plaid dresses, which she could have sworn had been powder-blue moments ago, were now coal-black. And not just their dresses – their smocks, their shoes, the blue ribbons that had been tied in their blonde pigtails – everything they wore was now black as pitch. The nun vigorously rubbed at her eyes, trying to clear her vision.

But the strange sight didn't disappear; it only worsened.

Tendrils of smoke unfurled from the girls' blackened clothes and bodies, imbuing the room with the acrid stench of singed hair. Their skin, once creamy white, was now scorched, and their flesh was falling off their bones in charred clumps.

Maggie let out a shrill, blood-curdling scream while Constance clutched the cross at her throat, struggling to remember the words to The Lord's Prayer, which she had recited twice a day for the last sixty-eight years, but now had somehow failed her completely.

"Bye, Elliot," the older girl waved at him, her tiny hand reduced to nothing more than blackened ligaments and bones.

"Bye, Kimmy," Elliot waved sadly. "See you tomorrow."

And then, in the blink of an eye, the girls were gone, though the stench of death lingered in their wake.

Maggie hadn't realized she'd been screaming until Father Isaac slapped her smartly across the face, making her teeth clack together painfully.

Her hand instinctively went to her stinging cheek, while her rounded eyes flew back to Elliot, who was once more seated at the table, casually chewing on his imaginary peanut-butter-and-banana sandwich, swinging his feet back and forth as he impatiently waited for the lunch bell to sound.

. . .

"Tell me again what you both believe you saw," Father Isaac said, rubbing his temples with his fingertips, "and this time, one at a time, please."

Maggie and Constance simultaneously broke into shrill, overlapping explanations, forcing him to once again clamp his hands against his ears.

"Enough!" he shouted.

The nuns' mouths snapped shut in unison.

Isaac rose from his chair, still massaging the growing ache in his temples as he made his way toward the large wooden cross beside the window. After brushing a moth from the corpus' thorny crown, he gazed out the window at the Whitman boy, who was listlessly sitting on the playground's single good swing, scuffing his heels in the dirt. Like a school of fish circumnavigating a shark, the other children had formed a wide circle around the rusted swing set and the strange little boy that occupied it, as though their instincts had warned them of what their conscious minds had yet to understand.

"Father," Maggie said, rising to her feet.

"Speak, my child," Isaac sighed, though he didn't turn to look at her.

"Father, you must send him away," she urged, wringing her hands. "Something dark lurks in that boy – something I fear not even the Lord himself can cleanse."

"Watch your tongue, Sister Maggie," Isaac chided. "Hysteria is no excuse for blasphemy." He ran a hand through his thinning white hair, disquiet pitting in his stomach, before retrieving a mint-flavored Rolaid from his pocket and popping it in his mouth.

"But, Father, she's right," Constance implored.

Isaac arched an eyebrow at her uncharacteristic impudence.

"He is the son of perdition, I am sure of it! The signs are all there: deception, illusions, denouncing the word of God—"

"It's true!" Maggie nodded fervently. "Why, just the other day he openly refused to thank the Lord before the evening meal!"

"You must cast him away, and quickly, before he can harm anyone else!"

"Anyone else?" Isaac interjected, turning around to face them. "As far as I know, Elliot Whitman has not harmed anyone at all. When I arrived at the boys' dormitory, all I found was a lone child plugging his ears against the screams of two hysterical women wailing about ghosts and evil spirits!"

"But Father—" Constance started.

He held up a hand. "This is what happens when worldly books are allowed into the convent. Just yesterday, I found Sister Jeanette reading from a…a…" the priest lowered his voice to a disparaging whisper, as though he were speaking an obscenity in polite company, "…a *fiction book* instead of bible verses." Isaac shook his head, muttering to himself, "*The woman was deceived and thus became a sinner…*" He cleared his throat. "I want you both to go meditate on the Pauline epistles, and when you feel you have fully regained your composure, we can examine the negative influences that have led you both astray, starting with those poisonous fiction books that I told you to dispose of weeks ago."

Maggie opened her mouth to argue – after all, *she* hadn't been concealing worn paperbacks of long-haired, shirtless men in the Lord's Book during Sunday Mass – but Constance put a firm hand on her elbow, silencing her.

"Of course, Father," the older woman cut in, shooting the novice a sharp look. "We will meditate on this and ensure those iniquitous books are properly disposed of."

"Very good." Isaac nodded, returning to his desk to jot a note in his leather bound journal of sermon ideas. He waved his free hand toward the door. "You may go."

Constance grabbed Maggie by the sleeve, tugging her into the hallway as the headmaster's door clicked shut behind them. Before Maggie could get a single word out, Constance clapped a wrinkled hand over her mouth. "While Satan has clouded Father Isaac's judgment, the Holy Spirit has filled me with clear vision on this matter."

The younger woman let out a long, muffled sigh against Constance's palm. "Oh, thank Heavens," she mumbled, the words partially smothered.

After wiping her hand on her robes with an appalled grimace, Constance quickly made the sign of the cross, kissing the crucifix dangling from her neck once she had finished. "Come. There is only one thing to be done at a time like this." She gripped Maggie by her slender wrist, leading her down the hallway and back toward the boys' dormitories.

"And wh-what's that?"

"In dire moments, the Lord may permit evil in order to draw forth some greater good."

"I don't understand," Maggie fretted, jogging to keep up with the surprisingly spry old woman.

Constance stopped abruptly, her expression darkening into a fearsome glower as she met

Maggie's wide-eyed expression. "Sometimes, the only way to vanquish evil is by means of a greater evil."

CHAPTER 2
CASE CLOSED

Lilah glanced at her watch, groaning inwardly, then withdrew another sour gummy worm from the crumpled baggie in her pocket to tame her growling stomach. She should have been back home scarfing down leftover pizza with her father over an hour ago, but Virginia Dobson, her last witness of the day, appeared to be as talkative as she was easily distracted. Lilah took a deep breath of lilac-infused air to take the edge off her impatience, grateful for the warm spring weather despite the darkening creep of evening.

The middle-aged woman sitting across from her frowned, and not for the first time that afternoon. "I'm sorry, Detective, but *how old* did you say you were?"

"Uh..." Lilah faltered as she dusted the residual sugar from her fingers and onto her jeans. "Nineteen?"

"Are you asking me or telling me?"

"...Telling?"

The woman's frown deepened. "That's a little young to be a detective, isn't it? And a *lady* detective at that!"

"I'm sort of a special case," Lilah explained – or rather, deflected. This wouldn't be the first or last time she would be grilled on her age or appearance by one of her case subjects. "Anyway, Mrs. Dobson, if we could just get back to last Tuesday, the night of April twelfth... Now, you mentioned seeing a woman in a yellow jacket standing on the corner of Eighth Street and Pine – do you remember what you were doing and what time that was?"

"I remember exactly what we were doing – trying to get out of the crazy weather! Snow and thunder all at once, can you imagine? And I remember the time, too, because I turned to Mr. Dobson and said, 'No respectable young lady should be standing alone, in the freezing rain, at ten o'clock at night!'"

"Elizabeth was a grown woman – not exactly a 'young lady,'" Lilah interjected mildly.

The wrinkles in Mrs. Dobson's forehead deepened. "To an old lady, *every*one under the age of fifty is young, which makes you practically a baby! Now where was I…? Oh, yes. I had just started marching over there to tell her how unseemly she looked when a man in a white Miata pulled up to talk to her."

Lilah jotted that down in her notebook excitedly. "You're absolutely certain it was a Miata?"

"I am, because Mr. Dobson sighed and said, 'If only the Postal Service paid me enough to afford that new Mazda MX-5 Miata,' and I elbowed him in the ribs and reminded him that even if they did, I was still waiting on the diamond tennis bracelet he promised me on our honeymoon thirty-nine years ago!"

"A Mazda MX-5 Miata?" Relief washed over Lilah like a warm fleece blanket. *This* was the big break in the case she had been waiting for. "Oh, Mrs. Dobson, I could kiss you right now!"

The woman let out a harrumph. "Well, I'm not sure what exactly I did to deserve that, but I'm happy I could help. Anyway, after she got in, the car peeled away so fast, she'd forgotten her jacket on the sidewalk."

"I wonder why?" Lilah frowned. "Did you happen to grab it?"

"Of course not. It was freezing cold outside and my dress was already soaking wet! Now if there's nothing else, I've got a pot roast in the oven and Mr. Dobson gets cranky if I let the edges get too crispy." She rose to her feet, turning to go, then stopped. "Is she alright? The girl in the yellow jacket, that is?"

Lilah hesitated, then smiled. "I'm sure she is."

Mrs. Dobson nodded once, looking thoughtful, then turned to walk away. As she did, her tailored blazer and matching pastel skirt dissolved into ashes, along with the rest of her. Lilah watched as her witness returned to her resting place beneath the soil, finally letting go of the breath she felt like she'd been holding for the past week. It immediately condensed into a swirl of icy crystals that rose into the darkening sky.

A red-winged blackbird landed on a nearby gravestone, cocking its head in her direction.

Sighing, Lilah reached into her pocket, retrieving a pink-and-green gummy worm, then tossed it to the bird. It deftly caught it in its beak, then flew away without so much as a grateful trill.

"You're welcome!" Lilah sarcastically called after it.

After zipping up her jacket against the returning chill of November, she rose to her feet, lacing her fingers high above her head to stretch out her lower back. Far more than the living, the dead loved to talk – even when they had long forgotten they were dead.

Sighing, she walked over to a pile of crunchy leaves where she'd propped the fancy gold watch she'd discovered while searching for her biological mother three years before. It had a shiny, royal blue dial with four smaller sub-dials embedded within, which gauged everything from the time of day, to the month, to the lunar cycle, to the calendar day – a true perpetual calendar watch. Because objects that touched her skin were immune to temporal distortions, Lilah would always remove the watch when combing through time to make sure she was exactly "when" she needed to be – down to the precise second, if necessary. Once the watch had properly re-synced with the current day and time, she replaced it on her wrist, beside the old analog watch her father had given her for her sixteenth birthday. Combined, she could always figure out what day and time it was, both inside and outside of her "chrono-bubbles" – as her father had dubbed them.

Brittle leaves and frozen dirt crunched beneath her Converse sneakers as she made the short trek back to the forest-green station wagon Sheriff Reid had generously gifted her after its previous owner failed to pick it up from the impound lot. After sinking into the driver's seat and slamming the door behind her, she took a moment to admire the last vestiges of the crimson sunset dipping below the grove of willow trees that lined the cemetery. Having just lost their leaves to the frost, the slender branches looked ghostly and pale – like icy phantoms lying in wait.

Lilah loved the sight of them, because they reminded her of her two mothers: Marie, the woman who had adopted her out of the love and kindness of her own heart, and now rested beneath them, and Willow, the teenage girl who gave birth to her, then disappeared shortly after.

There was a time when Lilah blamed herself for her biological mother's abrupt disappearance, believing she – or rather, her time-altering seizures – had been the cause. It wasn't until Lilah stumbled upon Willow's missing bones in the middle of the forest that she had learned the truth, simultaneously solving a sixteen-year-old cold case. Because of Willow's own testimony, Lilah was able to help Sheriff Reid track down the killer that had murdered her young mother, thereby cutting short his growing list of victims. Fortunately, she and Reid had been able to scrape together enough physical evidence for the case to be successfully reopened and sent to trial.

This case, on the other hand…

Lilah sighed as she started the car, rubbing at the wrinkle that had appeared between her furrowed brows. For this case, all she had was the testimony of a dead woman, and that wouldn't be enough to bring Elizabeth Simmons' murderer to justice. Security cameras hadn't yet been installed in the outskirts of Butte, Montana in 1990, so Lilah would have no way of digging up footage of the Mazda MX-5 Miata Mrs. Dobson had spoken of. But Sheriff Reid would have access to vehicle registrations for the State of Montana and would almost certainly be able to pull up the name of its registrant. And once she had the owner's name, all Lilah would have to do was go chrono-digging around the address on record, looking for the remains of Elizabeth Simmons that had yet to be found.

You are a veritable genius, she commended herself as she turned out of the long cemetery dirt drive and onto paved asphalt. *This has got to be one of your best ideas yet!*

. . .

"This has got to be one of your stupidest ideas yet!" Lilah's father snarled, slamming an empty pot on the stovetop.

The self-satisfied smile that was tugging at the corners of Lilah's mouth abruptly went lax. "What do you mean, stupid? It's brilliant!"

"Brilliant?!" Stanley Quinn rolled his eyes as he stabbed the can-opener into the family-sized can of Chef Boyardee he was clutching as though he had a personal vendetta against canned ravioli. "'Don't mind me, Dad,'" he sang in a high-pitched voice as he violently cranked the knob of the rusty can-opener, "'I might be just the teensiest bit late for dinner tomorrow night after I go poking around some serial killer's house looking for skeletons in his backyard!' 'Oh, sure, Li!'" he answered himself in a deep, fatherly tone. "'That's no problem at all, and if you happen to get yourself murdered in the process, I'll give Reid a courtesy call so he knows you'll be out Monday morning!'" He dumped the contents of the opened can into the pot, oblivious to the tomato sauce he'd splattered across his plaid shirt.

Lilah rolled her eyes as she gathered a handful of paper towels from beside the sink and started blotting at the stain on his shirt. "It is my *job* to solve crimes!"

"No, it is your job to talk to dead people so *Reid* can solve crimes!" Stanley barked, snatching the paper towels from her so he could belligerently scrub at the worsening stains. "And he will readily echo those sentiments!"

"But I'm a detective!"

"No, you are an *honorary* detective who has yet to complete actual detective training!" Lilah opened her mouth to offer a snappish retort but Stanley steamrolled right past her. "You don't even carry a gun! What are you gonna do – sweet talk a murderous psychopath into submission?"

At that, Lilah crossed her arms and gave him a pointed look.

Stanley stared back at her, dumbly, before mumbling, "Oh…right."

"I seriously doubt a baby or a pile of bones could do much damage to me." Lilah directed her attention to the bowl of crisp, red apples resting on the counter, which immediately turned into a pile of stinking slop.

Stanley tried and failed to suppress a shudder. "You know I hate it when you do that."

The festering mound of rot transformed back into six waxy apples, one of which Lilah took a zealous bite from. "And *I* hate it when you treat me like a kid!" she retorted between angry chomps of apple. "I'm not some toddler with seizures anymore, Dad! I'm an adult and I can look after myself!"

The vein in Stan's forehead bulged.

Lilah braced herself for the forthcoming explosion, only to find a manic grin unfurling across Stan's face instead.

Her eyebrow arched. "Uh, Dad…? Do I need to call Dr. Kreuter?"

"Oh no, I'm fine, just fine…" Stan's voice was cheerful as he wiped his hands on a towel, then strode across the kitchen to where the phone was hanging on the wall. "But I do wonder what Jace will say when I tell him the love of his life is planning to break into yet *another* cold-blooded murderer's house…"

Lilah's face blanched of all color. "You wouldn't."

"Oh, *wouldn't I?*" Stan's grin was teetering on vicious as he started casually punching in Jace's number, which he knew by heart.

"Dad, don't you dare!"

"Don't I dare what?" he asked, the question sopping with innocence. "I'm just calling my dear buddy, Jace, whom I've missed terribly since he left for UW—"

"Dad," Lilah growled, "if you rat me out to my own boyfriend, I'll…I'll…"

Stan's finger paused over the last digit. "You'll what?"

"I'll—*ugh!*" she groaned, knowing full-well she'd been beaten. "Fine! I'll let Sheriff Reid know what I found out and let *him* decide next steps. Happy?"

"Good girl." Stanley nodded, then punched in the last digit of Jace's number.

"Dad!" Lilah shrieked, lunging for the phone.

"I'm not ratting you out!" he shouted, spinning out of her grasp. "I'm just—oh hey, Jace!"

"Dad, give me the phone!" Lilah hissed.

Stanley ignored her. "Nope, she hasn't done anything stupid—*yet*." He gave his daughter a pointed look. "I was just calling to see how the game went! Uh-huh… No kidding!" He grinned widely, then clasped a hand over the receiver. "He hit a homer against the Beavers! A *pitcher*, hitting a home run! It's almost unheard of, unless you're

Mike Hampton! And because of that, they won, four-zip!"

"I know!" Lilah snapped. "Will you please give me the phone?"

He held up a finger. "So, who are you playing next week? …The Ducks? Oh man, you guys are gonna cream those suckers!" Cradling the phone between his chin and shoulder, Stanley went back to stirring his canned ravioli, grinning from ear to ear. "I know! I can't believe how spotty their pitching has been this season! They really need to bring back Martinez. …Wait, he got in trouble for *what?* No kidding!" He let out a low whistle. "I didn't even know you could smoke that!"

Lilah sank into the nearest kitchen chair, groaning into her palms. Still, the tiniest hint of a smile tugged at the corner of her mouth. Three years ago, Stanley had searched for any and every possible excuse not to like Jace, the boy Lilah had secretly loved since elementary school, and who had secretly loved her back. Most of the time, he'd found himself grasping at straws as Jace proved, again and again, that he was a truly decent young man despite the hardships he'd endured at the hands of his checked-out mother and alcoholic stepfather.

Last fall, when Jace went off to college at the University of Washington, Lilah wasn't sure which of them had been more distraught – her or her father. With no love to be found at his own house, Jace had found a home at the Quinn residence. Even though she'd never admit it out loud, especially when her father was hogging her boyfriend to himself, Lilah couldn't be happier that Jace and Stanley had forged their own special relationship over the years.

After all, as far as Lilah was concerned, there was nothing sadder than a child raised without love.

RED CROSS, THROUGH SHIELD

The minute and hour hands on the clock were both pointing straight up when Elliot was shaken awake in the middle of the night, a firm hand pressed against his mouth to stifle a yelp.

"We're going to go on an adventure," Maggie whispered, hushing him. "But you have to be very quiet or you'll spoil it. Can you do that for me?"

Wide-eyed, Elliot nodded.

"Good boy." She withdrew her hand and ushered him out of bed. "Don't worry about changing into your day clothes – you won't need them where we're going."

Half-lidded and yawning, Elliot followed the nun out of the boys' dormitory, his bare feet plodding against the cold tile. He cast a quick glance over his shoulder at Kimmy and Mari, who were once again seated at the play table, their make-believe tea cold and untouched. A striped column of moonlight shone through the barred windows, illuminating their crestfallen faces as they waved goodbye.

"Bye," Elliot whispered.

Hand clamped over her mouth to suppress a burgeoning scream, the nun hastened her step, making the sign of the cross as she did.

Constance was waiting for them outside the rusted front doors of the orphanage, clutching the keys to Father Isaac's Ford station wagon in one hand while fingering her rosary with the other. "Get in," she urged Elliot, quietly opening and closing the car door for him.

He climbed inside, rubbing his eyes tiredly as he lay down across the back seat to go back to sleep.

Maggie hurried over to the passenger side, holding her breath as she shut the door behind her as gently as possible. "The demons were back," she muttered to the old woman under her breath. "Both of them. Just sitting and… watching." She hugged herself, shuddering. "As soon as he stepped through the doorway, they disappeared, just like before. Oh, Constance, what if he summons them right here, inside the car?"

The old woman made a sharp gesture for Maggie to lower her voice, stealing a glance at the sleeping boy in the rearview mirror before turning over the engine. Both women winced at the noise, but the orphanage windows remained dark; miraculously, no one else had awoken. After slowly backing out of the long dirt drive, which was surrounded by shadowy evergreens, Constance turned the car onto the main road, steadily picking up speed. The dark silhouettes of soybean fields, silos, and cattle fencing went whizzing by like a hastening blur, while the street lights that illuminated them became fewer and farther between.

"His parents – both young and healthy – died in their sleep," Constance murmured to Maggie. "They never were able to figure out the cause."

Her younger accomplice clenched her trembling hands in her lap, muttering the Prayer Against Every Evil under her breath.

"Where are we going?" Elliot mumbled from the back seat, his head cradled in the crook of his elbow.

"It's a surprise." Constance tightened her already-white-knuckled grip on the steering wheel. "You'll see when we get there."

When the car turned onto the highway twenty minutes later, following the signs for White Pine Hollow National Forest, Maggie darted an anxious look over her shoulder, half-expecting a squadron of police cars to be following them.

By the grace of God, the road was completely dark.

Her eyes fell on the little boy who had curled into a ball in the back seat, fast asleep. The passing streetlights cast him in intermittent stripes of light and shadow, his features vacillating between cherub and fiend.

Maggie suppressed another shudder as she turned back around in her seat. "We're doing the right thing…aren't we?" she asked, rubbing her thumb in small circles around the wooden cross she wore around her neck.

Constance gave her a curt nod as she turned onto the unmarked, seldom-used service road that led deep into miles and miles of untouched forest. "The Lord took no pity on the Prince of Darkness, and neither will we. Just as it was necessary to cast Satan from Heaven, we must defend this place from the dark one's iniquitous agenda." She nodded again, this time to herself, firming up her resolve. "The Lord redeems the life of his servants; none of those who take refuge in him will be condemned."

"Amen," Maggie whispered.

• • •

Elliot jolted awake an hour or so after he'd fallen asleep, rubbing the fresh ache in his head as he yawned. A loud noise had started him awake, but there was no sound now – not even from the car engine, which had been switched off. Outside the car, the world was almost completely black, the faint outline of trees just barely illuminated by the setting moon.

"Where are we?" Elliot half-asked, half-yawned.

Both nuns were looking around in confusion, as though trying to remember. Finally, Sister Maggie cleared her throat and answered, "I…I think we're in a forest." She turned to Sister Constance, who was knuckling the deep ache in her wrinkled forehead. "But…how did we get here? Did Father Isaac—"

"I don't know," Constance interrupted with more than a touch of irritation. She turned the key in the ignition, but the engine didn't so much as sputter. "Open up the glove box and see if there's a map inside."

"What good will a map do if we don't know where we are?"

"Just see if there's one in there!"

While the two nuns bickered about maps, Elliot, who suddenly felt very tired and sore, turned the handle of the back door and stepped outside. A blast of hot air and smoke hit him in the face, making his eyes water, while the caustic smell of burning oil made him dizzy. He staggered away from the car, wincing as twigs and sharp pine needles poked at his bare feet. When the stench of smoke and burning rubber had finally dissipated, he cast a glance over his shoulder, where the car he'd been taking a nap inside had crashed head-first into a tree, immediately killing two out of three of its inhabitants. He watched as the fire and smoke rising from the crushed front end of the station wagon rose higher and higher, painting the surrounding forest in flickering stripes of crimson and orange.

Hugging himself tightly, he stumbled away from the smoldering wreckage and the nuns' flame-wreathed bodies, the ground pitching beneath his feet while towering trees spun all around him. Eventually, the soles of Elliot's feet found cold, smooth asphalt, which they followed until the plume of smoke was far behind them, and the first traces of dawn appeared above the jagged line of trees as a faint purple glow. When a car rolled to a stop beside him, he almost didn't notice.

"Excuse me – young man!" a voice called. "Are you all by yourself?"

Elliot turned around to find a middle-aged man in a tan business suit slamming his car door and jogging over to him.

"Son, are you alright?" the man asked, crouching in front of him. "Where are your parents?"

"Dead," Elliot answered.

The man muttered a sharp word Elliot had never heard before, then carefully scooped the little boy into his arms. "We need to get you to a hospital," the man said, gently placing Elliot in the front passenger-side seat. After taking off his suit jacket and tucking it around the boy like a blanket, he sank into the driver's seat, wrenched the transmission to "D," then hit the gas so hard the tires squealed in protest.

It was hard for Elliot to keep his eyes open, and as the movements of the car lulled him back into a heavy sleep, the man, the road, and the forest feathered in and out of existence. In their place, his mother's arms, his father's quiet sobs, and the nuns' screams appeared as flashbulb memories, each one brighter and more distressing than the last.

His eyes briefly fluttered open when the nice man scooped him out of the car and helped lay him atop a rolling stretcher while three men in ties and white jackets were asking him a rushed litany of questions.

"What's the boy's name?"

"How old is he?"

"Where did you say you found him?"

"Are you his father?"

"No, the boy says his parents are dead," the man replied. He was jogging behind the three white-jacketed people, who were wheeling Elliot into the garish lighting of the emergency room. "I don't know anything else about him. I found him wandering by himself along IA-3, just outside of White Pine Hollow thirty minutes ago. I'd've stopped to look for his family, but when I saw he was injured—"

"The lacerations on his feet and hands appear to be shallow," one of the three doctors said, pressing a cold stethoscope against Elliot's exposed chest, while another shone a bright flashlight in his eyes. "But given his body temperature, I'd say you made the right call. Shirley!" he called the curly-haired woman sitting at the receptionist's desk. "Dial up ISP and tell them to send a squad car over to IA-3"—he turned back to the good Samaritan—"you don't happen to know the mile marker do you?"

"About a quarter mile west of White Pine Lane."

Elliot began to whimper.

"Libby!" the flashlight-wielding doctor barked. "Damnit, Shirley, where's she gone this time?"

"Right here!" A frazzled young woman in a white physician's jacket jogged over to where the four men had clustered around Elliot. "I'm sorry, I was just—"

"What a luxury it must be, being able to take your third coffee break of the day! Now, if it's not too much trouble, perhaps you could go and clean this boy's wounds? After that, you can call in myself or Steve to take a better look at him."

The female doctor kept her gaze carefully schooled. "As I've reminded you before, Dr. Jacobs, I'm not a nurse. And I don't—"

"If you don't like the way my E.R. is run, *Miss* Shermann, take it up with the Chief of Medicine. Until then, either do your job or go home."

Biting back a retort, the woman blew a strand of blonde hair from her eyes, then turned to Elliot, her features softening. "Hey there, little friend." She smiled down at him as she wheeled him away from the bedlam and into a tiny room with a blue curtain instead of a door. "Can you tell me your name?"

"Elliot." He squinted his eyes against the bright light.

"It's very nice to meet you, Elliot. My name is Dr. Shermann, but you can call me Libby." She dimmed the lights, then gently removed his nightshirt. After performing a quick inspection – no bruises or signs of trauma, other than a small lump on his forehead – she wrapped a warmed blanket around his body. "What were you doing out in the woods all by yourself?"

"What's that for?" Elliot asked, crossing his eyes to look at the steaming washcloth she was pressing against his forehead.

"This is to help your body warm up, because you got a little too cold while you were walking around outside." She wrapped more warm towels around his legs, eliciting a contented sigh from her tiny patient, then withdrew a pocket-sized flashlight from her jacket, which she shone in his left eye, and then his right, before switching it off. "So Elliot, can you tell me why you were walking around all by yourself in the middle of the night?"

"Sister Maggie told me that we were goin' on an adventure so we got in the car with Sister Constance. But I had to be very quiet or else I would spoil the surprise."

Libby reached for a bottle of antiseptic on the counter, which she upended into a cloth. "And how old are your sisters?"

Elliot scrunched up his face in thought. "Well, Sister Maggie is kind of old, but also kind of young, like you. She just has one big wrinkle between her eyebrows, like this"—he pulled his eyebrows together in a stern expression—"and Sister Constance is really, *really* old, like trees, 'cause her face is wrinkly and she smells like old milk."

"Oh, Maggie and Constance are nuns?" Libby gently began blotting the bottom of Elliot's feet, making him wince. "Sorry, sweetie – I have to clean out these scratches so they don't become infected. So, what happened after you got in the car with Sister Maggie and Sister Constance?"

When he didn't answer right away, she glanced up at him, frowning at his paling cheeks. "You doing okay, Elliot?"

He shook his head.

"Do you still feel cold?"

He nodded.

"Would you like me to get you some hot chocolate?"

He nodded again.

"Okay." After cleaning out the worst of the lacerations, Dr. Shermann set the pink-tinged cloth and plastic tub aside, peeled off her gloves, and rose to her feet. "I'll go ask one of the nurses to bring you some hot chocolate, okay? Don't worry, I'll be right back."

Elliot watched her leave, then looked around the room, clutching the warm blanket against his trembling body. There were so many whirring machines with blinking screens and glowing buttons, reminding him of the last time he was in the hospital, after his parents had gone to sleep and never woke up. Remembering that, Elliot's heart began to thud loudly in his ears and the edges of his vision blurred.

A different woman appeared in the room, her face almost as wrinkled as Sister Constance's, though she thankfully didn't smell like sour milk. "What brings you in here today, young man?" she asked, taking a seat beside his bed.

"I hurt my feet and my body got too cold so Doctor Libby is making me hot chocolate."

"Oh, Dr. Shermann is a very nice lady. I like her."

"Why are you here?" Elliot asked shyly, half-hiding beneath his blankets. "Are you a doctor too?"

"Oh, heavens no – Dr. Shermann is one of the few ladies in this world tough enough to handle a job like that. My name is Carol, and I'm a patient here, just like you. And if you can believe it, I'm so old, my kidneys – that's these two organs right here"—she pointed to the left and right sides of her back—"have stopped working. So, I have to come in here three times a week and get my blood cleaned."

Elliot's eyes widened. "How do they clean your blood? With soap?"

Carol laughed. "Worse. They have to draw the blood right out of my body with a tube, filter it through this big, noisy machine, and then put it all back in."

"At least it's not soap." Elliot scrunched up his face. "Sister Constance once made me eat soap and it tasted even worser than brussel' sprouts."

"Oh dear." Carol clicked her tongue. "Did you say something naughty to Sister Constance to make her wash your mouth out with soap?"

"We're 'sposta thank God every night before dinner but I told Sister Constance I don't want to thank God because he made my parents go to sleep and never wake up so she got angry and made me eat soap."

Carol's expression softened. "I'm very sorry to hear that about your parents."

Elliot's eyelids were getting heavy again. "I hope my kidneys never stop working," he murmured as his eyes began to flutter closed.

"Me too, young man." Carol patted his arm. "Me too."

Libby returned to the room a moment later, pulling on a fresh pair of latex gloves. "Okay, sweetie, Shauna says your hot chocolate will be ready in a few minutes." She looked around the room, frowning. "Who were you talking to?"

"Carol."

Libby froze halfway into putting on her second glove. "Who?"

"Carol. She has to get her blood cleaned by a noisy machine three times a week."

The doctor's frown deepened. With her latex glove still only partway donned, she stuck her head out the curtain, calling, "Hey Shauna – do you have any patients named Carol?"

"Uh-huh!" a woman's voice answered.

Libby's shoulders relaxed.

Shauna, who was dressed in a starched white dress, white cap, and white nylons, stepped through the curtain. "You remember the widow I was telling you about – the one who had to take a taxi to and from her dialysis treatments?" She held out a Styrofoam cup of hot chocolate to Libby, eyeing her men's-cut physician's jacket with a flicker of disdain. "I used to head downstairs after my shifts and sit with her."

"Oh, right," Libby said, taking the steaming cup from her, "I remember her now."

"One of my absolute favorite patients." Shauna let out a long sigh. "I was devastated when I found out she passed away two days ago – poor thing collapsed right in the middle of treatment."

The cup of hot chocolate Libby had been holding toppled to the floor.

CHAPTER 4

BREADCRUMBS

"Well I'll be damned," Sheriff David Reid muttered to himself while thumbing through the pages Lilah had set in front of him. He scratched at his thinning brown hair, marveling at her notes. Behind him, his faithful hound dog, Bandit, was curled up in his dog bed in the corner, lounging in the warm rectangle of late afternoon sunlight that was streaming through the window. "How did you know Virginia Dobson and her husband had seen Elizabeth that night? I don't remember seeing their names on any of the witness statements..." He reshuffled the stack of papers he'd been perusing, adjusting his reading glasses as he did.

"I didn't," Lilah answered, a touch of smugness creeping into her voice. "The last time

Elizabeth used her debit card before her disappearance was at a bar called The Waterhole, which is located on the corner of Eighth Street and Pine. There are three different apartment complexes located on that corner, so I tracked down every person who was living there at the time – both alive and dead. And it just so happens Mr. and Mrs. Dobson were coming home from their anniversary dinner at the exact same moment Elizabeth stepped inside *this*"—she slapped down the vehicle registration she'd dredged up from the state archives—"Mazda MX-5 Miata. It belonged to one Anthony DeWitt, who's currently incarcerated at South Dakota State for unrelated drug and prostitution charges and set to go free next year – unless you and I nail him for first-degree murder, that is." She grinned.

"We've been over this, Lilah." Reid sighed. "Until he's been proven of murder – which usually requires both proof *and* a body, neither of which we have – Anthony is a *suspect*, not a murderer." Reid's eyes narrowed. "Furthermore, half of what you just rattled off is privileged information – which you accessed *how* exactly?"

Lilah's grin wavered the teensiest bit. "Uh…by using your log-in credentials and combing through state and penitentiary archives?"

Reid palmed the growing crease between his brows. "Kid, you know I could lose my badge for that."

"Why? I'm a detective!"

"No, you're an extremely well-paid *clerk.*"

"Who has solved more cold cases for Montana than any other 'clerk' in the state's history!" Lilah blustered. "Not to mention at least half a dozen cases from Wyoming, North Dakota, and Idaho!"

"Without a single certification, degree, or a badge!" Reid retorted loudly, rousing poor Bandit from what had been a particularly good dream about catching a squirrel that had long been eluding him.

The hound gave an irritable grunt.

"But—"

"Lilah, we – you, myself, and your father – have been through this time and time again. In order to become a *real* detective"—he held up a hand before she could sputter a word of protest—"you'll need to get yourself a criminal justice degree—"

"Which I am less than two months away from earning!"

"—attend and *graduate* Police Academy," Reid continued as though he hadn't been interrupted, "pass a strenuous written and physical exam, get several *years* of experience out in the field, first as a traffic cop, and then in law enforcement as a local beat cop, and *then,* after all of *that*, complete a detective examination and an interview process."

Lilah balked. "You would actually make me interview for the job?"

Reid palmed his eyes, sighing. "*That's* all you took from that?"

"Look, Dave—er, Sheriff Reid," Lilah amended, "if I waste all of that time – I mean, we're talking *years* – training for something I'm already doing, how will I keep doing…well, any of this?" she finished lamely. "I mean, I'm already solving crimes like any other detective – why go through the time and cost and aggravation for some lousy piece of paper?"

"Because that 'lousy piece of paper' is what grants you the right to do the things I am already putting my badge on the line to let you do!"

"Yeah, but—"

The radio on Reid's hip chirped. He held up a hand to silence Lilah's protests, then brought the walky-talky up to his bushy mustache. "Reid here. Go ahead, over."

"*Sir, we got another call about Patrick O'Malley drinking outside the pub without pants again. Should we bring him in or do you want to handle this time? Over.*"

Reid let out a rather coarse expletive. "I'm on my way!" He snatched his wide-brim hat from the edge of his desk and placed it squarely atop his head. "No arrests!" he barked into the radio as he fumbled with his jacket. "Repeat, do *not* arrest – but feel free to put him in the back of the squad car and put the fear of death in him 'til I get there. Over."

"But Sheriff, the man's not wearing pants!"

"Then lay a damned towel over the seat! Over!" Still muttering obscenities under his breath, Reid stood up and began hastily gathering his belongings.

"Patrick O'Malley – that's Annie's brother, right?" Lilah asked.

"Sure is – and if he gets arrested for public intoxication and indecent exposure again, *I'm* the one who has to deal with the aftermath…both here and at the dinner table."

"Right… Um, sir, just one more thing," Lilah started, rising to her feet. "At the time of Elizabeth's disappearance, Anthony DeWitt was living just a few miles from here. If I could just head over to the residence and poke around, I might be able to find—"

"The home's current owner standing on the front porch, cocking a shotgun at you," Reid cut in. "Just cool your heels, little lady. Once I'm able to pull together a plausible excuse for why we need it, since we can't exactly cite a dead person's witness statement, I'll work on getting a warrant for the DeWitt place. Until then, you've still got a whole mess of paperwork waiting to be filed from *last* week." He nodded toward a tall stack of papers teetering on the edge of his desk. "Besides, there's no rush – it's not like Miss Simmons can get any deader between now and next week."

Lilah bit her tongue, stifling a sardonic retort.

"And that's *if* she's dead," Reid grunted as he re-cinched his gun belt around his waist, sucking in his belly as he did. "For all we know, the woman has been living in the Cayman Islands for the last decade. Her neighbors said she'd been acting erratically in the years leading up to her disappearance – leaving her high-paying job, nailing up her windows, turning into a recluse—"

"None of which matches her character profile."

"Mental breakdowns seldom do. Oh, and on that note, I just dug up an ancillary file relating to her case that you're gonna want to look at before you go digging around. Wild stuff."

"What kind of—"

"Tomorrow." The sheriff let out a sharp whistle. "C'mon boy!" He jerked his head toward the door to his office. "We got a town drunk to escort home."

Bandit let out another aggrieved grumble as he rose to his paws, his old bones creaking and protesting with every movement.

"Good boy," Reid said, bending down to scratch him behind the ears.

Lilah opened her mouth to press Reid about the case, then sighed and closed it again. "Good luck with your brother-in-law." She smiled tightly. "In the meantime, I'll try to find something on Anthony DeWitt that doesn't rely on the testimony of a dead person."

"Atta girl." The sheriff smiled approvingly. "Even better, just set the whole thing aside for now. You've got an online Criminal Justice degree you should be focusing on, which will get you one step closer to becoming a real detective."

Lilah forced a smile that looked more like a pained grimace.

Nodding a curt goodbye, Sheriff Reid strode out the door, his faithful hound dog doddering at his heels.

The second he disappeared down the hallway, whistling some jaunty tune, Lilah sank into his chair and heaved a disgruntled sigh. "Stupid CFE," she muttered, absentmindedly blowing a stray lock of auburn hair from her hazel eyes. "What's the point of hunting down some stale breadcrumbs if I've already got a loaf of bread in the oven?" Her attention darted from the towering stack of paper to the pair of watches on her wrist – both of which read half past two – to the golden afternoon sunlight streaming in through the window.

If Elizabeth's remains aren't there, why bother coming up with a fake story and a warrant? It's just more time and paperwork. Lilah chewed on a candy-apple-green fingernail as she regarded the growing stack of unfinished paperwork she'd yet to file. *All I have to do is dig around for a few minutes and see if I can find her body – and maybe ask her a quick question or two, if she's in the mood. It's not like anyone would see me.*

Indeed, chrono-bubbles provide excellent camouflage; even from a relatively short distance, they appear as nothing more than a shimmering ripple in the air. It's not until an onlooker is standing a few paces away that the true nature of the time distortion is made plain: not a ripple, but a curved, mirrored surface with millions of tiny facets reflecting the surrounding area. When standing directly outside the distortion, the facets smooth away to reveal a transparent, undulating sphere, which rises from the ground with a surface like rippling water. Only *then* would she potentially be spotted. And, of course, if the spectator were to inadvertently step inside and get swept up in the time distortion in the process, that would eradicate the witness problem altogether.

But, for the moment at least, that was neither here nor there.

"Warrant *shmorrant*," Lilah muttered, her resolve solidifying.

As she rose to her feet, her eyes settled on one of the open manila envelopes resting on the corner of Sheriff Reid's desk, labeled COLD CASE #00219-2174551-MT.

Lilah picked up the file, her eyebrows arching in surprise. It wasn't a victim that stared back at her, but an alleged murderer. Her eyes scanned the faded picture that had been paperclipped in the top corner of the folder. A photo of a young man stared back at her in a coldly discomfiting way, his dark hair in disarray, and his pale, freckled face marred by deep purple rings beneath his eyes. Just before taking his own life at twenty-six years old, the man had apparently confided in a pastor, ultimately confessing to a dozen murders. Except none of the victims had been found, and he'd left no clues as to who or where they might be.

A sticky note written in Reid's hand had been stuck on the inside of the page – *Accompany L. to grave at First Presb. Church in Whitehall to interview for leads.*

"Huh." Lilah stared at the man's unsettling expression for another second before unceremoniously tucking the folder under her arm. After peeking her head out the door to make sure the coast was clear on both sides, she quickly darted out of the sheriff's office and through the back door before Pam – Reid's garrulous receptionist – could launch into a twenty-minute exposition about recent weather patterns.

Upon successfully making her undetected escape through the back door of the Tri-Forks

Police Department, Lilah jogged back to her car, kicking off the short journey to Anthony DeWitt's last known residence – where she had a sneaking suspicion she might finally get to speak to the missing woman in the yellow jacket.

Beneath the crook of her arm, the cold, dead eyes of Elliot Whitman stared blankly into the distance.

Chapter 5
Old Dogs, New Tricks

Elliot clutched his new stuffed rabbit against his chest as he looked around Dr. Libby Shermann's tiny, unused guestroom with wide-eyed rapture. The white walls were freshly painted and unadorned, and the only furnishings were a quilted twin bed, a small wooden writing desk and matching chair, and an antique, turtle-shaped Tiffany lamp.

It was the most beautiful room Elliot had ever seen.

"This…is mine?" he asked, his voice filled with wonder and disbelief.

"Yes." Libby smiled.

"I don't have to share it with anyone?"

She shook her head. "It's all yours, kiddo. I'm just sorry it's so bare. We'll get you some toys as soon as possible – this weekend, I hope."

So long as I'm not called into the hospital. She chewed on her lip with a sigh, working to dispel the tightness that knotted in her chest every time she thought about work. The chief of medicine himself had promised her greater flexibility in her schedule, given the extraordinary circumstances: namely that Elliot clearly couldn't go back to the orphanage from which he'd been kidnapped – the strange details of which were still being ironed out via an ongoing investigation – and refused to talk with any of the police officers or social workers who came to speak to him. Every time one of them tried, he'd cry for "Doctor Libby" instead, speaking to them only through her.

I'm happy to see your maternal side is finally poking through, her supervisor had told her three days before. *After Phil died, we weren't sure if you'd ever consider settling down again. As traumatic as his unexpected passing was, a young, pretty thing such as yourself should be at home caring for a husband and children, not working day and night at a hospital.* He laughed. *I mean, just look at what this place has done to Shauna – thirty-eight years old and well past her prime. I just don't want to see that happen to you.* The sentiment was voiced with genuine concern as he curled a finger under Libby's chin.

Libby bristled at the unpleasant memory, her hands clenching into fists, before letting out a resigned sigh. She didn't have to take Elliot home, of course. Female or not, she was still a medical professional, and could have treated the boy and then sent him on his way to be placed back into the system. No one would have thought twice about it. But something about Elliot's wide, dark eyes tugged at her heartstrings, and while she'd never planned on having a child of her own, with every day he'd remained in her care, she found it increasingly difficult to turn her back on him – especially after everything he'd been through.

Furthermore – unlike the other doctors and nurses, who seemed to instinctively shy away from the boy – Libby found herself inexplicably drawn to him. Elliot's strange stories and unsettling comments intrigued her; after all, he'd talked to her in detail about her newly deceased patients not once but thrice, citing specifics he couldn't possibly have known via casual hearsay. And while Libby was by no means a gullible woman – medical school had ingrained in her the pursuit of hard, science-backed facts over superstition – the idea that this boy could see the dead…well, what kind of knowledge-hungry individual would she be if she weren't at least a *tiny* bit interested? Regardless of whether he could or couldn't see those who had crossed into the spiritual plane, if such a place even existed, her detailed findings would make for one hell of a paper. All she had to figure out was whether to tailor it for a medical journal or a psychological one, depending on the kid's mental state.

The sound of Elliot's rumbling stomach roused her from her contemplations. "It's getting late, isn't it?" she muttered, glancing at her watch. "Um, I don't really have a lot of food in the house…" Her thoughts trailed to the half-empty bottle of wine and half-eaten turkey sandwich sitting in her otherwise-barren fridge. "How about we order a pizza?"

Elliot's eyes rounded with excitement. "Pizza?"

Nodding, Libby guided him through the narrow mahogany-paneled hallway that connected their two rooms, down the carpeted stairs, past the unused dining table in the cramped, puce-green kitchen, and to the sliding-glass back door, which led to a small fenced-in backyard. A towering oak tree – which had barely been a sapling when her late parents built this house more than thirty years ago – shaded the overgrown lawn from the retreating late-July sun.

"You go play outside, okay?" she told Elliot. "I'll go order us a pizza." She sniffed at the armpit of her work shirt. "Might take a quick shower too…uh, if that's okay?"

Elliot stared at her with a quizzical expression, which she mirrored back at him.

"Uh…right." She rubbed the back of her neck. "I gotta tell ya, kiddo – I'm not exactly the motherly type. I don't even really know what I'm doing, to be honest."

The little boy's shoulders rose in a shrug, brushing against the lobes of his slightly oversized ears. "Can we have pepperoni on our pizza? Like they do on the TV?"

The corners of Libby's mouth quirked into a smile. "Sure thing, kid. You can have all the pepperoni you'd like – it's my favorite topping too." She glanced around the backyard – her eyes settling on the rusted gate that led to the front yard, which led to the street, which fed into a bustling boulevard, full of speeding cars – and swallowed tightly. "I'll be back in fifteen minutes, okay? Just, uh… Just stay in the backyard 'til I get back. Okay?" she repeated, suddenly feeling unsure. *A five year old is old enough to be left unattended for a few minutes…right?* An anxious flurry of common pediatric accidents flipped through her brain like a Rolodex – deep splinters, broken bones, split lips, bloodied knees—

"Okay!" Elliot flashed her a thumbs-up, just like he'd seen the kids do in the pepperoni pizza commercial, then ambled outside, still clutching the stuffed rabbit she'd bought him from the hospital gift shop. Libby watched him from behind the sliding glass for a long moment, giving herself a reassuring internal pep talk as she did, then made her way toward the refrigerator, where a worn magnet for Tony's Pizza was calling her name.

After dialing the number into the rotary phone, she cradled the receiver between her chin and shoulder, still surveying Elliot from the kitchen window.

"Hey, Tony," she greeted the owner after he'd answered on the first ring. "Yep, it's Libby… Yeah, I'll take the usual, please – extra pepperoni, light on sauce… No, not a small." Her eyes darted to the little boy in her backyard who was squatting on his haunches to inspect an overgrown weed that ended in a lovely purple thistle. "Better make that a medium tonight."

• • •

While Libby embarked on her Thursday night ritual of pizza-wrangling and a steaming shower to wash away the grime and stress of the E.R., Elliot tiptoed around the backyard, carrying out his own peculiar ritual. In general, dead people – or, as he thought of them, "sleepers" – didn't bother him. In fact, they often made for better company than the living, since none of *them* acted as though he were strange or frightening. But some sleepers were crankier than others, and those were the ones who made him nervous – especially when they showed up unannounced.

To Elliot's relief, all he found in Libby's backyard were squirrel and dog bones. While the squirrel wasn't particularly interested in playing, the dog – *W-O-O-F-E-R-S*, Elliot carefully sounded out the letters on the collar the hound had been buried with – was all too happy to play a rousing game of catch with the old tennis ball Elliot had unearthed alongside his remains.

"C'mon, Woofers!" Elliot shrieked, using his stuffed bunny to lure the chocolate-colored lab into a spirited game of tag. "Catch me!"

Woofers, who had gotten a little too excited from finally being able to stretch out his stiff legs again, playfully jumped on top of Elliot, knocking him to the ground. The two of them rolled once, twice, three times – landing in a breathless heap in front of two slippered feet.

Clad in a mint-green robe, her wet hair gathered in a towel at the top of her head, Libby gaped at her childhood dog with wide, glassy eyes as she clapped a trembling palm against her mouth. "Woofers? How…?"

Her question was cut short by Woofers himself, who jumped into her arms and began furiously licking her salty face.

"Woofers," she sobbed against his fur. "I never thought I'd see you again!"

Her red-rimmed eyes darted to the flat, moss covered stone her parents had long ago placed beneath the oak tree to mark his grave. She'd been away at college some ten years ago when her dog was struck by a car; it wasn't until she had come home for winter break that her parents finally mustered up the nerve to break the news to her. Ten years later, the memory still made her throat twist into a painful knot.

After enduring a full minute of Libby's bone-crushing embrace, Woofers wriggled free from her arms. With a playful bark, he pressed his front paws to the ground in front of Elliot, who obediently tossed a slobber-covered ball to the other side of the yard for Woofers to chase.

Libby dropped to her knees beside the boy, clutching his shoulders. "I don't understand – *how* are you doing this?"

"Um..." Elliot chewed on his lip, the complexity of the explanation far too great for a five-year-old's limited vocabulary. "Well, if I stand real close to a sleeper, they sometimes wake back up."

"A 'sleeper'?" Libby swallowed, trying to and failing to collect her wits. "Do you mean... Do you mean, like...a person sleeping *underground?*"

"Uh-huh."

"But only...sometimes?"

He shrugged one shoulder, suddenly shy. "If they went to sleep a long time ago, it's harder."

Libby frowned. "You mean, if they died a long time ago, it's harder to bring their soul back?"

Elliot frowned back at her, each of them straining to understand the other.

"A soul…" Libby struggled to find the words without using complex medical jargon. "You know, the thing inside of people that makes them…them. The energy in their brains and bodies that makes them think and talk and move—"

"You mean awake people?" Elliot asked, cocking his head.

"No, not—" Libby's mouth fluttered open and then closed again. *He doesn't understand what 'dead' means,* she marveled. *To him, dead people aren't actually dead – they're just sleeping.*

She scrubbed a hand down her face, which was still damp from her dead dog's very real slobber. "So let me get this straight…if you're near a dead body—er, a *sleeping* body," she amended, seeing his confusion, "that went to sleep recently…it's easier to…wake them up?"

His expression brightened. "Right!"

"Of course," Libby breathed. "The mortuary is below the E.R. That's how you were talking to Carol, isn't it?"

Elliot nodded, even though he didn't know what a mortuary was.

The doctor's eyes trailed back to her childhood dog, who was busy chasing a squirrel around the base of the tree where his bones used to be buried. "H-How long—" She swallowed, then tried her question again. "How long can he stay like this – with us?"

"Until he doesn't wanna stay anymore… or I have to go inside to eat," Elliot said with an accompanying rumble of his empty tummy. "Is the pizza coming soon?"

As if on cue, the doorbell rang, eliciting an exuberant "Yippee!" from Elliot.

The moment he ran inside, Woofers disappeared into thin air.

Libby started, her wide, green eyes blinking rapidly for the span of a single, protracted second, before she darted inside after Elliot. After hastily tipping the delivery driver and inadvertently slamming the door in his face, she ushered Elliot to the kitchen table, where he eyeballed the long strings of gooey cheese dangling from the slice of pepperoni pizza she was serving him with wide-eyed reverence. Meanwhile, Libby was still shaking from the sight of her beloved, albeit decidedly dead, childhood dog running around the backyard – a dog that then disappeared into thin air the moment Elliot had skipped off.

She forced herself to wait for him to chew and swallow at least three bites before asking, "Do you *have* to be near the remains for it to work?"

Elliot stared at her in confusion.

"The remains – er, the sleeping bodies," Libby amended with the tiniest of shudders. "Do you always need to be near them to bring them back to life? Or can you do it from far away?"

Sadness flickered across the boy's face. "I tried talking to my mommy when I was at the orphanage but she was too far away. But Kimmy and Mari are there and I sometimes played with them and their friends."

Libby swallowed. "Kimmy and Mari are…dead?"

Elliot shrugged again, confirming her suspicion that he didn't fully understand the meaning of "dead." "They sleep under the orphanage with the other kids, from when the first orphanage burned down."

Libby leaned back in her chair, running a trembling hand through damp blonde hair. Try as she might, she couldn't keep her thoughts from trailing back to Phil – the charming, handsome EMT she'd met four years ago, back when she was toiling away as a fresh-faced, twenty-six-year old resident in a trauma center full of pinched-faced male physicians who refused to take her seriously.

But Phil did.

It took no time at all for the two of them to forge a close friendship, which was followed by a fierce, yet tender, romance. When he proposed six months later, no one at the hospital or in their circle of friends batted an eye; even the most cynical of cynics could see they were meant to be together. One year later – two weeks before their wedding – Phil was the first to arrive at the grisly scene of a multi-car crash. While he was struggling to free an unconscious driver from his mangled vehicle, a semi-truck collided with the upended bed of the driver's truck, killing all three of them.

She closed her eyes and pressed her fist to her mouth, forcing her rising emotions back where they belonged.

"Do you have a tummy ache?" Elliot asked, eyeing her untouched slice of pepperoni pizza.

"Oh, uh…no." She reached forward and shoved a big bite in her mouth, forcing herself to quickly chew and swallow, before leaning forward and asking, "Does anyone else know about this?"

"About pizza?"

"No." She took a deep, steadying breath. "That you can, um…that you can wake up people who are sleeping underground?

"Mommy and Daddy and Sister Maggie and Sister Constance knew, but I don't think they liked it very much."

Libby nodded to herself, wrangling her panic and grief into submission by instead focusing on pure logic – a coping mechanism she'd long ago developed as an emotional crutch. *If I could study him, gather enough evidence to write a scientific paper about his abilities, I could present my findings to The American Journal of Medicine.* Her eyes widened. *I could win a Nobel Prize in Physiology – me, a female! It would send all the chauvinistic physicians of the world into an uproar,* she thought, her lips curling into a giddy smile.

"This is the best food I ever ate!" Elliot exclaimed.

Pulled from her fanciful reverie, Libby's gaze settled back on the little boy, who was happily dangling his legs from his chair while he ate, the knees of his brown corduroy pants stained from rolling in the grass with Woofers.

Her buoyed spirits slowly began to deflate.

If I parade Elliot in front of the AJM, his face will be plastered on the front page of every newspaper in the country. People would be terrified of him... He'd never be able to act like a normal kid ever again. Her shoulders rose and fell in a heavy sigh as she remembered her own curtailed childhood, which had been cut short the moment her younger sister had been born with a long list of health problems that eventually claimed her life, just before her fifth birthday. Libby was eleven years old when Peggy died.

The poor kid wouldn't even get a say in the matter. He'd just get whisked away for experiments…or locked up in a mental institution. She swallowed. *Hell, we* both *might get locked up, which would be the end of my medical license and my career.*

No. She shook her head, pushing away the frightening thought. *I'll just have to keep him close. Study him. Write up all my findings… And then, when he's old enough, we can publish it together: Shermann and Whitman, et al.* Her heart fluttered in excitement. *Hell, we could travel to all the Ivy League schools and top medical programs to discuss the implications – maybe even do a paid lecture series!* She exhaled sharply through her nose, shaking her head in wonder at all the possibilities that lay ahead. *Just like Dad.*

Libby's eyes darted over to the mantle in the living room, where a faded black and white photo of her parents on their wedding day was resting just beside her and Phil's cobweb-covered engagement photo. Her father had been considered one of the top neurosurgeons in the state of Iowa before the death of his youngest daughter – and the persistent tremor in his hands he'd developed as a result of it. Libby's immaculate school record notwithstanding, her father's reputation had been the only reason she'd been accepted into medical school as one of four women in a class of nearly four hundred. But he'd suffered a stroke a year before she graduated, and her mother – a lifelong smoker who had increased her intake to two packs a day after Peggy's death – had succumbed to a pulmonary embolism a year and a half into Libby's residency. Neither had lived long enough to see her pass her board certifications. They, her baby sister, and her fiancé were all buried in the same cemetery, which Libby went fifteen minutes out of her way to circumnavigate both to and from the hospital, rather than having to pass it.

"Do you miss your parents?" she asked Elliot softly.

He stopped chewing mid-bite, the tears in his eyes catching both him and Libby by surprise.

"Oh!" She abruptly rose from her chair and scooped him into a tight hug. "Hey – it's okay," she murmured, patting his back. "I miss my mom and dad too." She felt Elliot wipe his nose on her robe, and while that might have irritated her twenty-four hours ago, at that moment, it didn't faze her.

"Are you going to leave me too?" He sniffled against her shoulder.

"Never," Libby answered fiercely, her decision to protect him from the rest of the world solidifying into stone. She pulled away from the hug, extending her pinky towards Elliot.

He stared at it, unsure what to do.

"You give me your pinky, like this"—she hooked her pinky around his—"and then we both make a pinky promise, which can't ever be broken."

"Ever?"

"Never, ever." Libby shook her head. "So, you gotta believe me when I say I *pinky promise* to never leave you, okay?"

He sniffled, scrubbing the tears from his eyes with his free hand. "Okay."

"And now I need you to make a pinky promise to me. Do you think you can do that, Elliot?" When he nodded, she continued, "You can't ever tell people about Kimmy, Mari, Carol, or even Woofers. What you can do – waking up dead people, I mean – you can't tell anyone about that, *ever*. It'll just be our special secret…okay?"

"Our special secret," Elliot repeated, a shaky smile stretching his freckled cheeks. "Pinky promise."

"Good boy." Libby ruffled the wild mop of dark hair atop his head. "Now, hurry up and finish your pizza. I'm gonna run outside real quick, and when I come back, we'll watch *Bewitched* together." She nodded to the brown couch and small antenna TV in the living room, nestled in the corner beside the mantle. "Sound good?"

"Okay!" Elliot beamed, even though he had no idea who or what "Bewitched" was.

Thirty minutes later, after Elliot had changed into one of Libby's oversized t-shirts, which she had given him to use as temporary nightclothes, and Libby had put away the shovel she'd removed from the garage and changed out of her muddy robe, the two of them settled in on the couch with a big bowl of popcorn and Libby's resurrected childhood dog, who sat between the two of them, basking in warmth and an endless supply of vigorous head scratches.

ONE FOOT IN THE GRAVE

When Lilah pulled up to the last known residence of Anthony DeWitt, the main suspect in her ongoing investigation of Elizabeth Simmons' disappearance, she let out a relieved sigh. The neighborhood was relatively well-kempt, with neat front yards and painted fences that had only begun to peel from the recent frost. The old DeWitt house, however, stood alone at the end of the cul-de-sac, as though the other houses were afraid to catch whatever disease was ailing it. Not only was there no shotgun-wielding owner waiting for her on the porch, but there was hardly any porch at all. The concrete slab had long ago crumbled into disrepair, along with the rest of the house, which sported a massive FORECLOSURE sign tacked to the front door.

With a quick glance over her shoulder to make sure no one was watching, Lilah trotted around the side of the house, where several planks of wood had been haphazardly nailed over a broken window. As she fixed her gaze on it, her eyes became distant and glazed. A moment later, the weathered planks had transformed into polished hardwood, the rusted nails were shiny and new, and broken glass shards had flown up from the ground, reforming themselves into a smooth pane. Eventually, the wooden planks fell away altogether, revealing a brand-new, intact window that Lilah easily pushed open and hoisted herself inside. When her Converse sneakers made contact with the other side, she found herself standing in the middle of a dilapidated living room with torn-up hardwood floors, a couch with bare springs and protruding stuffing, and a fireplace surrounded by charred bricks and a rusted set of wrought-iron fire pokers. Broken picture frames lay scattered across the fraying area rug, which reeked of sulfur and ammonia – the overpowering stench of which made Lilah's eyes water.

Crinkling her nose, she removed her perpetual calendar watch from her wrist and set it on one of the drink-stained wooden end tables. Her eyes once more focused on something unseen and faraway, and the dials of the watch began spinning backward. As they did, the picture frames on the floor flew back up to their respective nails, the peeling yellow wallpaper adhered itself back to the mahogany wood panels, and the hardwood floor resolidified, its jagged splinters smoothing back into place as the planks parsed themselves back together.

Over the years, Lilah's internal clock had gotten more and more attuned; she could feel the decades passing, could differentiate between one year and the next, could sense the passing of months, weeks, even days. As with any physical ability, the more she practiced, the better she was able to calibrate that internal clock, so much so that her perpetual calendar watch had become more of a safety net than a necessity. That said, she still needed work on navigating the minutiae of minutes, accepting that *that* type of precision might take a lifetime to hone.

Lilah let out a deep breath, her eyes once more refocusing as she glanced at her watch on the table, noting the year: 1980. She brushed her fingers across the DeWitt family photos, which rippled and shimmered from the disturbed time dilation. She recognized Anthony DeWitt's much-younger, adolescent face in several of them, along with a handful of other faces that appeared to be his mom, dad, and siblings. Based on the parents' straight-laced, bookish demeanors, Lilah hazarded a guess that Anthony had inherited the house from them before setting up what smelled like a homemade meth lab, if her single prior experience with such a crime served her nasal memory correctly.

Shuddering, she made her way around the increasingly messy house as the next ten years rapidly ticked by like ten minutes, leading up to the week of April twelfth, 1990. She wasn't nervous about the previous owners popping back into existence, since her abilities only affected the age of the materials that were present within the radius of her chrono-bubble. In other words, she couldn't conjure up anything or anyone that wasn't presently there. After all, she didn't travel *through* time, she merely reshaped it around her.

When the dials on the watch marked the last evening Elizabeth Simmons had been seen, Lilah turned in a slow circle, took a deep breath, then anxiously made her way toward the typical burial places – the basement and backyard. This was the part of her job she both anticipated and dreaded: the moment the victims' remains would momentarily come back to life, creating a play-back recording of their final moments on Earth. Oftentimes, the victims were distressed, spurring Lilah to try to comfort them. It was during these upsetting moments that Lilah repeatedly reminded herself that their souls had long since left their bodies, leaving nothing but a photocopied husk, whose memories were limited to the moment of their resurrection. Without their souls, resurrecting the victim's bodies in such a way meant nothing in the past would have changed – for better or worse – nor would the moment of their deaths be prolonged or exacerbated in any way.

Nevertheless, her palms were clammy as she peeked out the kitchen window and into the overgrown backyard, then made her way down the stairwell that led to the basement, where a furnace was humming and a puce-green dryer was thumping loudly on the concrete floor. Apart from that, nothing – and no one – stirred.

With a sigh of both disappointment and relief, Lilah made her way back upstairs and into the living room, where she was surprised to find a woman in a pink robe and hair curlers gaping at her with bulging eyes.

"Who in the Lord's name are you?" the woman shrieked, hurling a frying pan in Lilah's direction.

Lilah yelped, covering her head as she dove out of the way. As she did, the time bubble abruptly popped, plunging her back into the present – albeit with a frying pan sailing over her head and the ceramic jar teetering on the opposite end table now crashing to the ground.

A plume of ashes enveloped Lilah, sending her into a coughing fit that quickly morphed into an infuriated groan. She'd learned long ago to search for things like urns before creating a bubble, as rogue remains always proved an unpleasant surprise.

What a rookie mistake! she chided herself, fumbling to put the pieces of the urn back together.

It was a futile effort, of course. While her time bubbles were ephemeral, the consequences of them were not. She'd learned that the hard way when she accidentally sent a self-proclaimed "shaman" – one Michaelangelo Z. Hastings – into the past, where he promptly got skewered by a tree that had been innocently growing in that exact spot twenty years before. Sheriff Reid and Lilah's father had repeatedly assured her that Mike had had enough tainted mushrooms in his system to kill an elephant and likely wouldn't have lasted through the night regardless, but the experience had permanently shaken her. Luckily, it had taught her something as well: No matter how well she could manipulate the passage of time, death was death. Both inside and outside the confines of a time bubble, once a soul is ripped from its body, it can't be put back.

With a sigh and a silent apology to their previous owner, Lilah gently scooped the ashes back into the lower portion of the broken urn, then set the lid haphazardly on the top jagged edge.

For the next half hour, Lilah carefully walked through the house, fast-forwarding and rewinding the years leading up to, and well after, Elizabeth Simmons' disappearance, combing through every inch of space and time. But her efforts were in vain. For better or worse, there were no other remains in Anthony DeWitt's house.

Discouraged, Lilah let herself back out through the window, letting time fall back into place behind her. When she slumped into the driver's seat of her car, her eyes darted first to the late afternoon sun, from which the frosted shadow of the abandoned DeWitt house was darting farther away, then landed on the manila envelope she'd borrowed from the sheriff's desk.

Accompany L. to grave at First Presb. Church in Whitehall to interview for leads.

"May as well learn *something* today," she muttered as she retrieved the folded map from the glove box. The idea of going to the graveyard by herself to interview a self-proclaimed serial killer made her heart thump heavily against her sternum, but as she'd repeatedly told her father, bones and ashes never hurt anyone…

Or so she thought.

• • •

Between the icy roads and the fact that nearly everything in Montana is scattered and sprawling, it took the better part of an hour for Lilah to reach the First Presbyterian Church on the westernmost outskirts of Whitehall, behind which an untamed grove of trees and a private cemetery lay. When she found no one inside the church, Lilah walked over to the rusty gate, unlatched and propped it open with a rock, and then got back in her car to drive through. The cemetery was too small to navigate by vehicle, so she parked her car on the side of the narrowing dirt road to search for Elliot Whitman's grave on foot. Unpruned pine trees and overgrown weeds had snarled over much of the gravel footpath. Lilah treaded lightly, careful not to trip over upturned roots or tilted gravestones – most of which appeared to mark deceased pastors and church congregants, she noted.

Was Elliot one of them? She glanced at the manila envelope she was holding. Apart from his name, little was known about the perpetrator, who had confessed his crimes to a pastor shortly before taking his own life ten years ago.

Did he kill himself here? she mused, a fresh shudder seizing her as she thumbed through the multitude of papers. *Is that why he was buried —*

Her foot caught on a broken stone, sending her pitching forward. With a startled gasp, she barely managed to catch her balance on a crooked maple tree that had become stooped and gnarled with age. Lilah's eyes widened as they fell on the worn gravestone nestled just underneath it. Unadorned and unkempt, it had a large crack running through the center of the inscription, which read, simply, "ELLIOT WHITMAN, 1964 – 1990."

"So young." Lilah muttered, inspecting the stone with a grimace.

The grave didn't list the exact date of Elliot's death, and the stack of papers she'd given naught but a cursory glance hadn't prominently listed it, either – which meant timing her interview would be trickier than usual.

Of course, she could have just *read* the file, which Reid had repeatedly chided her about, reminding her that ninety percent of detective work was paperwork. But there was just *so much* of it. And today was more of a preliminary endeavor to gather basic info, anyway – namely, figuring out how cooperative the subject was willing to be so she and Reid could come up with an appropriate strategy to coerce the information from him later.

With a grunt of irritation, she settled in beside the grave, placing her jacket under her bottom to protect it from the icy ground, and carefully set her gold watch atop the gravestone. The air shimmered around her as time became displaced, and two decades of seasons came and went like a sped-up movie montage. Eventually, the dial of her watch struck December 31, 1990. With decreasing speed, the dials slowly ticked backward. Winter turned to Autumn. Autumn turned to Summer. Summer turned to Spring.

And, finally, just as Spring was turning back into Winter, Elliot appeared.

Tall and lanky, but with labor-hardened muscles showing through his form-fitting black t-shirt, he closed his eyes and took a long, deep breath, filling his lungs for the first time in over ten years. He didn't seem startled or confused like so many of the other deceased people she had interviewed over the years. In fact, when he opened his eyes again, they immediately landed on her, narrowing into coolly appraising slits... as though he'd been expecting her.

Don't be ridiculous. Lilah shook her head roughly, then scrambled to her feet, her heart thumping and her mouth going dry. "H-Hello," she stammered. "U-Um, my name is Lilah Quinn... Can you tell me your name? Do you remember what year it is?"

Elliot didn't answer. He just stared at her, sending a cold shiver down Lilah's spine. She felt as though he could see directly into her soul.

She crossed her arms over herself as though they were protective armor, rubbing at the fresh goosebumps that appeared on her skin. "Hello?" she asked again, her voice coming out shriller and weaker than she would have liked. She cleared her throat. The lump embedded in it didn't budge. "C-Can you hear me?"

The young man cocked his head at her, his dark hair falling across his storm-gray irises. "Lilah Quinn?" he whispered. The surprise that flickered across his face was quickly replaced by an unfurling smile that turned her blood to slush.

"Y-Yes," she forced herself to answer. "A-And I came here to ask you about a confession you made—"

Elliot took a step closer to her, which made her take a reflexive step back.

"Lilah Quinn," he whispered again, his raspy voice scraping against her ears like dried leaves as he took another step forward.

Her eyes darted to his muddy boots, which were no longer rooted to the narrow confines of his grave.

That had never happened before.

"H-How are you doing that?" she spluttered, backing away until her shoulders were pressed against rough bark. With every step the murderer took from his grave, from his own remains, Lilah's eyes became rounder and rounder.

Elliot extended his arm in her direction, his bloodless fingers straining and grasping as though they meant to wrap around her throat.

"Stop!" Lilah cried out.

The bubble wavered alongside her mounting emotions, making Elliot's age flicker alongside the unstable, swirling seasons.

"Lilah Quinn," he whispered again, now a little boy with wild, dark hair and unsettlingly pale cheeks. Oblivious to his vacillating years, he stalked toward her with time-stiffened legs.

"Get away from me!" she pleaded.

Without warning, the boy's icy fingers abruptly shot forward to snatch Lilah's wrist. He should have reverted to bones the instant his flesh made contact with hers. But Elliot Whitman remained, the bone-dry heat of late summer filling the rapidly shrinking space between them.

Lilah squeezed her eyes shut, blinking away frightened tears. At her silent plea, the time vortex snapped like a rubber band, inviting the frosty bite of winter back with a vengeance. Lilah let out a sigh of relief as a fresh yet welcoming chill snaked down her spine.

The boy was gone.

"Thank God," she muttered, dropping her hands to her thighs to catch her breath. The cold air was already burning her lungs; it felt as though the graveyard had cooled twenty degrees in two minutes. After retrieving her jacket from the ground, Lilah snatched her watch from the grave, double-checking the time and date as she slowly and shakily rose to her feet. When she turned around, a bloodcurdling scream shattered from her throat.

Elliot Whitman was standing in front of her, his face as pale as ash.

"Lilah Quinn," he rasped, reaching for her.

Instinct replaced thought as Lilah shoved past him with all her might, her sneakers sailing over broken headstones and snarled roots as she raced back toward the car. Her hand reached out to yank open the door, then hurriedly slammed and locked it behind her as she sank into the driver's seat. Without stopping to see if the boy was still following her, she turned on the ignition, slammed on the accelerator, and shot up the dirt drive, sending a spray of dust and gravel in her wake. It was only when she had shot past the gate, her front passenger wheel knocking aside the rock that had been holding it open, that she eased her foot from the gas pedal, risking a glance in the rearview mirror.

Standing still as a statue, his two bone-white hands clutching the rusted bars of the gate, was Elliot, his cold eyes narrowing as he watched her car disappear around the bend.

CHAPTER 7
STAIRCASE TO HEAVEN

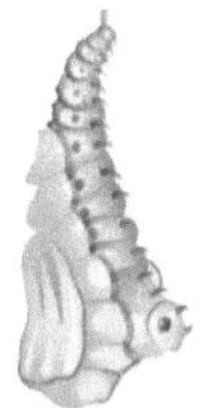

After leaping between the sliding doors of the school bus before they had even fully opened, Elliot dashed the entirety of the two blocks between the bus stop and home, raced up the narrow walkway leading to the porch, then burst through the front door with a breathless *"Ma!"*

"I'm upstairs, El!" Libby hollered back. "Just got home!"

Pausing only to dump his backpack on the floor and rouse Woofers from his "nap" inside his special paw-engraved urn atop the mantle, Elliot bounded up the stairs two at a time, skidding to a stop that bunched up the hallway runner underneath his shoes, then did a sliding hairpin turn into Libby's bedroom, where she was tiredly changing out of her work scrubs. The moment she saw Elliot, breathless and flustered, her bloodshot eyes brightened.

"Well?" she demanded, trying to contain her own excitement. "What did she say?" When Elliot didn't immediately answer, she let out a groan. "Don't do this to me, kid! I've been so nervous all day! Now come on – spill!"

Elliot's already-wavering poker face broke into a wide grin. "She said yes!"

"Get outta town!" Libby shoved his shoulder. "Marsha Summers said yes? As in, you two are officially going steady?" She bit her lip, trying to keep from laughing at the notion.

"Uh-huh!" Elliot's impossibly wide grin grew even wider. "I did exactly what you told me to. I complimented her dress, telling her how it brought out the color of her eyes—"

"Perfect." She nodded approvingly.

"—then I showed her this really cool caterpillar I found at recess—"

"Gross, but innovative."

"—and then I asked her if she wanted to be my girlfriend."

"What did she say when you asked her? Tell me word for word!"

Elliot scrunched his face, trying to remember exactly how Marsha had put it. "She said, 'Well, Tyler Nelms asked me to be his girlfriend too, but he has bad breath and you don't. I can't get married until I'm at least thirteen, though.'"

"Discriminating *and* pragmatic – I like her already!" Libby beamed, then pulled Elliot into a tight squeeze. "My little ten-year-old Cassanova. I'm so proud of you! When can I meet her?"

"I was thinking maybe I could invite her over for dinner tomorrow?" he asked, plopping on her bed beside Woofers, whose head was resting on his paws.

Libby ducked into her closet, where she quickly tugged on a loose-fitting Beatles t-shirt and torn bell bottom jeans. "For our sacred Thursday Night Pepperoni Pizza Party?" she asked. With a grimace, she yanked the elastic band out of her messy bun, turned her head upside down, and ran her fingers through shoulder-length blonde hair before putting it back up into a high ponytail that removed at least five years from her face. "Are you sure you're ready to take such a big step in your relationship?"

Elliot's nod was solemn. "If I'm gonna marry her someday, then she has to know all the different sides of me – including the Thursday-night pizza side."

Libby's heart skipped a beat, but she kept her face carefully schooled. "But not *all* sides of you…right, little man? You haven't told her about…well, you know." She gestured her head at Woofers, who was curled up in a tight ball, snoozing. She frowned slightly. Was it just her imagination, or had he been sleeping a lot more these past few days?

Elliot looked confused for a moment, then heaved a big sigh when he understood her meaning. "I didn't tell her about that. But, Mom—"

"No buts," Libby said sternly. "When you're an adult and in a long-term, committed relationship, it will be your choice, not mine—"

"But Marsha and I are getting married!"

Libby did her best to guise her laugh as a halfway-believable cough. "Well, when you two get married – as adults, that is, not during recess – you can choose what to tell Marsha. But in the meantime, you made me a pinky promise… And above everything else, pinky promises are what?" she prompted.

"Unbreakable," Elliot intoned, rolling his eyes. "I know."

"That's my boy," she said, kissing the top of his head. "Now run downstairs and get started on your homework. I put out some peanut butter crackers for you on the table. I'll be downstairs in a few minutes to help you with your fractions, okay?"

"Okay." After rousing Woofers from his nap – which took two tries – Elliot pushed himself up from the bed and walked out of the room, yawning hound dog in tow.

Libby watched them leave, biting her lip. It had been five years since Woofers had been brought back to life. And while he had always eaten and barked and played like any other dog, as of late, his demeanor seemed…different. Tired. Less enthusiastic. In truth, the more time Woofers spent here, in his second life, the more lethargic he became. It was as though…

Libby swallowed. *As though he's too far past his expiration date.*

In the recesses of her mind, she had long wondered if it had been right to keep Woofers around for so long. Not only for her languishing dog's sake, but for Elliot's. At ten years old, he finally understood death to mean that the soul had left behind a lifeless husk – and that for everyone else in the world, that was the end of the road. The body's soul, perhaps, would move on. But the body itself…well, the body doesn't get second chances. What was she teaching him, allowing him to circumvent the very laws of nature in such a way? How would he ever understand grief and loss – to be able to properly process such definitive, inevitable things – if she allowed him such a crutch?

A weight settled in her chest, making it harder to breathe. It wasn't healthy, what he was doing. What *they* were doing. Death wasn't meant to be circumnavigated. And loss – well, for everyone else, at least – was simply a part of life.

To continue to pretend otherwise would be developmentally and psychologically damaging to them both.

Libby's thoughts drifted to her last patient of the day – a young woman who suffered from Manic Depression, which, chief among many complex factors, stemmed from a debilitating fear of abandonment. The woman's boyfriend had broken up with her earlier that day, prompting her to swallow a bottle of acetaminophen in an attempt to stifle what she had described as the "indescribable, insurmountable pain" of his abrupt departure. They had been dating for six weeks.

It was an extreme case, to be sure. But it solidified Libby's resolve: Elliot couldn't run from loss his entire life. Nor could she. As much as it broke her heart, it was time to let Woofers go – and for both her and Elliot to sit with that passing, acknowledging their shared grief instead of running from it. She took in a deep, steeling breath, running through the words in her head to get them just right, then turned and walked out of her room.

We could spread his ashes in the backyard, where his grave used to be. And maybe after a few months, we could adopt a new puppy from the shelter. Libby sighed, chewing on her lip. *Except puppies have to be housebroken, and who has time for—*

She let out a muted gasp as blackness flickered in front of her vision. For one brief, startling moment, she found herself standing both at the top and bottom of the steps, as though she somehow existed in two places at once. Blinding white light exploded in her eyes. *Hypotension?* Libby squeezed her eyes shut and shook her head roughly, trying to clear the overlapping visions from her mind.

At that same moment, her toe caught on the runner that had been left bunched up in the hallway, sending her sprawling face-first down the stairs. As her head struck the bottom step, her neck snapped, killing her instantly.

The pencil Elliot was chewing on dropped to the floor. Slowly, his breath caught and held, he turned around in his chair to find Libby's body lying in a crumpled, unmoving heap at the bottom of the staircase.

"Ma?" Elliot whispered, rising to his feet. Tears pricked at his eyes, though he didn't fully understand why. "Mom?" he tried again.

No answer.

He took a step closer. The lights in the room flickered and dimmed. With a soft yip, Woofers reverted back into a puppy, then disappeared altogether.

Another step. A moth fluttered by, then turned to dust. The wallpaper sloughed off the walls like dead skin, and the shag carpet in the living room became matted and brown with age. Behind the tattered drapes and furls of flaking wallpaper, the drywall began to crumble, exposing rotting studs underneath. The rickety planks vibrating beneath Elliot's feet splintered and cracked, while cobwebs and dust settled over everything in the house like freshly fallen snow.

Elliot took another step, his feet landing on grass instead of wood. The sounds of the prairie were all around him: crickets, birds, and a warm, fluttering breeze. The house had disappeared, reduced to glittering piles of nails, shattered glass, broken bricks, and crumbled slabs of concrete that were neatly arranged inside the small patch of otherwise-untouched grassland.

In the center of it all, partially hidden among tall grass and gently swaying purple thistles, Libby still hadn't moved.

"Mom?" Elliot knelt beside her body. When he saw the unnatural angle of her neck, the house snapped back into place, sending a violent jolt ricocheting through his teeth. "Mom!" He shook her shoulder roughly, just as he'd done to his biological mother when he'd found her cold, unmoving body lying in bed five years ago.

Libby's head lolled limply to the side, her eyes unseeing.

"MOM!" The word tore from Elliot's lungs like a primal roar. Time seized and convulsed all around him. The house and furniture flickered in

and out of existence; where carpet and wood once lay, trees sprouted and toppled, snow fell and melted, and flowers bloomed and withered. Animals reappeared from the soil and momentarily lived again, only to return to the ground where their bodies disintegrated into blossoming mushrooms.

And then, all at once, everything stopped.

Libby sat bolt upright with a wheezing gasp, her hands flying to her throat. Whites shone all around her green eyes as she looked around the room, her shoulders rising and falling alongside her hastened, shallow breaths. When her wide, frightened gaze fell on Elliot, it held.

The two of them stared at one another for a long moment, frozen in mute horror.

And then the real screaming started.

CHAPTER 8

STRANGERS IN THE NIGHT

Lilah burst through the front door of her house, breathless and sobbing. "Dad!" she shouted. *"Dad!!"*

Stanley came barreling out of the downstairs bathroom a split second later, boxers hastily yanked into place but trousers still bunched around his ankles. "What is it?" he bellowed, tripping and again righting himself as he staggered into the living room, fumbling to clasp his belt. "What happened?"

"I'm being followed!" Lilah screeched as she flung herself at him.

Stanley caught her in his arms, momentarily rendered speechless. It had been more than a decade since his little girl had come running into the house, crying for her dad. And now here she was, a grown woman, gazing up at him with frazzled hair and terrified, red-rimmed eyes.

"Who's following you?!" he demanded, his own eyes bulging with feral intensity as he gripped her by her narrow shoulders.

"E-Elliot W-Whitman!" Lilah half-sobbed, half-hiccupped, her rushed words stringing together with nary a space or pause in-between. "H-He's supposed to be dead b-but he's not! And I t-tried to tell him to go away b-but he wouldn't and then he t-touched me and he *still* wasn't dead so I drove away as fast as I could and came straight here but I think he's still following me!"

Stanley had only made out about a third of what Lilah was hysterically trying to tell him, but when she said "he" and "following me" he gently shoved her aside, marched over to the front door, and yanked it open, nearly ripping out the hinges as he did. Belt unfastened, shirt flapping, and feet bare, he leapt onto the front porch, teeth bared and fists clenched.

"Where are you, you little punk?" he snarled, his head swiveling wildly from left to right.

There was no one outside, save for Mrs. Hendrickson, who was walking her three poodles and quickly averted her eyes when they fell on Stan's foamy-mouthed state of undress.

After doing a full, frantic lap around their house, searching the shed top to bottom, and even crawling under Lilah's car to ensure it was free of creeps, Stanley stomped back toward the house, giving Mrs. Hendrickson – who was now covertly spying on them through slatted blinds – the stink eye.

"What are you looking at?!" he bellowed in her general direction before slamming and locking the door behind him.

Lilah was sitting on the edge of the couch, hugging her knees against her chest and rocking slightly.

Stanley closed the distance between them in three strides, resting an arm around her shoulders as he sank beside her. "Li, what happened out there? Who was following you?"

"A dead murderer I was trying to interview."

Before the bulging vein in her father's temple could burst, she quickly filled him in on what had happened, too shaken to try to sugarcoat any of the grisly details.

"And then he…he *grabbed* me," she finished a few minutes later, shuddering. "But he didn't revert back into bones or disappear when he did. He…He just stood there, saying my name over and over. When I looked back, he was standing at least a hundred feet away from his grave, just…watching me."

Stan's hands were clenched so tightly, his knuckles were white. Lilah tensed, expecting him to erupt like the Strawberry Fanta and Mentos-fueled volcano she'd made in third grade, but when he finally opened his mouth to speak, his voice was terrifyingly calm.

"Go upstairs and get yourself cleaned up. I'll have dinner whipped up for us by the time you're done."

"But I'm not—"

"Whether you feel hungry or not, you need to eat. You're in shock."

Lilah nodded mutely as she rose from the couch, then made her way to the stairs.

"And Li?"

Her hand stilled on the banister. "Yeah, Dad?"

"After dinner, either you can call Reid and tell him you're off the Whitman case, or I will. Up to you."

Lilah nodded again. She didn't have the strength to argue; at that moment, in fact, she couldn't have agreed with her father more.

. . .

Dinner had involved a long series of follow-up, rapid-fire questions from her father, some of which had to do with Elliot's unusual chrono-bubble behavior, but most of which had to do with Lilah herself – namely, her powers. Many years ago, Stanley had believed Lilah possessed some rare, supernatural form of epilepsy, and therefore insisted she took a daily pill that suppressed both her seizures and her powers. Now that Lilah was openly embracing her abilities, rather than repressing them, she had been entirely seizure-free for three years. During that period of time, her powers had grown, though their scope and limitations remained consistent. Chief among those consistencies: anything – or anyone – directly touching Lilah had always been shielded from her time-bending abilities. In other words, if a dead murderer reached out and gripped her by the bare wrist, he should have immediately reverted to bones. And yet when Elliot had done that, he remained unaffected.

Did that mean the specifics of Lilah's abilities were shifting, and if so, what did that mean – both for her, and for those in her immediate vicinity?

To help answer that question, Stanley mustered up the courage to suggest she conjure a time bubble while holding his hand to see if the manifestation of her powers had shifted. Lilah rewound the clock two complete decades, but as always, Stanley – his hand firmly latched onto her wrist – remained unaffected. The two of them repeated the experiment with whatever else they could find in the vicinity: apples, newspapers, a slice of pizza – even a daddy longlegs that Stanley had plucked from the kitchen corner. Beneath the umbrella of Lilah's time bubble, the rotten apple Stanley was holding in his left hand reverted back to a fresh apple the moment he placed it in Lilah's palm. Even the daddy longlegs – which Lilah forced herself to hold in her bare hand, her face contorted into a scrunched-up grimace as she did – was shielded from her time-bending effects.

So why was Elliot immune to them?

It wasn't even eight o'clock when Lilah crawled into bed less than two hours after dinner, too tired even for the latest episode of *Buffy the Vampire Slayer*. And yet, as exhausted as she was, her mind was racing as she lay wide awake in bed, staring at the bare branches of the elm tree clawing at her window. She clutched her lavender bedspread against her chin, trying to push aside the chilling memory of Elliot's pale, cold fingers wrapping around her wrist.

Even as she squeezed her eyes shut, his piercing gaze bore into the backs of her eyelids.

Despite Lilah's quickened heartbeat and the shrill gusts of wind that rattled the shutters, fatigue eventually managed to overtake her. She drifted into a fitful sleep, where her dreams continued to be marred by the boy, who diligently stalked her from nightmare to nightmare. When Lilah started awake several hours into the night, rubbing the sleep from her blurry eyes, she let out a sharp gasp.

There, silently watching her from the shadows of a darkened corner, was Elliot.

She recoiled from the sight with a stifled cry, praying she were somehow still asleep.

"Lilah Quinn," he whispered, his voice as cold and raspy as the wind whistling through her shutters.

She clutched the covers tighter against her body, as though they were a shield. "This is just a dream," she whispered, her voice catching on the lump in her throat. "You aren't real. Ghosts aren't real."

Elliot stepped out of the shadows, his pale face illuminated by the column of blue moonlight trickling in from the window.

A scream rose and froze in Lilah's throat. *Wake up!* she silently pleaded with herself. *Please, wake up!*

Someone rapped against the window, making her and Elliot's heads simultaneously jerk in that direction. When two hands reached from outside to push the window open, Lilah tumbled out of bed, her arm flailing for the light. She fumbled until she found the switch, bathing the room in color.

The moment the shadows disappeared, so too did Elliot.

As the window slid open, and a tall, lanky figure stepped inside, Lilah flung herself across the room.

"Jace!" she sobbed.

He caught her in his arms, pulling her into a tight embrace. "Did I scare you? I'm sor—"

"Not you, him!" She pointed to the empty corner beside the window, where Elliot had been standing moments ago.

Jace stiffened. "Who?"

Her heart still crashing against her ribcage, Lilah gently pushed away from Jace and sank into the bed. "You wouldn't believe me."

"Try me," he countered.

Lilah took a deep breath, trying to loosen the knots in her chest. "A dead guy I was trying to talk to earlier today. He was standing right there. I…I'm positive."

Without hesitating, Jace wordlessly dropped to the ground to search under her bed, then pulled open the closet door and yanked on the light. There was no one in there, or under her desk. He stuck his head out the window, searching for any sign of movement below, but apart from the swaying tree branches he had used to hoist himself up to the window sill, nothing else moved in the night.

"I'm sorry." Lilah felt a warm flush creep up her cheeks as she rubbed the dull throb in her temples. "I know you probably think I'm crazy, but—"

"I don't think you're crazy at all." Jace cut in. "If you say someone was in here, I believe you." A wave of relief flooded through Lilah as he sat down on the bed beside her, pulling her close. "Should we call the Sheriff?"

She shook her head.

"Do you want to talk about it?" he asked.

Her head shaking intensified. Gently pushing away from Jace's embrace, she frowned up at him. "Jace, what are you doing here? And what's with the window? We're not a couple of high schoolers sneaking around anymore. You can use the front door."

"Um, well…" The tips of his ears turned pink as he ran a hand through his sandy blond hair. "I was so worried about you after your dad called, I finished my last midterm and then drove straight here." He grinned sheepishly. "As for the dramatic window entrance, I had an extra-large slushie back in Idaho and all those extra pit stops I had to make got me here later than I was hoping. I didn't think Stan would appreciate me ringing the doorbell at one a.m."

"You're insane," Lilah marveled, hugging him so tightly the air rushed out of his lungs in a *whoosh*. When she let go a few moments later, her eyes darted to the corner where Elliot had been standing. "Stay with me? Please?"

"Of course I will." He brushed a soft kiss against her lips, then pressed his forehead against hers. "Fair warning, though – I told your father I was on my way, but I don't know how thrilled he'll be to see me strolling out of your room tomorrow morning."

Lilah couldn't help but smile at that. "Oh, please. He'll be so happy to see you, I doubt he'll even notice."

Jace snorted as he wriggled out of his purple and gold Huskies baseball jacket, leaving a form-fitting white t-shirt, unbuckled and stepped out of his jeans, then climbed into bed with Lilah. She immediately wrapped her arms around him and nuzzled against his warm chest.

"You have no idea how happy I am to see you," she breathed against his neck.

He kissed the top of her head. "Oh, I think I have some idea." He tightened his arms around her trembling body, pulling her closer.

Lilah took a deep, full breath, comforted by his scent and his touch. But as she switched off the lamp beside her bed, her eyes immediately darted back to the shadows.

"There's no one there," Jace reassured her. "It's just you and me. And I'm not going anywhere."

Nodding, Lilah managed to pull her eyes away from that corner of the room, settling into the comforting warmth of Jace's embrace.

Outside, standing near the base of the elm tree, Elliot stared up at Lilah's darkened bedroom window, his eyes narrowed. As another gust howled against the rattling shutters, he disappeared in a puff of ashes, carried by the wind into the night.

CHAPTER 9
OVER MY DEAD BODY

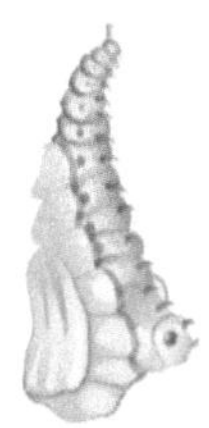

Libby gaped at Elliot, her eyes brimming with tears. "El…" she whimpered, still clutching her throat. "Am I…?" She tried to swallow, to put some moisture back in her mouth, but her tongue had gone completely dry. "Am I…dead?"

"No!" Elliot cried, the ferocity of his words catching her off-guard. "You promised me! You pinky promised you'd never leave me!" He was screaming at her now, his small hands balled into tight, trembling fists. "You can't leave me! You *can't!"*

He stamped his foot and the entire house flickered, its floors and paint momentarily reverting to far newer, pristine states, while Libby flickered into a frightened little girl, no older than seven. It happened so fast – in the blink of an eye – that a casual spectator might have shaken his head and rubbed his eyes, swearing off the drink for good this time.

"I don't want to leave you either," Libby whispered, once more fully grown and holding back tears. "I don't want to leave at all. But I… I…" She trailed off as she pressed her fingers against the side of her neck, where her pulse was fluttering. "I don't understand what's happening. The last thing I remember was my vision going black, followed by the sensation that I was somehow standing in two places at once… And then I…I must have tripped." She frowned, trying to find the words to explain as she pulled herself into a sitting position at the bottom of the stairs. "It was the strangest feeling, El…like I could see myself as it happened."

Elliot hadn't moved from his spot; as his adoptive mother spoke, he tugged at a thread on his shirt, not quite meeting her eyes.

"I saw myself falling"—she swallowed roughly—"and…*dying*. I felt like I was hovering just above myself, watching as you tiptoed over to my body. I was rising higher and higher, drifting farther and farther away…and then something yanked me back"—she looked behind her warily—"back to the top of the stairs. And then I blinked…and I was here. Staring up at you."

Elliot was chewing on his lip, wringing the hem of his shirt in his hands. "I couldn't let you leave me."

Libby blinked slowly, still processing what had happened. "Am I... Am I like Woofers now?" She found herself clutching her wrist, silently counting her heartbeats as she spoke, comforted by every pulse. "If you leave me...where will I go?"

"Um..." He rubbed the back of his neck anxiously. Despite Libby's wide eyes and trembling voice, Elliot could feel the tendrils of fear that had been tightening around his chest slowly begin to loosen. He didn't know what would happen to her or where she would go when he left for school tomorrow morning. But he knew she would still be there when he came home. And to a ten-year-old, that's all that matters. "I'm not—"

Libby shook her head and held up a hand. "Actually, you know what? I don't want to know. I don't want to think about any of that right now. If I do, I...I might fall apart." Indeed, she could feel the familiar chains of panic and grief digging into her ribcage. She shoved the feelings away, relegating them to the deep, walled-off place she'd long ago constructed to carry the heavy burden of losses she'd suffered over the years. If she forbade herself from grieving, from processing their deaths, or even passing by their graves, perhaps, somehow, her loved ones could still be alive. In the same vein, if she just continued living her life as though she'd never died…maybe she hadn't.

Maybe it was all a bad dream.

"Enough crying," she huffed, scrubbing at her tears as though they were a fresh wine stain on white carpet. "It's almost dinner time, and I'm hungry. What do you want to eat? TV dinner? Mac and cheese? Because I'm dying for—" She gulped, darting a glance in Elliot's direction. "Um, I'm starving. How about you? Are you hungry?"

Elliot nodded, scrubbing at his own tear-stained face as he did.

"Mac and cheese it is." Libby forced a reassuring smile that bordered on manic. "After dinner, we'll straighten up the house, since Marsha is coming over tomorrow evening."

Elliot opened his mouth, presumably to cast doubt on that decision "But—"

"Nope!" Libby cut in hastily. "Over my dead body are we going to cancel your very first date! …Get it? *Dead?* Ha ha!" She laughed loudly, gripping her stomach, where it felt as though a lead brick had been firmly lodged. "When that's done," she continued, wiping fresh tears from her eyes, "we'll make a big bowl of popcorn and stay up late and watch *Bewitched*. Everything will be *fine*," she added sternly, noting the fresh quiver in

Elliot's bottom lip. "Hell, everything already *is* fine. Totally fine." She clapped her hands together. "Where's Woofers?"

Before Elliot could answer, she swept past him and into the kitchen, where she grabbed a pot from under the counter and slammed it on the stovetop with a forceful clang that made both of them jump.

Libby cleared her throat. "Go wake Woofers and then get yourself washed up." The grin on her face was frozen as though in plaster. "And you know what? Forget homework. And forget cleaning! Tonight we're eating dinner in front of the TV, got it? And after that, we're making brownies! With marshmallows!"

Elliot's eyes widened. "And ice cream? Can we have that too?"

"Yep." Libby nodded. "Heck, we can have ice cream for dinner if you'd like!"

In spite of himself, a wide grin appeared on Elliot's face. "I'm gonna change into my pajamas first!" he yelled over his shoulder as he ran up the stairs. "Be right back!"

Tears blurred Libby's vision as she watched him go.

And then blackness overtook her.

• • •

The following morning, Libby called in sick, promising the chief of medicine she'd be back on Monday while knowing deep down it was a lie. Elliot went to school as usual, though he took the bus instead of Libby dropping him off. He did his best to keep his thoughts firmly planted in his classroom, but every so often, the memory of his mother falling down the stairs, and the sickening crack that accompanied her landing, punctured his thoughts. The longer the day wore on, the more his stomach twisted itself in knots. By the time he'd trudged home from the bus stop and was reaching to unlock the front door, his stomach was hurting so badly he thought he might be sick. To his relief, the door swung open before he'd even withdrawn the key from the handle, and Libby was standing there, arms crossed and foot tapping.

"I've been waiting for you all day, little man!" she admonished him as he swung his backpack to the floor. "What took you so long? I've just been waiting and waiting, with nothing to do! I haven't even had a chance to clean or start dinner and Marsha will be here in, what—" She glanced at the clock. "Two hours?! That's not nearly enough time!"

"Sorry!" Elliot called as he squeezed past her. "I stopped to look at some tadpoles when I was walking home. There's a whole bunch of them down the street, just swimming around in a big puddle—"

"Well, don't do that again!" Libby snapped, then winced. "Sorry, El. It's just…without you here…there's nothing. Just haze and shadows and endless…time," she finished, clearing her throat roughly. "Um, will you help me clean up the living room? The carpet smells weird, probably needs a good vacuuming." With a soft gasp, her eyes darted to the staircase.

Dried blood still stained the bottom step.

She swallowed tightly. "Um…El?"

"Yeah?" he asked as he hung his jacket across the back of the couch, his attention firmly rooted on the zipper he'd taken a sudden interest in.

"Where…" Blood was rushing in Libby's ears and her head was swimming, making her stomach lurch. She clutched her wrist tightly, silently counting the steady beats of her heart until her labored breathing began to slow and blurred edges of her vision came back into focus.

"Ma?" Elliot asked, concern creeping into his voice. He glanced at her, then quickly returned to the jacket zipper he was fiddling with. "Are you okay?"

"Um…" She tried again. "M-My body…" Her eyes darted to the mantle, where Woofers took his "naps" inside his urn when Elliot wasn't around. She was clutching her wrist so tightly, her hand had gone numb. "When you're not here…wh-where…I mean, what…" Her knees were shaking, so she promptly sat on the floor, her eyes glued to the crimson stain at the bottom of the staircase. "Where's my body?" she asked, her voice barely a whisper. "My real body."

Elliot blinked rapidly to keep his vision from turning blurry. "In the basement."

"Oh." Libby pressed her forehead to her knees, forcing herself to take a series of slow, deep breaths. "Okay… Okay." She slowly exhaled through her nose, finding her bearings. "Um, why don't you get started on vacuuming? I, um…I have to make some phone calls. But don't go too far, okay?" Her voice cracked on the last word.

He nodded mutely.

While Elliot quietly straightened up the living room, Libby took out the phone book, thumbing through the yellow pages until she came across her own hospital listing. Her shaking finger ran down the various departments until it settled on "Morgue." She dialed the number, pacing back and forth across the kitchen until she was forced to untangle herself from the cord, then breathed a sigh of relief when Stephen – the morgue worker who'd had a crush on her for years – picked up on the fourth ring.

"H-Hey, Stephen – it's Libby… Yes, Libby Shermann," she said, balancing the phone against her shoulder as she rooted around the cabinet for paper plates and Kool-Aid mix. "I'm fine, how are you? …Yes, it has been a while, I know. Um, I have a favor to ask you, but I'm wondering if we can keep it between us?" When Stephen heartily agreed, Libby grimaced, forcing the words between gritted teeth. "Um…do you happen to know any morticians who, um…who might happen to have a, uh, 'flexible' moral compass?" She pulled out a pen and jotted down several of the names Stephen was casually rattling off on the back of a paper plate, then sighed. "Which of these guys would you say is the most…um, *flexible* in the morality department?" She circled the name he repeated, that of his roommate, Craig. "Okay, thanks. Um, last thing – is this guy trustworthy? That is, can Craig be discreet?" Her face blanched as Stephen listed off an uncomfortably long list of all the dubious and unsavory things Craig – and he – had done and kept quiet about over the years. "Okay, okay – I…I get the point. Thanks, Stephen." She went to hang up the phone, then paused as his nasally voice continued to drone through the speaker, ending on the very question she had been hoping he wouldn't ask. "Trust me when I say you wouldn't believe me if I told you. Have a nice night, Stephen."

With that, she hung up the phone with a shudder.

. . .

Dinner went off without a hitch. Marsha's father dropped her off at promptly 5:00 p.m., though he did linger in the doorway, his eyes flicking to the bare ring finger on Libby's left hand, until she eventually gave him an awkward finger-wave goodbye and shut the door in his face. Pizza arrived twenty minutes later. Neither Libby nor Elliot spoke much as they ate, their eyes darting to the locked basement door more than once. Luckily, Marsha talked more than enough for the three of them, nattering on about school and all the subjects she liked best, the pony her father had recently bought her, and the white polka-dotted dress she was planning on wearing for school picture day tomorrow. Libby smiled and nodded, forcing down bite after bite of cold pizza as the girl regaled them all with the latest fifth-grade drama.

When Marsha and Elliot ran upstairs to play with his brand-new Magna Doodle, Libby found herself trailing behind him as though tethered by invisible rope. With the muffled sounds of laughter trailing from the next room, she ducked into her own bedroom, pressing her back against the wall she and Elliot shared and slid to the ground. Woofers plodded through the doorway a few minutes later, licked the salt from her cheeks, then curled up in her lap to sleep. She hugged him tightly as she buried her face in his fur and let herself cry – really cry – for the first time since Phil had died five years ago.

Not long after that, Marsha's father arrived to pick up his daughter, casually suggesting to Libby that they arrange another playdate for tomorrow evening – this time, with both adults present and a bottle of wine to share between them. Libby politely shut him down, shutting and locking the door before he could protest further. She had more important things to do than entertain the town's most eligible widower, including a whole catalog of errands she would have to rush to complete during her fleeting hours of Elliot-centric existence: making a list of groceries they desperately needed, digging up her outdated will, and figuring out how to pay the bills if she was unable to return to work – to name a few.

But more important than any of that, she first had to dispose of her own remains.

Just as Lilah had predicted, her father was so happy to see Jace the following morning, he'd completely forgotten to threaten to kill him for spending the night in his daughter's bed. Stanley was so elated, in fact, that he sat them both down at the table and began arranging all the ingredients needed for his late wife's famous chocolate chip flapjack recipe.

"Buttermilk…no buttermilk… Regular milk should do the trick, right?" Muttering to himself, he slammed the refrigerator door, balancing a carton of milk, two eggs, and a bottle of Hershey's syrup (since they were also out of chocolate chips). "We don't have any baking powder – wonder if doubling up on the baking soda will work? …Yeah, that'll be fine," he answered himself before Lilah had the chance to open her mouth.

She and Jace exchanged nervous glances.

"So, did Lilah tell you about the zombie that followed her home?" Stanley asked Jace as he dumped what was *probably* eight ounces of milk into a measuring cup, sloshing half of it on the counter as he did.

"Yeah." Jace put an arm around Lilah's shoulder, drawing her close. "She did."

Stanley nodded, then sneezed, as a cloud of flour tickled his nostrils. "I was thinking you and I could head down to the graveyard and rough him up a bit – teach him not to mess with our girl. What do you think?"

"Dad," Lilah cut in, sensing Jace's impending enthusiastic response, "that's not how it works. Elliot's soul has moved on, so you'd just be 'roughing up' an empty vessel. And besides," she added quickly, rubbing at the fresh goosebumps on her arms, "We agreed to stay away from his grave – remember?"

"Probably better not to antagonize the undead," Jace agreed.

"I made it clear that *you* shouldn't go anywhere near his grave – I, on the other hand, am more than happy to pay the creep a visit." Stanley squinted at the bottle of vanilla he was holding, then upended what was supposed to be a teaspoon of it into the lumpy batter.

"Dad, can I help with th—"

"Nope, I've got it!" Stanley violently whisked at his concoction before spooning a large pile of Hershey-stained brown mush into a hot oiled skillet. The batter splattered all over the stovetop and the front of Stan's apron, though he didn't seem to notice. With his tongue caught between his teeth and his bushy eyebrows scrunched in deep concentration, he flipped the skillet with two hands, catching about two-thirds of the half-cooked flapjack as it came sailing back down. After repeating that process several more times, he slapped two plates down in front of Lilah and Jace several minutes later, beaming with flour-dusted cheeks. "Eat up!"

Lilah warily prodded her stack of spongy brown flapjacks with a fork, while Jace instinctively shoved a big bite in his mouth. His eyes narrowed, then bulged, as he chewed.

"Mmm," he mumbled through tearing eyes. "These are *so* good."

Biting back a grin, Lilah cut herself a dainty piece while Stanley watched with bated breath. "So, so good," she agreed, working her features into what she hoped looked like an approving smile.

"Excellent!" With that, Stanley set about making his own plate of flapjacks, humming cheerfully.

It took the better part of a minute for Lilah to muster the strength to swallow the lump of "food" she'd been diligently chewing, and when she finally did, she had to chug a glass of milk to wash the taste away. Meanwhile, Jace had doused his own plate in syrup, shoveling the tooth-aching slop into his mouth like a champ.

"Does your mom know you're in town, son?" Stanley asked as he flipped the skillet, this time only sending a quarter of the batter splattering across the stovetop.

"No, sir," Jace replied after a long swig of milk. "And I'd like to keep it that way, if that's alright. The last time I came to visit, my stepdad and I had a…disagreement."

Lilah stiffened at the memory.

"Oh?" Stanley asked gruffly. "About what?"

"Well, when he offered me a ripped blow-up mattress to sleep on for the week, I argued that I should be able to sleep in my old room—"

"—which Frank has since turned into a second closet to store his clothes and Playboy magazine collection," Lilah cut in.

"—and he disagreed with me," Jace finished. "Heartily."

Stan's eyes narrowed. "Did he hit you?"

"No, but several of his rolled-up Playboy magazines did."

A muscle in Stan's jaw tensed. "Today seems like an excellent opportunity to leave an anonymous tip at the sheriff's office about the lemons that Frank Wainwright has been peddling as 'certified used cars.'" He turned to Lilah. "Speaking of which, have you told Dave that you're off the creep case?"

Technically, he doesn't even know I'm on it. Lilah winced, then muttered, "Uh…yeah."

Her father arched an incredulous eyebrow. "Are you lying?"

"Nope." She shook her head. "Here, Dad, you sit down and eat. I'll clean up."

"I'll help," Jace offered. Lilah flashed him a grateful smile as the two of them darted over to the sink, where they hurriedly dumped the contents of their plates down the disposal before Stanley could notice.

"You guys really wolfed those down," Stanley remarked as he took his seat with a grunt. "I should make flapjacks more often!"

Lilah stifled a groan as she surveyed the disaster area that used to be their kitchen with a pained grimace, then sighed. "Sounds great, Dad."

. . .

"So," Jace started nonchalantly as he and Lilah headed out the front door, "I take it you *haven't* told Sheriff Reid anything about what happened yesterday?"

Zipping up her red down jacket against the rapidly plunging autumn temperatures, Lilah shook her head. "Nope. Your car or mine?"

"Yours." He couldn't bear to look at the hideous orange truck he'd been forced to drive for the last five years, but after tuition, boarding, books, and food, his meager college baseball scholarship didn't leave nearly enough left over for a new car – especially one of the overpriced "lemons" his stepfather kept hounding him to buy at full price. Jace's lips curled into a small smile. If he ever did save up enough for a new car, he'd be sure to buy it from Dealin' Doug, Frank's car-dealer nemesis across the street.

"Would you mind driving?" Lilah asked, pulling him from his gleeful reverie. "I want to read through this guy's file." She patted the manila folder with Elliot's case details inside, then tossed Jace the keys.

Jace nodded, catching them easily. "Where are we going, Detective Quinn?" His eyes narrowed. "Not back to that creep's grave, right?"

Lilah opened her mouth to answer, then closed it again as a cold gust tore through the neighborhood, whistling through shutters and whipping her hair against her cheeks.

Tap tap tap.

The back of Lilah's neck was tingling as though a spider had crawled into her jacket collar. She slowly turned around, where the wind was making the branches of the massive oak tree outside her bedroom window rap against the glass. There, leaning against the tree, was Elliot, his black hair and clothes blending in perfectly with the shadows, untouched by the wind.

Lilah clapped a hand against her mouth, stumbling into Jace.

"Who are you?" Jace snarled, placing himself between Lilah and the stranger. "What do you want?"

Elliot didn't answer, didn't even spare him a glance; he was too busy staring at Lilah with a piercing gaze that cut to her marrow.

"What do you *want?*" Jace repeated, taking another step forward.

A rueful smile tugged at the corner of Elliot's mouth, but he said nothing. As another frigid gust of wind lashed at the branches above, he disappeared back into the shadows.

Lilah was clutching Jace's hand so hard, her knuckles hurt. "Y-You saw that, r-right?" she whispered. "I'm not crazy?"

"I saw him." Jace's voice was as rough as gravel.

A long moment of silence passed between them. Finally, Lilah shook her head roughly, then tugged on his hand. "Come on. We've gotta go."

"What about your dad? We can't just—"

"He's not interested in my dad, or in you." Lilah swallowed tightly, suddenly grateful for her empty stomach. "It's me he wants." With that, she started for the car, resolution hardening her soft features.

Jace had half a mind to go back inside and employ Stan's help in the matter, but against his better instincts, he jogged after her. After slamming the driver's side door shut and locking it, he reached across Lilah and locked her door as well. "Tell me everything you can about this guy," he ordered as he turned the key in the ignition. To his relief, the car started without so much as a sputter. He flipped a narrow U-turn to turn out of the cul-de-sac, his eyes lingering in the rearview mirror as they sped down the road.

Lilah was thumbing through the pages of Elliot's file, her face pinched with consternation. "Right before killing himself, he confessed his crimes – a string of murders – to a pastor. But we don't know who his victims were or where their bodies are now." She fell silent for a moment, quickly reading through the preliminary case notes. "He was born in Iowa almost forty years ago. His parents died in their sleep when he was five – suspected carbon monoxide poisoning – so he was sent to live at an orphanage." Her eyes widened. "Two of the nuns apparently *kidnapped* him after he'd been there a few months, then died in a car accident that same night. He was the only survivor."

"Jesus." Jace's hands tightened around the steering wheel.

"A Good Samaritan picked him up, brought him to a hospital. He was fostered by one of the doctors who treated him, a woman named Libby Shermann…" Her voice trailed off, her mind still stuck on the two nuns. Elliot's situation hit just a little too close to home. After all, she too had been whisked away by two women in the dead of night – two women who were never heard from again. Different circumstances, of course; Willow had been killed and Celeste, Lilah's grandmother, was never found. Still, it was the motivation for the nuns' bizarre actions, not the result, that interested her.

"Maybe they weren't kidnapping him," she muttered, almost to herself. "Maybe they were trying to get rid of him."

Jace glanced over at her. "But why?"

"Because he scared them." Lilah had no evidence to back up her hypothesis, of course. Still, the words rang true. "I think we need to call the orphanage. See if we can learn anything about his time there."

"After everything that's happened, you still want to mess around with this guy's case?" Lilah didn't answer, so Jace pressed, "But why? His victims are dead. *He's* dead. There's no justice to be served here, Li."

"It's not about justice."

"Then what's it about?" Impatience was creeping into Jace's voice. "Because if you ask me, we need to tell Sheriff Reid what's going on and figure out how the hell to get this creep off your back… You know, like a ghost restraining order." He tried to force out a weak laugh.

"But that's just it." Lilah chewed on the inside of her cheek, unsettled by the words she hadn't even spoken yet. "I think Elliot's trying to tell me something. And I don't think he's going to stop following me around until I figure out what that is."

CHAPTER 11
GONE WITH THE WIND

"Elliot!" Libby hollered from the kitchen. "Come set the table!"

Pulled from his reverie, Elliot released the dead moth he'd found on the bathroom window sill, which fluttered out the open window and into the backyard. It wouldn't make it very far – only about twenty feet or so before dying again, this time for good – but Elliot couldn't bear the sight of death, even in a creature so small.

"El! Did you hear me?"

"Coming!" He took one final look in the mirror to tame the dark waves of hair that spilled across his forehead before shutting the bathroom door behind him. His head ached from maintaining their connection from afar, but it was an ache he had grown accustomed to; the alternative was far worse. He jogged down the stairs two at a time, clutching the banister for dear life as his mom had always reminded him, then skidded to a stop at the bottom. "How do I look?"

Phil glanced over the top of the newspaper he was reading, smiling. "You look like a million bucks, my guy! Are you nervous?"

"Of course he's nervous. He's had a crush on this girl since the fifth grade!" Libby strode out of the kitchen, stirring a bowl of cake batter nestled in the crook of her arm. Phil wrapped an arm around her waist as she approached the kitchen table. "You look so handsome," she smiled at Elliot, her eyes shining. "Mom, doesn't he look handsome?"

Libby's mother, Jean, looked up from the crowded mantle she was carefully sweeping clean with a feather duster, her plump face breaking into a wide grin. "That Marsha is one lucky gal! How long has it been since the two of you went steady the first time around?"

Her husband, George, clicked his tongue from the sofa he was lounging across. "Ten-year-olds can't 'go steady,' Jean – they're just pipsqueaks!"

"True." Elliot grinned. "We weren't exactly making out beneath the bleachers four years ago."

"You'd better not be doing that now, either!" Libby barked from the kitchen as she poured the batter into two prepared cake pans. "You're way too young for that!"

George flashed his grandson a knowing wink.

"Anyway," Elliot continued, squeezing past his mother to grab some cutlery from the drawer, "Marsha and I fell out of touch when she went to a different middle school."

"They're right on the county line," Libby explained to her parents.

"Right. And our high school is so big, I didn't even realize she'd come back until she sat next to me in algebra!"

"And then it was love at first sight all over again, eh?" Phil asked, batting his eyelashes at Elliot playfully. "Just like your mom and me."

"Don't be silly!" Libby chided, slamming the oven door with a little too much gusto. She dusted her hands off on her apron with a *harrumph*, then plopped down at the kitchen table Elliot was setting. "They're not in love. El's just having a good time."

"I…well…" Elliot's hand faltered as he went to set a fork atop Marsha's placemat. He could feel the tips of his ears heating up. "I-I dunno, Ma… I mean, I really like her."

"Oh." Libby's mouth pressed into a tight line. "I see." Her hand crept toward her wrist, where she began counting her fluttering heartbeats beneath her breath. As they often did, her thoughts drifted to the distinct possibility that Elliot might one day settle down with a family of his own, leaving his adoptive family in the literal dust.

Phil scooted his chair closer to hers to wrap an arm around Libby's shoulders.

Seeing the change in her demeanor, Elliot kissed the top of his mother's head. "Hey, I'm not going anywhere," he reassured her. "I promise."

Still, her grip on her wrist tightened.

"Oh, stop smothering the boy already!" Jean scolded her daughter as she dusted the purple-glazed ceramic urn she had picked out for her own ashes. "You'll make the poor thing neurotic, and Lord knows we have enough of that in this house."

"Amen," George, a retired neuroscientist, chimed in.

Humming to herself, Jean carefully set down her urn and moved onto the next one, which was adorned with a single pawprint. "Where has Woofers gone to?" she asked, tapping the ceramic lid of his pot. "I feel like I haven't seen him in ages."

Elliot and Libby exchanged the briefest of glances before Libby cleared her throat. "He, uh...hasn't woken up in some time."

"Some time?" George arched an eyebrow. "How much time?"

"About a week or so."

"Oh dear." Libby's mother glanced at Elliot over her shoulder. "And why do you suppose that is?"

Elliot glanced at Libby, who was glancing at her father, who was rubbing the bridge of his nose tiredly.

Again, Libby cleared her throat. "Well, based on the research Dad and I have been doing—"

"Can you believe their dissertation just passed the hundred page mark?" Phil interjected, pulling her in for an enthusiastic smooch on the cheek. "I'm so proud of you, honey!"

Blushing, she flashed him a smile. "As I was saying, Elliot has always maintained that it's harder to rouse people if they've been dead a long time. Woofers died, what – twenty years ago?"

"Yes, but Peggy passed well before that!" Jean protested, jerking her chin at Libby's baby sister, who had scooched all the way up to the TV and was straining to hear *The Flintstones* over the racket.

"Shh!" The little girl held a finger up to pursed lips.

"As I was saying," Libby continued, obediently lowering her voice, "the amount of time that's passed since the initial death is important, but I'm beginning to wonder if there's more to it than that. For example, when Elliot leaves the house and our physical bodies return to ashes—"

"Oh, I hate it when you talk like that!" Jean shuddered. "It makes me feel like some sort of ghoul or something!"

"Sorry, Mom, but I'm a scientist, and I have to deal in facts – even if those facts make some of us uncomfortable." Libby gave her mother a pointed look. "Anyway, Dad and I have been researching Elliot and his ability to affect cellular age through the temporal progression and regression of organic matter – all of which all takes place on a physical level. But what about consciousness? How is it that we all continue to exist even when he's not around? How are we thinking and making memories during that time without a cerebral cortex or hippocampus to store them?"

"Certainly turns the traditional hippocampal-mnemonic model on its head," George groused.

"Right. Which means we need to move away from the traditional model and start looking at consciousness less as a brain function, and more of a spiritual state that exists outside the physical vessel."

Her father made a disparaging grunt. "I've warned you about treading into the metaphysical, Lib. Mysticism and conjecture won't win us a Nobel prize."

"Forget about the accolades for once!" Libby shot back, her voice uncharacteristically shrill. "This is so much bigger than—"

"Shh!"

"Sorry, Peg." Libby took a deep, centering breath for the span of ten heartbeats, then blew it out in a slow exhale. "Look, we've all retained our pre-death memories while continuing to make new ones – which indicates that our consciousness has persisted even after our deaths. Not only that"—she rose from her chair and began to pace back and forth—"but from the moment Elliot leaves for school to the moment he returns in the afternoon, we continue to persist, fully aware of ourselves and our surroundings—"

"But not each other," Jean interjected. "To not be able to interact, or even see one another…" She shuddered again. "That's the worst part, truly. The loneliness and boredom, in particular."

"It's definitely unsettling," Phil agreed, ruffling the edges of his newspaper. "Wandering around like ghosts, surrounded by warbling images that fade in and out of sight, unable to even pick up a book or newspaper to pass the time…"

"At least you can watch the TV – when Elliot remembers to turn it on, that is," George grumbled. "For me, the images are just a whizzing, nonsensical blur when I'm not in my body."

Elliot took that opportunity to start polishing their dinner glasses, meticulously focusing on the nearly imperceptible fingerprints and smudges while actively tuning out everyone else.

"It's awful. It feels…wrong, somehow." Libby stopped pacing, meeting Phil and her parents' solemn expressions. "Which makes me wonder…what if our consciousness – our souls, for lack of a better word – were meant to go somewhere else when we died?"

"Like Heaven?" Phil asked, setting down the newspaper.

"Heaven, another life, another universe…my point is, when Elliot pulled us back, so to speak, where exactly did he pull us *from?* Furthermore, all this constant pushing and pulling into and out of our bodies has got to be causing some strain on us, be it physical or spiritual or both."

"Conjecture!" George barked. "Scientists work with facts, not speculation."

Libby rolled her eyes. "I'm merely *hypothesizing* that over time, it may become harder for our souls to continue moving back and forth between some hypothetical astral plane. I mean, we've all noticed that Woofers has been acting increasingly tired and depressed." She opened her mouth to add that she, too, had started feeling more lethargic, but upon seeing Elliot furiously polishing perfectly clean glasses, she decided against it. "I guess I'm just wondering, will there be a point when the rest of us are unable to come back at all?"

Everyone fell silent, save for Fred Flintstone, who had just gotten his toes rolled over by

Barney's heavy stone car. *"Yabba-dabba-d'OWWW!"* he was hollering as he hopped up and down on one foot.

Peggy let out a gleeful laugh.

"Do we have to talk about this right now?" Elliot demanded, slamming his glass on the counter.

The lights in the kitchen flickered.

Phil leaned over and whispered something in Libby's ear that sounded something like, *"Not today, darling. It's his birthday."*

Elliot's stomach twisted into uneasy knots as he turned away from them, but he shoved his anxious thoughts deep down, where they would be smothered until he was able to forget they'd ever existed. What was the point of obsessing over frightening, hypothetical "what-ifs" anyway? Part of him resented Libby for bringing it up – for even thinking about it, really.

"Marsha should be here any minute," he muttered, glancing at the clock. "Can we all just pretend to be normal for a few hours?"

"You're right, of course." Libby's smile was tight. "I'm sorry, honey." Rising, she made her way to the kitchen to tend to the meatloaf. "This is an important day for Elliot, so please, everyone, no slip-ups—"

"Shh!" Peggy cut her off sharply.

"Margaret," George coaxed his youngest daughter gently, "what's a nicer way of saying 'shh'?"

"Daddy, be quiet...*please!*"

Elliot bit his lip. "Maybe it would be better for Peggy to take a nap? Otherwise Marsha might wonder why she's calling you two 'Mommy' and 'Daddy' when she's supposed to be my little sister."

George ran a hand through thin gray hair. "Well, couldn't you just make Jean and me younger?"

"And then who would you be? *My* brother and sister?" Libby cut in. "No, that's just making things even weirder and overly complicated than they already are. Just put Peggy down for her nap early."

"Okay, okay... Come here, baby," Jean said, abandoning her dusting efforts to scoop Peggy into her arms. "Is it okay if we put you to sleep a little earlier than usual tonight?"

"No!" Peggy tried to squirm away from her. "I wanna watch *The Flintstones!*"

The doorbell rang.

"Sorry, Peg," Elliot said softly. A moment later she was gone, with the smallest urn on the mantle teetering from her abrupt return.

Jean plopped on the couch beside George with a heavy sigh. "What a 'life' we live."

Libby shot her parents a stern look as she accompanied Elliot to the front door. As if to compensate, she swung it open with a wide smile, greeting their guest with a little too much enthusiasm. "Hi, Marsha, come on in!" She waved at Marsha's father and very pregnant stepmother before ushering the girl inside. "It's so good to see you again!" she enthused, leading her in by the elbow. "Don't worry about taking off your shoes – we're a very laid-back household!"

"Mom," Elliot muttered under his breath.

"Oh, right." Libby grinned sheepishly. "I'll just, uh…give you two a moment." She turned around, her wide smile promptly evaporating as she headed to the kitchen.

"Hi, Marsha," Elliot stammered, giving her the briefest of hugs. "Um, come on in."

"Thanks." She smiled, her eyes rounding when she saw the crowd of people watching them expectantly. She tucked a strand of strawberry blonde hair behind her ear, the blush creeping up her cheeks masking her freckles. "Oh, gosh! I didn't know your whole family was going to be here!" She cast them a shy finger wave. "Hello!"

"Sorry," Elliot whispered apologetically, then cleared his throat. "Marsha, this is Phil, my, uh, dad—"

"Hello!" Phil waved.

"—and these are my grandparents, George and Jean."

"Nice to meet you, dear!" Jean waved from her seat beside George on the couch.

"Nice to meet you, too," Marsha replied as she awkwardly minced into the room. "So, uh, do you all live here together, or…?"

"No, no…" George cut in with a wan smile. "Just visiting."

• • •

Despite some initial awkwardness, dinner went off without a hitch. When Libby brought out the homemade cake she had baked for Elliot – "Double chocolate with raspberry filling, Elliot's favorite!" she announced, giving Marsha a pointed look – his eyes lit up like a little boy's. After that, the whole family sang "Happy Birthday," with Phil prolonging the final notes of the song in an absurd operatic rendition that made Elliot's ears turn pink and Marsha giggle uncontrollably.

Libby stood behind Elliot's chair, squeezing his shoulders. "Go ahead and make a wish, El!"

Scrunching his eyes shut, he blew out all the candles.

"What did you wish for?" Marsha asked, batting her eyelashes at him.

"For all the people I love to always be together, just like this." He cast her a shy smile that she returned with warmth.

"Hear hear!" George called, raising his glass.

"I can't believe our little boy is fourteen years old already," Jean said, dabbing at her eyes with a napkin. "Before we know it, he'll be all grown up and making his way in the world!"

Libby shot her a dirty look. "Can we focus on one birthday at a time please, Mother?"

"You've got some frosting right here," Marsha smiled at Elliot, pointing to the corner of his mouth.

"Here?" Elliot asked, scrubbing the right side of his face with a napkin.

"No – here." Marsha reached over to gently brush her thumb against the left corner of his mouth, then licked the frosting from her finger without breaking eye contact with him.

Elliot was caught so off-guard, the rest of the family briefly flickered into much younger versions of themselves, with Libby and Phil appearing as toddlers. Elliot's heart skipped a beat at the sight, though – thankfully – no one else seemed to notice. Sucking down a deep breath, he hurriedly excused himself from the table to splash some cold water on his face from the kitchen faucet.

After dessert, when the plates had been cleared and the adults were sitting around the kitchen table drinking coffee, Elliot joined Marsha in the living room, where she was inspecting the family photos that had been nailed to the wall and placed among the urns on the fireplace mantle.

"Aren't there any baby pictures of you?" she asked. "I was hoping to see what you looked like with fat little baby cheeks!"

"Oh, uh…no." Elliot dropped his voice so Libby couldn't overhear. "I was adopted."

Marsha's eyes widened. "You were?"

"Elliot, open the back door, would you?" Phil called. "It's too hot in here."

"Says the human furnace," Libby clucked, pinching the collar of his flannel shirt. "Just put on a t-shirt!"

"You were adopted?" Marsha pressed, lowering her voice to a suitably conspiratorial whisper.

"I'll tell you about it some other time," Elliot whispered back. Pushing the sliding glass door open, he flashed his mom an innocent smile. A cool autumn breeze fluttered through the open door, ruffling Marsha's hair.

"That's what I'm talking about!" Phil grinned, leaning back in his chair.

"Don't lean so far back, you'll break the legs right out from underneath you!" Jean chided.

"Who's this?" Marsha asked, pointing to a black and white photo of Peggy at age five, shortly before she died.

"Who, her?" Elliot faltered. "Um…that's Peggy. Mom's—er, well…my sister." He could feel the blush in his cheeks creeping up to the tips of his ears.

"She's so cute! How old is she now? She's gotta be much older than you, right?"

"Um…well…"

"Oh, wow!" Marsha breathed, running her finger over Jean and George's wedding photo. "This photo looks so old!" Her eyes narrowed slightly. "Like…really old."

"Um, yeah, my grandparents are pretty old," Elliot answered, his eyes darting back to the kitchen table, where Libby had stopped talking and was watching their hushed interaction with a wary expression.

"They don't look that old." Marsha frowned. "What's in all of these jars?" she asked, reaching for Peggy's pastel-pink urn to inspect it.

"Don't touch that!" Libby barked.

Marsha jumped, knocking over Peggy's urn in the process. It tumbled from the mantle, end over end, before smashing to the ground like a detonating grenade. Half of the ashes exploded on the tiles just in front of the fireplace, coating Marsha's legs in a plume of fine gray powder; the other half blew out the open door, where a fresh gust of wind carried them up and away.

"Peggy!" Jean screamed, leaping to her feet.

Phil toppled backwards in his chair as Jean shoved away from the kitchen table, shrieking. George was at his wife's heels, bolting toward the living room. Libby slowly rose to her feet, one hand clenching the inside of her wrist as she watched the horrifying scene unfold with wide, unblinking eyes.

"What have you done?" Jean screamed at Marsha as she fell to her knees, frantically scooping Peggy's ashes into a small pile that kept getting blown about by the wind. "Close that damn door!" she screeched at her husband, who was already in the process of slamming it shut.

"I...I..." Marsha took a step backwards.

"Move!" George snarled at her, dropping to the ground beside his wife. "Do something!" he shouted at his grandson, clutching the broken fragments of ceramic in trembling hands. "Fix this!"

"I don't know how," Elliot whispered, stricken.

Marsha took another step backwards.

"Peg..." Libby blinked rapidly, trying to break free of her paralyzed trance. She felt as though she were eleven years old all over again, witnessing her parents' howling grief at the loss of their youngest daughter. With effort, she took a step forward, the floor lurching beneath her as she did. Her hand groped for the nearest chair for support.

Phil staggered to his feet, rubbing the lump on the back of his head. His eyes darted over to Libby, and then Elliot, before landing on poor

Marsha, who was covered in ash and choking on a sob. Stumbling into the living room, Phil put a protective arm around the girl as he gently pushed her away from the scene.

"It's not your fault," he whispered, casting another glance over his shoulder at Libby, who had sunk to the kitchen floor, her face as white as a sheet.

"I don't understand!" Marsha wailed, craning her neck to find Elliot. "El, what's happening? What did I do?"

He didn't answer. He could only stand there mutely as Libby's father groped at the bottom of his soot-covered shirt, shouting, "Do something, boy! *Anything!*"

"Come on, I'll take you home," Phil said, hurriedly ushering Marsha outside. As the front door slammed behind them, he took two long strides, then abruptly froze on the bottom step of the porch. His eyes went wide.

Marsha had already bolted past him, hugging her body for warmth and blinking away tears. When she realized Phil wasn't following, she whirled around to find him rooted to the porch, his face contorted with what appeared to be chagrin.

Marsha clapped a hand over her mouth, suppressing a scream.

He flashed her an apologetic grimace. "Sorry, kiddo. Tell Elliot and his mom I love them, would you?"

Marsha could only watch with bulging eyes as Phil dissolved into ashes, swirling alongside the clusters of snowflakes that had just begun to tumble from the dark clouds above. She stood in her spot, paralyzed for the span of a single, ragged breath before Jean's howl of anguish sounded from inside the house, draining the remainder of the blood from Marsha's face. As she bolted down the driveway, too frightened to hazard a second glance behind her, the wind howled through the trees, carrying the ashes of Peggy and Phil along with it.

CHAPTER 12
THE SECRET LIVES OF TREES

Lilah and Jace darted inside the phone booth just outside the Tri-Forks Public Library, a crumpled piece of paper with the phone number for the St. Nicholas of Myra Orphanage – now a private Catholic school – clutched in Lilah's hand.

As a cold gust of wind rattled the doors, Jace scooched closer to Lilah for warmth. "Remind me why we can't just use the phone at the police station?" he muttered, blowing several long strands of Lilah's hair from his mouth.

"Because then I'd have to explain the whole situation to Sheriff Reid and I really don't feel like doing that."

"Uh-huh."

"Besides, this is more of an off-duty endeavor anyway." Lilah punched the orphanage's number into the phone, letting out a groan when the payphone's automated voice requested an additional two dollars. "Stupid long-distance calls," she muttered, feeding more quarters into the coin slot until the line began to ring.

"Won't Reid wonder why you aren't in the office this morning?" Jace pressed.

"He'll probably assume I'm still working on the Simmons case."

"Simmons?"

"Elizabeth Simmons, yeah – she disappeared over a decade ago," Lilah added. "I thought I was close to solving it after chatting with my last witness, but then I hit a dead—"

"St. Nicholas of Myra School for Wayward Youth, this is Sister Janine. How may I direct your call?"

"Oh, hi!" Lilah squeaked before hastily adopting her best "professional" voice. "Uh, my name is Detective Lilah Quinn—"

"Nice," Jace whispered.

"—and I was wondering if I might speak with someone who was working at your orphanage in"—she glanced down at the open manila file she was balancing on her palm—"uh, March of 1969."

"This is a Catholic School, not an orphanage!"

"I know," Lilah replied, "but at one point you *were* an orphanage, so I was hoping—"

"Please hold."

"I—er, okay." She darted a sideways glance at Jace, who flashed her a cramped-yet-encouraging thumbs-up.

A full minute later, another, much older-sounding woman picked up the phone. *"St. Nicholas of Myra School for Wayward Youth, this is Sister Catherine. What is the nature of this call?"*

"Yes, hi, my name is Detective Lilah Quinn, and I was calling—"

"Speak up child, I can't hear you!"

"My name is Detective Lilah Quinn," she repeated loudly, "and I was calling to see if—"

A computerized voice cut her off. *"Please deposit another two dollars."*

"Oh for Pete's—hold on!" Lilah began frantically shuffling around her pockets, searching for loose change.

"Hello?" the nun demanded. *"Is this a prank call? Because if it is—"*

"No!" Lilah shouted, then flashed Jace a grateful look as he hurriedly put another three dollars' worth of quarters in the slot. "I'm calling from the Tri-Forks Police Department. I have some questions about one of the children who was living at your orphanage in 1969. Did you happen to work there at the time?"

The nun was silent for a long moment before answering, *"I did... What exactly is it you want to know?"*

Lilah spoke fast, noting the increasing frostiness of the woman's tone. "I'm wondering what you can tell me about Elliot Whitman, and what might have prompted the two nuns to kidnap him—"

"Kidnap?!" the nun spat into the receiver. *"That wasn't a kidnapping, that was a mercy! One my dear friend Maggie sacrificed her life for, God rest her soul!"*

Lilah blinked. "A mercy?"

The nun didn't appear to have heard her. *"Why, I remember my last conversation with Maggie as though it were yesterday! She firmly believed the boy was the Beast himself and was raising the dead through Satanic agency in a vile attempt to convince the world he could do as Christ does! Her sacrifice saved us all!"*

"What do you mean, Elliot was 'raising the dead?'" Lilah pressed, a cold chill spider-walking down her spine.

"Sister Catherine, is that you?" another woman's voice filtered through the receiver. *"I heard you shouting! What's the matter?"* The sounds of muffled discussion could be heard, and

then, after some shuffling, the new voice demanded, *"Hello? Who is this?"*

Lilah took a deep breath, working to conserve her dwindling patience. "As I've already explained several times, my name is Detective Lilah Quinn, and I'm calling to get some information about Elliot Whitman—"

Click.

"Hello? Ma'am?" Lilah gaped at the phone in her hand, her mouth fluttering open. "They hung up on me!"

Jace was knuckling the crease in his forehead. "You get why, right?"

"Because they think Elliot was bringing people back from the dead?"

"Because they think he's the Antichrist. Or 'was,' I guess I should say."

Lilah arched a quizzical eyebrow. "How do you know that?"

Jace let out a long sigh. "My stepdad has always been a bit of a bible thumper – literally." He rubbed the back of his head sub-consciously. "But a few years ago, he'd gotten it in his head that Y2K was gonna bring about the Rapture."

"As in, the end of the world?"

"Yeah. Frank was convinced Bill Clinton was the Antichrist and would go on and on about all the 'signs' that proved his theory. He had a whole list of them. And anyway, one of the so-called characteristics of the Antichrist is that he'll be able to perform a bunch of tricks that look like miracles in order to deceive the world into thinking he's Christ reborn – tricks like raising the dead."

"Oh, wow," Lilah breathed. "If Elliot really can raise the dead, that might explain how he's been following me around…which means I gotta find those nuns!" She shoved open the doors of the phone booth, producing a fresh blast of frigid air, and quickly made her way toward the parking lot, thumbing through Elliot's file as she did.

"Which nuns?" Jace asked, jogging after her. "The ones you just spoke to?"

"No, the dead ones! Sister Maggie and Sister, uh…Constance," she finished, locating the name on the page. "Of course, they're probably buried in Iowa," she muttered, coming to an abrupt halt. "That could be a problem."

Jace's eyes widened. "*Could* be? Isn't there someone here in Montana we could try to talk to first?"

Lilah shook her head. "The guy was a recluse. See?" She pointed to a highlighted paragraph in the open file. "He lived all by himself in some cabin in the middle of nowhere." She skimmed the page silently, adding, "It says he was born and raised in Iowa, but fled to Montana after he'd been accused of…" Lilah's face blanched. "Oh, my God."

"What?" Jace asked. "Lilah, what's wrong?"

"He…" She licked her lips, trying to put moisture back in her mouth. "It says here he— *aah!*" A violent gust of wind swept across the parking lot, scattering the pages from the open manila envelope across the asphalt. "No!" Lilah cried, bounding after the papers, arm outstretched. But the moment her fingers brushed one, the page crumbled apart. Lilah skidded to a stop, watching in mute horror as *all* of the pages of the file, including the folder that had housed them, dissolved into ashes, swirling higher and higher into the darkening sky.

Jace appeared beside her, his jaw hanging open. "What the—" His question cut off in a sharp hiss.

A little boy had appeared several yards away from them, his pale face half-hidden by the shadow of the library building.

"Elliot," Lilah whispered hoarsely, fear gripping her by the windpipe.

He cocked his head at her, saying nothing.

Forcing down the lump in her throat, she managed to rasp, "Why did you do it?"

The young boy slowly shook his head from side to side, his reproachful storm-gray eyes glued to hers. When he finally spoke, his words were scarcely louder than the wind: "Wrong question."

"What do you mean—" Lilah started, taking a step forward.

But the boy was already gone, claimed once more by the shadows.

Lilah's shoulders slumped and her hand flew to her chest, clutching the front of her jacket. Her breaths were coming in short, shallow bursts, and the edges of her vision were turning black. Just as her knees buckled, Jace was there to catch her.

"I've got you," he said, pulling her against his chest, his arms tightly wrapped across her back as if shielding her. "What was it he didn't want you to see, Li? What did he do?"

She squeezed her eyes shut, pressing her face against his chest. "He was accused of forcing himself on an underage girl."

"Son of bitch," Jace hissed, his grip on Lilah tightening.

"When the girl's mother reported it, he fled north, to Montana. That's why he spent the last few years of his life cloistered up in some cabin in the middle of nowhere." Lilah pulled away from the embrace, her hazel eyes darkening. "I saw the address, Jace. He didn't want me to see it, but I saw it anyway." She lowered her voice to a whisper. "I have to go there. I have to see what he was hiding."

Jace slid an arm around her shoulder, his eyes darting across the parking lot as he guided her back to the car. Once safely inside, he locked the door, did a thorough search of the back seat, then slumped back in the driver's seat. He ran his fingers through his hair, palming his eyes with a sigh. "Li, you said it yourself – the police never found any of his victims. If they knew the address of his cabin, don't you think they'd have already searched it for bodies?"

"Murderers don't always leave their victims' bodies whole," she muttered darkly.

Suppressing a shudder, Jace turned the key in the ignition and cranked the heat to full blast. "Look, Li…"

"I have to find them," she whispered, scrubbing the tears from her eyes. "This guy, he was – *is* – a monster. Right before he died, he confessed to a dozen murders, Jace. A *dozen*. Think of those victims' families. Their loved ones. And what he did to that poor girl! Even if it's too late to bring *him* to justice, I have to help them."

Still massaging his forehead, Jace let out a long, slow breath. "Help them…because you want to bring their families closure – or because this creep is sabotaging your case and you want payback?"

Lilah opened her mouth to argue, then closed it again, pressing her lips into a tight line. "Both," she finally admitted. "But more than that, I-I can't keep living like this – being frightened of the shadows. I have to figure out why he's been following me. And how to make him stop," she added, doing her best to keep her voice from cracking. "Will you help me?"

Jace chewed on the inside of his cheek for a long moment before abruptly shifting the car into gear. "Fine. I'll take you to the cabin…on one condition."

"What's that?" Lilah asked warily.

Jace backed out of the spot and drove toward the parking lot exit, his expression grave. "The second we get back, we tell Sheriff Reid the story – the *whole* story."

"But—"

The car jerked to a stop, making Lilah's mouth snap shut. Jace was gripping the steering wheel so tightly, his knuckles were turning white. "I'm proud of the work you do," he whispered, his eyes locked on the icy patch of asphalt separating them from the main road. "But I worry about you, Li – all the time."

"I…" Lilah faltered, the emotion behind Jace's words catching her off-guard. "I don't want you to worry about me."

He turned toward her, his blue eyes glassy and red-rimmed. "It's getting harder and harder to go back to school after these visits, Li… I-I don't want to leave you here."

Then don't go back. Lilah bit her tongue to keep the words from tumbling out.

After a long moment of heavy silence, Jace cleared his throat. "All I'm asking is that you let me make sure you're safe before I go back to Seattle. I can't just leave you here with some dead psychopath following you around. So unless you're willing to come with me—"

Lilah's heart skipped a beat. *Is he inviting me to come live with him in Seattle?* She opened her mouth to ask, then closed it again, afraid of his answer if she'd misunderstood.

"—we have to tell Reid and your father so we can all sort this out together, okay? If not for you, do it for my peace of mind." He cupped her cheek in his hand. "Please."

"Okay," Lilah whispered, resting her hand atop his. "We'll tell them – right after we go to the cabin to look for answers."

With a slow nod and a heavy sigh, Jace turned the car onto the road.

. . .

They drove west on I-90 for an hour – making a pit stop along the way for gas, snacks, and detailed directions – before turning onto I-15 for nearly an hour more. Once they'd passed Elk Park, the turnout for the Haystack Mountain Trailhead appeared within a few minutes, just as the gas station attendant had told them it would. After parking in the nearly empty gravel lot, using the park facilities, and replenishing their day bags with food, gear, and a few extra bottles of water, Lilah and Jace set out on a short hike. By that point, the sun was high in the sky, albeit obscured by swollen purple storm clouds and towering evergreen trees. Between the trail map, the folded roadmap from Lilah's glove box, and the directions they'd gotten from a few hikers along the way, it only took about forty-five minutes for them to find the lone cabin standing in the middle of the sprawling woods, several hundred feet off the beaten path. Small and inconspicuous, with dead, creeping vines trailing up the sun-bleached logs, the structure looked as though it hadn't been touched in the decade since it had been abandoned.

Jace and Lilah approached the front door, which was still cordoned off by faded and fraying police tape. Lilah's heart was thumping heavily against her breastbone.

"Are you sure you want to do this?" Jace asked, squeezing her hand.

She nodded, took a deep breath…and turned the knob before she could talk herself out of it. The front door swung open with a remonstrating creak, revealing a cabin that was completely bare, save for some empty bottles and cans that had been left there by various trespassers over the years. Graffiti marred the interior walls, the window over the rusted utility sink in the kitchen was broken, its screen in tatters, and the far corner of the room housed a charred spot surrounded by a ring of fist-sized rocks that smelled faintly of urine.

After doing a brief sweep of the room, Lilah peered inside the wood-burning stove in the center of the cabin, where only a pile of ashes remained, then shut it with a sigh. "Are you okay if I start doing a deeper dive for clues?"

"Sure." Jace moved closer to Lilah, who had just taken off her fancy gold watch and placed it atop the stove. At her nod, he reached out and took her bare hand, tensing for what he knew would happen next – and what he hoped wouldn't.

"Ready?" Lilah whispered.

He nodded reluctantly.

Reality flickered, the walls of the cabin becoming a fluttering blur as time itself shifted around them. Wincing, Jace clutched Lilah's hand tighter as the hour hand of the gold watch began spinning faster, the dials for the day, month, and year ticking backward. The scorched circle of rocks in the back corner reignited into a roaring fire, then extinguished, the flames blinking in and out of existence like a traffic light. Inside the wood-burning stove, ashes turned to wood and back to ashes again, while the broken window above the kitchen sink became whole once more. Outside, the bare branches of a small grove of oak trees sprouted dry brown leaves, which faded to orange, then yellow, then deep green, before turning into buds and continuing the cycle again.

Meanwhile, Lilah's eyes had become glazed and far-away, reminding Jace of the first time he'd experienced her unique time-bending ability: at the rock concert they'd attended together three years ago, when Lilah's triggered seizure had caused the very balcony they'd been standing on to revert into a pile of wood planks and unused screws, sending both of them plummeting to the ground fifteen feet below.

His grip on her hand tightened.

The furrow between Lilah's brows deepened as the watch dials continued ticking backward. Weathered logs became polished. The rusted exterior of the stove deoxidized into gleaming black cast iron. Moths fluttered and fell, their wings turning to dust. Within a few minutes, more than ten years had passed.

Lilah held her breath…but no one appeared.

After several tense moments, she let out a frustrated sigh, her eyes blinking back into focus as she looked around the room. "Guess I was wrong – again."

Jace opened his mouth to offer her some words of comfort…then closed it again. His eyes flitted to the clean and intact kitchen window, where, outside, the grove of oak trees had disappeared entirely. In their place, a cluster of people had appeared.

Jace's Adam's apple bobbed as he wordlessly lifted his hand and pointed at them.

Lilah's eyes widened, then hardened, as her gaze settled on the small crowd standing outside the kitchen window. "Damnit," she muttered, snatching her watch from the stove. Still gripping Jace's hand, she pushed open the back door and strode outside.

The line of people stood side-by-side atop the soil, their spacing and orientation perfectly matching the line of trees that had superseded them. Though they were all looking in Lilah and Jace's general direction, they didn't appear to see them. A gray-haired man and woman stood an arm's length from one another, each of them staring straight ahead. The man wore a sweater vest and high-waisted slacks that were belted well above his navel, while the woman wore a collared black dress with a wide skirt. She was clutching a cracked pink jar against her chest. A younger couple, perhaps in their mid-thirties, stood beside them, unmoving and unblinking. They, too, wore anachronistic clothing that looked to be at least forty years outdated. A few feet away, two young girls in matching powder-blue dresses with puffy sleeves and white pinafores stood, unblinking. Between them sat a chocolate-colored hound dog, his tongue lolling out of his mouth, yet frozen. At the very end of the line, two nuns – one at least eighty years old and the other perhaps a third her age – stared blankly ahead, their eyes focused on something long ago and far away.

"Hello?" Lilah called out as she and Jace drew closer.

No one answered. No one even seemed to notice their approach.

"What's wrong with them?" Jace whispered, fear creeping into his voice.

"I don't know." Lilah frowned, kneeling down to inspect the dog. He was breathing, blinking even. But he didn't react to her.

None of them did.

"It's like they're just…husks." Jace waved his free hand in front of the smallest girl's face. "Is that normal?"

Lilah opened her mouth to answer but was cut off by a low, gravelly voice. "Let the dead sleep."

She whirled around with a gasp, inadvertently letting go of Jace. He let out a yelp as he reverted to his eight-year-old self, his Huskies jacket swallowing up two-thirds of his shrunken body.

Elliot emerged from the shadows of the surrounding forest, his face unshaved and his cheeks sallow. At twenty-six years old, this was the oldest Lilah had ever seen him – the oldest he'd ever lived to be.

"You killed all these people?" Lilah demanded, her mounting anger momentarily usurping fear. "How could you?" She took an emboldened step forward. "Did you know them, or were they just some poor, unsuspecting strangers you murdered for kicks?"

The man stepped out of the shadows, his bloodshot eyes narrowing as he closed the distance between them.

Jace, stumbling over his oversized pants and sneakers, attempted to position himself in front of Lilah. "Get away from her!" he shouted shrilly.

Elliot didn't spare the boy a second glance; he merely waved a disinterested hand, causing the air around Jace to shimmer. A split second later, Jace blinked out of sight, leaving nothing but a large pile of rags and buttons in his wake.

A scream shattered from Lilah's throat. "Jace!" she cried, dropping to her knees. Her head jerked toward Elliot. "What did you do to him?"

"Let the dead sleep," he repeated, taking another step closer. The line of people that Lilah had unearthed still hadn't moved. They merely "watched" the interaction with distant, unseeing eyes.

Lilah clapped a hand over her mouth, stifling a sob. "What do you want with me?" she choked out, tears streaming down her face.

Elliot knelt in front of her, his haggard face contorting with what appeared to be pain as his hand reached out to cup her chin. "You must let the dead sleep," he whispered, his expression softening.

"Why?" she demanded, recoiling from his touch. "So monsters like you can get away with murdering them?"

An expression resembling remorse flickered across Elliot's face, carving out every premature line and wrinkle. Without saying another word, he rose once more to his feet, turning his attention back to his line of unseeing spectators: his victims. With another casual wave of his hand, their bodies turned to ash.

"No!" Lilah gasped, scrambling back to her feet. "Bring them back!" She watched wordlessly, helplessly, as the air in the clearing shimmered, and the line of oak trees reappeared where his victims once stood.

Elliot approached the two oaks, where the couple in their thirties had just been standing, and pressed his forehead against the snow-dusted bark of the woman's tree. Then, without another word or glance in Lilah's direction, he disappeared into the forest.

Lilah's red-rimmed eyes lingered on the shadows between the trees for the span of a single, ragged breath, then dropped back to the ground beside her, where a baby's muffled cries could be heard from beneath the pile of rags. With a frantic cry, Lilah sifted through them, letting out a sob of relief when she found the infant safely swaddled in Jace's jacket. She reached forward to help him, her eyes darting back to the line of trees – Elliot's victims, whose voices would never be heard again.

Chapter 13

Paradox

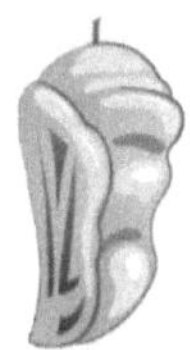

Libby leaned back in her desk chair, rubbing the stitch between her brows with the pad of her thumb. Her head had been aching for months now, and the fog that had long ago settled upon her brain refused to lift. Her joints ached. Her bones ached. Her *soul* ached. But what was the alternative? To simply cease to exist, as her parents had chosen six months ago? No. She wouldn't abandon Elliot the way they had, leaving him parentless – not once, but twice. Elliot needed her. And of course, Libby needed him. Every time Elliot left for school, Libby was forced to sit in the interminable, suffocating silence, during which the seconds ticked by like hours, and reality rippled and warped in and out of her darkening vision. She often found herself nodding off, slipping into that dreamless sleep of nonexistence, which was becoming harder to wake from. Eventually, the thought of him leaving – even for a few hours at a time – filled Libby with a fear so raw and primal, it was at times crippling.

What if she never woke up again?

It wasn't an unreasonable thought. Everyone else – Woofers, Libby's mother, and then her father – had just stopped waking up. Peggy and Phil, of course, had been lost well before that, their ashes stolen by the wind.

Now, once again, it was just Elliot and Libby.

Shortly after his seventeenth birthday, Elliot had decided it would be better if he switched to homeschooling. Initially, Libby protested the decision, albeit half-heartedly. But he reassured her that it was better this way; her body wouldn't be forced to revert to ashes when he left, and he wouldn't have to spend the day worrying about whether she would be there to greet him when he got home. It wasn't a perfect system, of course, since Elliot did have to rest for a few begrudging hours every night. But he'd gotten so good at keeping his concentration – even in sleep – that more often than not, Libby would make it through the night without reverting.

This was one of those nights.

Libby glanced at the clock – 4:15 a.m. – then back to the stack of papers beside her typewriter: her four-hundred-page dissertation on death and consciousness. The culmination of her afterlife's work. Pages upon pages were tacked to the walls and scattered across the floor of her bedroom, which had been repurposed into an office last year, shortly after the paper's co-author had stopped waking up. The bed had been the first thing to go, followed by the vanity and dresser. Since Libby never aged, she never needed – or wanted – to sleep. And what did it matter if she wore the same clothes every day? After Phil's sudden "departure" three years ago, she didn't bother changing them, instead resigning herself to the same outfit she'd died and been cremated in: a loose-fitting Beatles t-shirt and torn bell bottom jeans.

She reached down to pick up the last page she'd typed, unsure whether it had been minutes or days since she'd written it. In spite of the ever-present fog that had been plaguing her, she had recently made tremendous strides on her dissertation, which not only focused on Elliot's ability to bend time backward and forward, at times bypassing cellular death altogether, but on consciousness, the soul, and the plight of the human condition. Sure, she had strayed from hard science in recent weeks – or had it been months? – veering dangerously close to what her father would have derided as "metaphysical hokum." But he was no longer here to harp on her.

Sighing, Libby's bloodshot eyes quickly scanned the page as she read the concluding passage under her breath, *"In this paper, we've thoroughly examined the ways in which the subject's temporal manipulation has recurrently and reliably resulted in the advancement, regression, and cessation of cellular aging. We've also studied the apparent limits of this temporal manipulation, which appear to be tethered to the genetically ingrained age limitations of the living organism itself. Consider the squirrel test subject in Temporal Trial 03-23-78-004 (Appendix: D.14). A squirrel's natural lifespan is around five years. However, when pushed outside the natural confines of this limited lifespan – e.g., temporally progressed ten years instead of two, thereby terminating the squirrel in the process – the squirrel failed to revive at the conclusion of the trial, even when its decomposing remains reverted to its intact, temporally-unaltered form (see Dissection Notes 03-23-78 in Appendix: D.22). After numerous trials of a similar nature, using a variety of insects and rodents as test subjects, we have come to hypothesize that once an organism's soul (previously defined as 'consciousness,' 'awareness' and/or 'neurological responsiveness to stimuli') has been wrenched from the natural confines of its mortal coil (forgiving the self-indulgent Shakespeare reference), it cannot be returned.*

For this reason, it is necessary to do more research on the soul itself – that which has long been thought to separate the living from the dead—"

Libby rubbed at the growing knot in her left shoulder, discomfited – as she always was – by the topic. There was, of course, the rational fear her father had instilled in her that such "wild presuppositions" might incur the collective derision of the entire scientific community were she to stray too far from the established scientific method. But beyond that, the very notion of a soul – or rather, a lack thereof – frightened Libby to her core. Whether referred to by its scientific moniker of "consciousness" or its religious appellation of "spirit," the soul was one of the few concepts both science and religion agreed on: that living people possess one, and dead people do not. Sure, she'd retained her consciousness. But what about her spirit? If Libby's soul had indeed been lost in the process of dying, what would happen if Elliot did fail to rouse her? Would she simply cease to exist? Is that what had happened to Woofers and her parents? And what about Peggy and Phil?

"Cogito ergo sum," she muttered, absentmindedly counting the dull flutters of her heartbeat beneath her wrist. The phrase had become something of a mantra in recent months, a chant Libby repeated over and over in her head.

"I think, therefore I am. And if I am here, pondering my own existence, then one must presume my soul has persisted even through death." Libby leaned back on her chair, teetering on its two hind legs as Phil always had done. "No longer rooted inside my body, perhaps, but still tethered to my ashes…for now, at least."

She chewed on her lip, begrudgingly allowing her thoughts to drift to that terrible moment she had always actively worked to repress: the moment just before her death. In that split second, during which time itself seemed to have slowed to a trickle, Libby had experienced a brief cessation of consciousness. Immediately after that, she'd had the strangest sensation – one that could only be described as simultaneously existing in two places at once: both at the top of the stairs, where her foot had caught on the runner, and at the bottom of the stairs, where she had…

She cupped her throat, shaking her head to clear the memory.

Whether she was willing to say the words or not, the fact of that matter was that she had died. But why had she blacked out immediately beforehand? Libby had never experienced anything like that in her life. In fact, it was her sister, Peggy, who had suffered from seizures—

A sharp gasp slipped from her throat as the front legs of the chair landed sharply on the floor.

"Peggy," she whispered, shoving her chair away from her desk. "*Peggy* had blackouts. Mom and Dad, too, near the end." She snatched a medical textbook from the closest bookshelf, quickly thumbing through the pages. "Cardiac syncope," she muttered, running her finger down the list of symptoms. "The doctors suspected it ran in the family. But if that's true, why wasn't there a detectable arrhythmia in any of their test results?"

She snapped the book shut with a loud *clap*. As she did, a random memory jolted through the bleary haze of her mind – the day she returned home from college to find out Woofers had died. *"The driver said he reached into his glove box to retrieve something, and when he looked up, Woofers was standing in the middle of the road, unmoving. The man said he slammed on his brakes and honked, but Woofers didn't even turn his head – he didn't react in any way."* Her father squeezed her shoulder, trying his best to muster a reassuring smile. *"We think it might have been a seizure, which means he felt absolutely no pain or fear at the moment of death."*

A hysterical giggle burst out of Libby's lips, which quickly devolved into peals of uncontrollable laughter. Soon, she was laughing so hard her stomach hurt and her breaths were coming as short, wheezing gasps that turned the edges of her vision white.

When Elliot knocked on the door a few minutes later, still rubbing the sleep from his bloodshot eyes, he found Libby sitting on the floor, hugging her knees to her chest and rocking back and forth on the paper-strewn floor. Her eyes were wild and tears stained her sallow cheeks.

"Mom?" he asked, taking a tentative step into the room. "Are you—"

"We killed them, El," she whispered, half-laughing, half-crying. "We killed them."

Elliot stopped dead in his tracks. "Huh?"

"All of them – my parents, my sister, my *dog*…" Another peal of laughter slipped from her lips before she clamped them shut. "Hell, for all I know, we might have killed Phil too."

Elliot's eyebrows drew together as knelt in front of her. "What are you talking about?"

"Don't you get it?" she wheezed, rocking faster. "The soul can only exist in one place at a time! When you brought me back to life, you had to pull my consciousness from somewhere, right? And what better time than the moment right before I died?"

Elliot's breath caught in his chest.

"Peggy, Mom, Dad – all of them suffered from some form of seizures at the very end of their lives. You know why?" Her voice was growing louder and shriller. "Because you ripped their souls from their body so we could bring them back from the dead!"

"No." Elliot was shaking his head firmly. "No, that's not—"

"In order to bring me back to life, you yanked my soul out of the last living version of myself." Libby licked her lips, trying to put moisture back in her mouth. "I blacked out. That's why I tripped. *That's* why I fell down the stairs."

All of the color blanched from Elliot's face. "No," he whispered again, sitting back on his haunches.

"And Woofers!" White shone all around Libby's irises. "My father said he must have had a seizure right before he died! But no!" She shook her head wildly, violently. "*We* killed him! Because if we hadn't brought his bones back to life, he wouldn't have blacked out. He wouldn't have stood there, frozen, right in front of oncoming traffic!" She stood up shakily, using the wall for support.

"No." Elliot was shaking his head slowly from side to side. "I didn't... I mean, I couldn't have–"

She let out a sharp gasp. "Oh my God, Elliot, the nuns! The two nuns who died in the car accident! We assumed the older one had fallen asleep at the wheel, but what if it's because she blacked out?" She knelt and grabbed him by the shoulders. "Didn't you tell me you revived them right after they died? Didn't you?" she demanded, shaking him roughly.

"Ma!" Elliot pleaded.

Libby released him, her eyes wide and unseeing as she stumbled back to her feet. "They say Peg died of heart failure. That Mom died of a stroke and Dad died of a pulmonary embolism. That Phil was hit by a truck. But what if we killed them? What if Mom's stroke wasn't a stroke? What if it was us, pulling her soul away? What if Phil had blacked out right before that truck came barreling down the road, and just sat there paralyzed, like Woofers, instead of leaping out of the way? What if…" Her voice dropped to a rasping whisper. "What if he died because of us?"

Elliot gazed up at her, tears pooling in his eyes for the first time in years. "Are you saying…I'm a murderer?"

Libby wasn't listening to him. She was busy pacing the room, crumpling and kicking up papers with her slippers as she hugged her frail body for warmth. "I can't bear it," she whispered. "I…I just want to sleep…"

"Mom—" Elliot rose to his feet.

"Please!" she screamed, sending him staggering backward. "Just let me sleep!"

He sucked in a deep breath, forcing back the sob that had lodged itself in his chest. The muscles in his forehead, which had been furrowed for years, abruptly relaxed. Libby disappeared, the urn sitting on her desk rattling as she returned to ashes.

Elliot slumped to the ground, pressing his forehead to his knees. For years, he'd doggedly held back his tears, telling himself that if they never fell, the events that had invoked them had never happened. But tonight, they came without impediment or restraint, flowing like water through cracks in a dam. And as that dam crumbled, Elliot crumbled along with it, his body gripped by sobs as he wept alone in the darkness.

CHAPTER 14

FROZEN IN TIME

It had been a full minute since Lilah and Jace had finished their dumbfounding story, yet Sheriff Reid still hadn't said a word. He sat in his chair, motionless, save for the throbbing vein in his forehead – a harbinger of the verbal onslaught yet to come.

Lilah and Jace exchanged several nervous glances.

Finally, Reid cleared his throat, sucked a sharp breath of air between his teeth, then said, "I need you two to be completely honest with me." He paused, locking both of their eyes in his. "Have either of you been drinking today?"

Jace shot him an affronted look. "Seriously?"

"Drugs? Hallucinogens? Sniffing glues or solvents of any kind?"

Lilah rolled her eyes, not bothering to dignify his question with a response.

The sheriff abruptly stood from his chair, tipping his wide-brimmed hat to the side as he scratched the top of his head. "So, let me get this straight: you came to a dead end on the Elizabeth Simmons case, and instead of tackling the paperwork I've been asking you to file for weeks"—he jerked his finger at the teetering pile of forms haphazardly stacked on the corner of his desk—"you decide to *steal a case file* from my desk—"

"Borrow," Lilah interjected. "And it had my name on it."

Sheriff Reid's eyeballs bulged and his nostrils flared. "*Borrow* a case file without my permission, and then go lollygagging about some church graveyard to talk to a dead murderer that then *followed you home?*"

"Yes," Lilah answered, pointedly avoiding his narrowing gaze.

"And despite the fact this aforementioned zombie *has been stalking you for two days*, you not only *didn't* inform me, but decided instead to pop inside the murderer's cabin and pay his victims a visit?"

Lilah blew a strand of hair from her eyes. "Correct."

Reid's puffed-out cheeks turned several shades redder. "And instead of bringing me evidence – or even snapping a photo of the victims – you let all eight bodies—"

"Nine, if you count the dog."

"—all *nine bodies* disappear?!" Sheriff Reid exploded, the vein in his temple pulsing with ire. "What in the devil's name were you *thinking*, Quinn?"

"Now wait just a minute!" Jace stood up from his chair, earning himself a death glare from the sheriff that made him take a half step backwards. He cleared his throat. "What I mean to say, *sir*, is that Lilah couldn't possibly have known any of this would happen. I mean, how the heck could she have predicted a dead guy would follow her around and destroy her case files?"

Lilah winced.

"What?!" Reid exploded, whirling toward her. "How the hell did he—"

"The important thing to remember," Jace hastily interjected, "is that *none* of us could have guessed this would happen. And even if you *had* accompanied her to Elliot's grave, what good would that have done? The creep doesn't seem to care who's hanging around her anyw—"

"Li!" Stanley burst through the closed door, panting and red-faced. "Oh, thank God!"

"Hi, Dad," Lilah muttered, her cheeks flushing several shades of pink.

"And to think I actually trusted you to do the responsible thing for once!" Stanley barked, garnering an approving nod from Sheriff Reid. "And you!" He jabbed a finger at Jace. "I'm *doubly* disappointed in you!"

"I—" Jace's shoulders slumped. "I'm sorry, Stan. I should have taken better care of her."

Lilah's head swiveled in his direction. "I'm not a child, Jace! And I don't need *any*one—"

"Did she tell you?" Stanley asked Reid, steamrolling past her. "About the undead pervert who's been following her around?"

"Yeah, just now." Reid sighed.

"Well?" Stanley demanded. "What are we gonna do about it? We can't just have some murderous psycho stalking my daughter!"

Reid held up his hands in a pacifying gesture. "I agree. I'm thinking a twenty-four hour patrol around your neighborhood, plus a chaperone accompaniment. And of course, she'll be limited to desk work until we figure this out—"

"What?" Lilah gasped. "You can't—"

"As for the chaperones," Reid continued as though she hadn't spoken, "I can't spare more than two guys right now, but maybe you can lend me a couple guys from the fire station?"

"Hold on a minute—" Lilah started.

"Martinez and Smith can help patrol the neighborhood." Stanley nodded. "That's sixteen hours right there."

"I can help with the last shift," Jace volunteered. "That way we can have guys around the clock. I'll need a gun, though," he hedged.

"Absolutely not," Reid snapped.

"Besides," Stanley added, "the guy's already dead."

As their discussion devolved into the supernatural logistics of subduing a zombie who could melt into the shadows like a vampire, Lilah buried her face in her hands, doing her best to tune them out. As much as she hated being treated like a child – and worse, having the men in her life swoop in and take over – the fact of the matter was, she *had* messed up, botching every step of a case that hadn't even been formally assigned to her. She'd taken the files without thoroughly reading them, woken up a self-ascribed serial killer, and then abruptly lost the case files. Worst of all, she'd lost her victims. Their accounts, their clues, their remains…all of it was gone.

She had failed them.

Lilah rubbed her stinging eyes with the palms of her hands, the inside of her ears tickling; the room had gone silent. She lifted her head, her breath catching in her chest.

Sheriff Reid stood on the other side of his desk, his hand clutching a phone to his open mouth. Jace sat beside her, as still as a statue. Concern was etched into his frozen, unblinking expression as he reached a motionless hand in Lilah's direction as though to comfort her. Her father stood a few inches behind them, his head half turned as though to look over his shoulder. Lilah followed his gaze to the far corner of Reid's office, where a man was watching her from the shadows.

"Elliot." Lilah slowly rose to her feet, balling her hands into fists as she turned to face him. "The pages turning into ashes, Jace reverting to a baby… You're…" She faltered, unable to bring herself to say it: *Like me.*

"A chronomancer," Elliot supplied, inclining his head in a nod. "Indeed."

Lilah opened her mouth, but no words came. She had never met another person like her – someone who could bend time with a mere thought. Her gaze darted back to her father and Jace, both immobilized, before turning back to Elliot.

She took a step forward, swallowing tightly. "Don't hurt them, please. Whatever you want, I'll do. You want me to stop investigating your case? Fine. You already destroyed the case files and evidence. There's nothing left for me to do."

Elliot stepped out of the shadows, the light from Reid's desk betraying the splash of freckles on his cheeks and the dark circles beneath his eyes.

Steeling herself, Lilah held her ground, though her brain was screaming at her to run. "Please," she repeated, straining to keep her voice level. "Whatever it is you want from me, I'll do it." A tear rolled down her cheek. "Just don't hurt them. Please."

Elliot took another step forward, studying her expression with cunning, storm-gray eyes. He was taller than Lilah by at least half a foot – taller, even, than Jace. Perhaps twenty years old in this iteration of himself, he wore the same tight-fitting black tee he'd been wearing when he awoke in the graveyard. It made his ashen skin look all the more pale and lifeless.

"How are you doing this?" The question slipped through Lilah's lips, surprising even her. Swallowing tightly, she gestured around the office. "How are you freezing time for everyone but us? How are you even…alive?"

His eyes narrowed slightly, as if he were trying to decide how best to answer. When he finally spoke, his voice was surprisingly calm. "I need your help."

Lilah blinked, taken aback. "To do what?"

Elliot turned around and started for the door, gesturing for her to follow. "To fix the past." With that, he stepped through the doorway, disappearing into the inky shadows of the hallway.

Lilah chewed on a ragged thumbnail, darting an anxious glance between the door and the two people she loved most in this world. Both were still frozen. With a heavy sigh, she brushed a gentle kiss against Jace's parted lips, then squeezed her father's motionless hand. "I love you," she whispered. "And I'm sorry."

She squeezed her eyes shut, blinking back tears, and took a deep, steadying breath. Then, without another look back, she spun on her heel and walked out the door.

. . .

PART
II

. . .

WHAT'S GOOD FOR THE GOOSE...

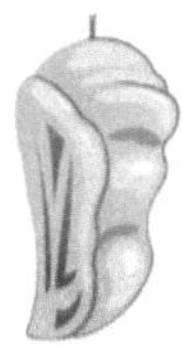

"Hey June – think fast!"

The assailant's target let out a loud shriek as a snowball went whizzing past her ear, exploding on the sidewalk in a shower of white powder.

"Oh yeah?" June shouted, bending down to pack a grapefruit-sized ball of snow between her red mittens. As she straightened, poised to hurl the icy missile at her pimple-faced aggressor, a second snowball hit her square in the rump, eliciting an even shriller scream. "Dillon Harold, I'll kill you for that!" she screeched, chucking the snowball in his direction. It went careening through the air, exploding on impact in the center of Dillon's upturned pug nose.

"You may have won the battle, but the war shall be ours!" Dillon crowed as he and Nicholas Weisse retreated to the transient safety of their crumbling snow fort.

"Yeah, you'd better run!" June shouted after them, waving her mittened fist in the air.

Violet clapped a blue-mittened hand on her shoulder. "You do know that Dillon has had a massive crush on you since the eighth grade, right?"

"Eww!" June wrinkled her nose in disgust. "He's so…gross."

Laughing, Violet fell into step beside her oldest friend, linking an arm through hers as they strolled away from the school bus stop, freed from the tedious confines of Scarville High School for the entire winter – well, three weeks of it, anyway. The bus had dropped them in front of the neighborhood park, which was blanketed in a heavy layer of sparkling snow. The swings sagged from the weight of it, and the slide was entirely covered in it – at least until Dillion flung himself down the slide face-first, sending a plume of white powder sailing into the sky. He landed in an ungainly pile of limbs at the bottom, having eaten nearly as much snow as he'd displaced.

"Aren't you a little big to be playing on the slide?" Violet shouted at him.

"Never!"

June rolled her eyes as they started on the path that circled around the frozen neighborhood lake. Bare silver maple and white oak trees lined the grassy shore, with the occasional park bench nestled in-between. It only took about fifteen minutes to circle the whole thing, or five if you decided to brave the ice and walk directly across it. But as warm as it had been leading up to the first snowstorm of the winter, only an idiot like Dillon would be dumb enough to traverse it. June and Violet were more than happy to take the sidewalk to the opposite side of the lake, where their two houses were nestled side by side – one an illuminated beacon of festive Christmas spirit, the other dull and muted in comparison.

"I am so *sick* of high school boys, Vi." June sighed. "Do they ever grow up?"

Violet snorted. "According to my mother, no… Speaking of which, she wanted me to ask if you and your mom are coming over for charades tonight?"

"I'll ask, but…" June chewed on her lip. "I don't know. My mom's been acting so weird lately. Last night she was up at one in the morning, placing all of these gross-smelling candles around the house to rid it of negative chi or something."

Violet arched an eyebrow. "Chi?"

"Yeah, I don't know. She's been reading a bunch of books by some shaman or something.

It's pretty much all she talks about these days." Her footsteps slowed as they drew closer and closer to their houses. "Hey, do you want to walk around the lake one more time before going home?"

"Sorry, I promised my mom I'd come home right after school to help set up for game night." Violet gave June a tight squeeze. "See you later tonight, I hope!"

"Yeah." June gave her friend a tight smile. "I hope so, too." She waved goodbye, then watched as Violet opened the wooden gate to her backyard and sprinted into the kitchen, where her mom was waiting for her with a big hug.

With a sigh, June shoved her hands in her jacket pockets and hurried past her own house, head down, to continue her lap around the lake. The sky was already getting dark, though most of the houses in the neighborhood had been strung up with colorful Christmas lights to help combat the winter blues. June glanced wistfully over her shoulder at Violet's house, which had been decked to the nines with mechanical reindeer, blinking icicles, and gingerbread-style rainbow lights that lined every window. It was a stark contrast to her own dismal house, which bore no Christmas decorations whatsoever. *"Unlike Violet, we don't have a man around the house to climb ladders and hang Christmas lights...or pay bills, for that matter,"* June's mother had been griping just that morning. *"Besides, Christmas is just a stolen pagan holiday. Now help me string these garlands of thyme across the doorframes. They'll help repel the* sha chi *looming in the house – like all the negative energy rolling off this sourpuss right here,"* she said, pinching June's cheek so hard it hurt.

June rubbed at her cheek absentmindedly, continuing her dawdling march.

Her attention was drawn to several honking geese that had crowded around a nearby park bench – or rather, the hooded man who was sitting alone at the park bench, tossing them hunks of bread from behind the curtain of bare willow trees. A small smile crossed June's face. She had always loved geese, to her mother's vocal dismay. To *her*, geese were just nasty, hissing things that left filth all over their backyard – which is why she'd put out fake fox silhouettes to scare them all away.

June swept aside the bare branches of willow trees that formed a curtain around the park bench, brushing the falling snow from her knitted hat as she sat beside the man.

"Hi," she said shyly.

He started, as though surprised by her greeting, then quickly turned back to the geese, who were eating crumbs directly from his hand.

June watched, transfixed. "That's so neat," she breathed. "Can I try?"

The man glanced at her from under the shadow of his hood, shifting uncomfortably. "Um…sure." He reluctantly handed her the heel of bread from the very bottom of the bag. "Just don't make any sudden movements. They startle easily."

She nodded, breaking off tiny bits of bread to feed to the tiny flock that had gathered.

The man leaned back against the bench with a heavy sigh. As he did, his hood fell away, revealing a much younger – and handsomer – face than June had been expecting. He couldn't have been that much older than her – a few years, at most. Wavy black hair fell across his forehead, and eyes the color of storm clouds gazed across the frozen lake, where the boys from June's ninth-grade class were horsing around on a playground built for children half their size.

"Morons." June rolled her eyes.

"Sorry?" the boy said, casting her a sideways glance.

"Oh, just those guys over there. They're all idiots. I was just telling my friend that all high school boys are… No offense, of course," she added, tucking a loose strand of deep auburn hair behind her ear. Her heart was racing so fast, she could feel it thudding against the front of her jacket.

"No offense taken." The boy exhaled softly through his nose. "I've been out of high school for…wow. More than a year, I guess." He blinked with what appeared to be surprise.

"Really?" June frowned. "But you don't look that old."

"I dropped out when I turned seventeen so I could take care of my mom." Sadness crossed his features, tugging at June's racing heart.

"Oh, I'm sorry," she said. "Is she sick?"

He was quiet for a long moment before answering, "Something like that."

"I'm sorry," June repeated. "My dad was sick too. He passed away when I was twelve."

"How long ago was that?" he asked with a furtive glance.

"Almost three years ago."

"I'm sorry," he said softly, and June could tell he meant it.

"It's okay." She dusted the crumbs off her hand before extending it in his direction. "I'm

Juniper, by the way. But my friends call me June."

The man looked at her palm warily. "Elliot," he finally said, clasping her hand in his before quickly withdrawing it. He ran his fingers through his hair nervously. "Did, uh… Did your dad ever suffer from blackouts?"

June frowned. "Not that I know of…why?"

"Just curious," he muttered, his eyes once more locked on the geese he was feeding.

The two of them sat in companionable silence, each quietly feeding the handful of geese that had gathered around them. When the last crumb of bread had been emptied out of the bag, June rose to her feet, casting Elliot a shy smile. "Do you, um, think you'll be here tomorrow?"

He stared at her for a long moment, then blinked as if to rouse himself. The Adam's apple in his throat bobbed up and down as he nodded. "Yes…I come here almost every day."

"Great." June's smile brightened. "Maybe I'll see you tomorrow, then." With that, she slung her book bag over her shoulder, waved, then made her way to the cluster of houses on the north side of the lake.

Elliot watched her leave, his own heart thudding in his chest, before shaking his head roughly. Muttering self-directed admonitions beneath his breath, he shoved his empty bread bag in his pocket and stood up, casting one last glance at the girl's shrinking figure.

Then, with a sigh, he turned to go.

As he did, the handful of geese that had gathered around the park bench disappeared, returning once more to algae-covered bones at the bottom of the lake.

. . .

Against his better judgment, Elliot returned to the park the following day, this time with a paper bag full of cracked corn. Bread, while fine for an already-deceased goose, wasn't a particularly healthy option for their living brethren – or so he had read the night before. Elliot sat on the same bench he'd been sitting yesterday, casting a glance in the general direction June had run off. His heart was racing as though he'd sprinted the entire three-mile trek from his front door to the park. Of course, he hadn't *run* the whole way, necessarily; it was more of a brisk jog.

Several geese paddled up to the edge of the lake, then plodded over to him. Elliot absentmindedly tossed a handful of corn in their general direction, though his attention kept drifting back to the houses on the other side of the lake. Luckily, geese aren't particular about the conversation or the company they keep, so long as their host has a steady stream of food, which Elliot did. Time ticked by slowly. He found himself tapping his foot impatiently as the growing flock of water fowl continued pestering him for handouts.

"Oi – take it easy!" he snapped, yanking his hand away from a particularly aggressive goose. "Sheesh." As he shook out his assaulted fingers, his eyes darted back over his left shoulder. He wasn't looking for *her*, per se, just observing his surroundings.

"Hi!"

Elliot jumped, nearly knocking over the bag of corn that he'd been balancing on his bouncing knee.

June stood in front of him, hands planted on her hips and a wide smile stretching her freckled cheeks. She was wearing the same cherry-red parka as the day before, as well as a matching knit cap and mittens. They brought out the streaks of crimson in her long, auburn hair and the flush in her cheeks.

"H-Hi," Elliot said, standing. The bag of corn toppled off his lap and spilled on the ground, causing a veritable feeding frenzy among the geese. "Aw, shoot," he muttered, dropping to his knee to grab the upended bag just as June did the same. Their foreheads met with an audible *thunk*, sending each of them tottering backward on their hunches.

"I'm so sorry!" Elliot stammered, but June was laughing too hard to hear him. "H-Here, let me help you." He clamored to his feet, extending a hand in her direction.

She took it without hesitation, letting him pull her to her feet. After dusting fresh snow and goose droppings off her pants, she plopped down on the bench, motioning for Elliot to do the same. "It's okay. I won't bite."

He forced out a weak chuckle as he sat back down, keeping a solid foot between their bodies. "Uh…here," he said, thrusting the half-empty paper bag in her direction. "I brought this for you—er, for the geese," he quickly amended. "For you to feed the geese, that is…if you want to."

"Thank you." She smiled at him as she took the bag from him, her vivid green eyes twinkling mischievously.

Elliot's heart skipped a beat.

"So…" June flashed him a sideways glance. "Do you live around here, or…?"

"Uh, no. I live about three miles that way," he said, pointing east.

"Did you drive here?"

He shook his head.

June raised an eyebrow. "You walk six miles out of your way to come here every day? Why?"

Elliot shifted. "Um, I only recently started doing that." He hadn't planned to say anything more on the subject, but the kindness in June's eyes made him feel strangely at ease – as though he could tell her anything and she wouldn't judge or belittle him for it. "I live alone, mostly. I mean, my mom, uh, comes around from time to time. But it's just me, for the most part…" He ran a trembling hand through his unkempt black hair. "Anyway, I guess what I'm trying to say is I have a lot of time to kill."

"So your mom's doing better?" June asked, tossing a handful of corn toward the nearest geese.

Elliot raised a quizzical eyebrow.

"Yesterday, you said she was sick." Her eyes suddenly went wide. "Oh, so she stays at the hospital, then? When my dad was sick, they put him in hospice for the last few months of his life. She's not in hospice, is she?" Her eyes shone with sympathy.

"I…uh," Elliot faltered, inwardly railing at himself. *This* is why he avoided talking to people. Why he wandered out of his small, nosy neighborhood every chance he got…Well, that and the fact that he was a danger to others.

"I'm sorry," June said, reaching down to place her mittened hand on top of his. "You don't have to talk about it if you don't want to."

Elliot's gaze lingered on her hand before gently pulling his away. He cleared his throat roughly. "I see her once or twice a week, unless she's too depressed for a visit… Like this week…" He turned his face away from June to inspect the zipper of his jacket. "And last."

"I'm sorry," June said softly. "So…who takes care of you? And pays the bills, for that matter?"

"After my mom stopped working, we were able to live off her parents' trust fund and her fiancé's life insurance." He faltered, his stomach twisting into knots – as they always did – when he thought about Phil.

"Her fiancé died?" June brought her hand to her mouth. "How?"

Me. Elliot cleared his throat. "Uh, car accident. Anyway, that money ran out earlier this year. So I've been working at the grocery store to make some extra money." His smile was tight. "It's not a big deal, really. The house is already paid off, so it's just utilities and groceries, which I get at a discount now. And I don't eat much, anyway." When he finally turned his head to look at June, he was taken aback by the sorrow on her face. "H-Hey, it's okay – really! I'm fine."

"I'm just so sorry," she whispered, scrubbing at a rogue tear on her cheek. "I can't even begin to imagine how hard it must be, living all on your own at seventeen."

Elliot's eyes widened. "Please, don't cry – I'm okay, really." He forced a wide, goofy smile to his face. "See?"

June laughed, rubbing her nose with the back of her mitten. "Sorry – I don't know what came over me."

A knot appeared in Elliot's throat. He'd gotten so used to solitude and loneliness those past few years, he'd all but forgotten what it felt like to have someone genuinely care about him. The urge to reach out and brush the sympathetic tear from the girl's lashes was almost overpowering. He clenched the paper bag between two trembling fists, not trusting himself to speak.

June fell silent, her eyebrows knitting together as she tossed another handful of corn to the geese. Her mouth was pressed into a tight line, reminding Elliot of the expression Libby always wore when she was working out a complex problem.

What's wrong with me? Elliot grimaced, his ears burning. *Any other guy would have just made casual small talk, and I had to go off on some depressing tangent and make her cry.*

"Do you want to come over for lunch?" June asked suddenly.

Elliot started. "Sorry?"

"My mom's out for the day and said she won't be back 'til after dinner." June's mouth broke into a wide smile. "She left me twenty bucks, so I was thinking of splurging on Pay-Per-View and ordering a pizza. Do you like pepperoni?"

Elliot's mouth went dry. He nodded, trying to swallow the lump of emotion that was caught in his throat.

"Great." June rose to her feet, dusting off her hands. "I live just over there." She pointed to an unadorned gray house on the other side of the lake.

Elliot nodded again, clearing his throat roughly. "Are you sure your mother won't mind if I come over?"

June snorted. "Are you kidding? She'd lose her mind if she found me home alone with a boy! But that's what back doors are for." June grinned at him. She extended a hand to Elliot, which he tentatively took, and hoisted him to his feet. "But in all seriousness, it'll be fine." Hands shoved in her pockets, she started walking toward the house. "She's like four hours away at some shaman's book signing."

Elliot fell into step beside her. "A shaman?"

"Yeah, a new age whack job who goes on and on about 'sacral-cleansing enemas' and a bunch of other astrological baloney. My mom is completely obsessed." June rolled her eyes in disdain. "Honestly, she's so preoccupied with the guy, I doubt she'd even notice if you were in the house." She gave Elliot a playful push. "Anyway, I'm not worried. I mean, it's not like you're some serial killer, right?"

Elliot stumbled over a crack in the sidewalk, fumbling to regain his footing. "Right," he croaked. His ribs constricted around his lungs, squeezing the air from them, as his thoughts trailed back to the line of urns collecting dust atop the mantle.

If only she knew.

CHAPTER 16

YOUNG LOVE

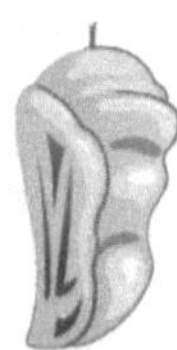

Weeks passed, and the new year came and went.

Elliot found a way to see June every day, whether walking her home from school, helping her with her homework on the park bench, or coming inside for pepperoni pizza and a movie when her mother was out. Sometimes they'd listen to records for hours on end, with June cheerfully singing along to Michael Jackson's newest album. Elliot had never felt so happy, or as safe, as June made him feel. And while he never forgot the pinky promise he'd made to his adoptive mother long ago, he felt compelled to share every part of himself with June that he could, spurred by her kindness, her compassion, and her unwavering empathy. She didn't just listen to Elliot, she *heard* him, understanding him in a way no one else ever had.

And he understood her.

Unlike the boys at June's school, Elliot would listen to her for hours at a time, asking questions and offering comfort whenever and however he could. When June's mother left her alone for the evening, a once-rare event that was occurring with increasing frequency, Elliot would come over and keep June company. They would cook together, play games until late in the evening, and then whisper a hushed goodbye when the garage door alerted them of her mother's return.

Elliot didn't know exactly where he and June stood as far as their relationship was concerned – after all, he'd never so much as kissed her on the cheek, out of fear his growing feelings for her were unreciprocated. But there were times, especially when Elliot had to leave at the end of the evening, that June would look up at him, biting her lip as though she were hoping he might... Well, Elliot wasn't sure, exactly. But with more than three years separating them in age – not to mention a total lack of romantic experience that might have otherwise helped him gauge the situation – he wasn't going to risk scaring her off. If all she ever wanted was friendship, then Elliot would be the greatest, most loyal friend June would ever have. Period.

Their friendship continued in this way for several months, until late one February night.

After a particularly explosive fight with her mother, June called Elliot in tears, asking him if he could meet her. After running the entire distance from his house to hers, he found her waiting for him at their bench beside the lake, her vibrant auburn hair set aglow by the light of the streetlamp. When she looked up at him, her green eyes shining with emotion, something stirred deep in Elliot's chest, stronger than it ever had before – something all at once wondrous and terrifying.

"Are you okay?" he asked, approaching the bench.

Without saying a word, June stood and flung her arms around him in a tight embrace. "Thank you for coming," she whispered against his chest.

He pressed his cheek to the top of her head, breathing in her sweet fragrance. "I'll always come when you call me… Always."

She pulled away with a muted sob, gazing up at him with eyes that were overflowing with tears.

Elliot's breath caught in his chest. "June, what's wro—"

His question ended in a startled gasp as June pressed her lips against his. Eyes widening, and then squeezing shut, Elliot wrapped his arms around her, returning the kiss gently, tentatively.

After a moment, he pulled away, rasping, "Are you sure about this? You're not—"

His sentence was once again interrupted, this time by a much deeper kiss. "I love you, Elliot Whitman," June whispered fiercely. "And I couldn't wait another moment to tell you that."

Upon hearing those words, Elliot crushed his lips against hers, the knot of repressed emotions in his chest unraveling, with him unraveling alongside it. When he finally mustered the strength to pull away from the kiss, he whispered, "I love you too, Juniper Brown – more than I could ever say."

With a small cry, she sank against his chest, cradled into the safety of his loving arms.

. . .

Spring returned, bringing Elliot's nineteenth birthday with it. That evening, he took June to meet his mother, who – to Elliot's immense relief – was sitting on the couch waiting for them when he opened the door.

"Ma," he whispered, scooping her in for a tight hug. Her skin was ashen as he'd ever seen it, and her cheeks were sallow, but for the first time in months, she was smiling.

"June, this is my mother, Libby," Elliot smiled, scrubbing a stray tear from his cheek.

"It's very nice to meet you," June started to say before being interrupted by Libby's tight hug, which smelled faintly of sulfur.

"It's so nice to finally meet you too," Libby murmured against June's hair. "I have heard nothing but wonderful things about you." She took a step backward, appraising her. "Elliot said you were beautiful, but I had no idea you looked like a Hollywood starlet." Libby's eyes crinkled, deepening the lines that had been born not by age, but by fatigue.

June, smoothed out her blue dress, blushing. "Oh, gosh, thank you… Um, would it be okay if I used your restroom?"

"Of course," Libby said, pointing toward the staircase. "It's upstairs – first doorway on the right."

"Thank you," June said again, casting Elliot a demure side eye as she turned to go.

"Oh, El, she's beautiful," Libby whispered, wistfulness creeping into the edges of her voice. "But she's so young…"

"I know. She turned fifteen in February, but she acts so much older, I sometimes forget." Elliot sighed. "And I already know what you're going to say—"

"If she makes you happy, son, then that's all I care about."

Elliot's eyes widened. "I…" He swallowed. He'd been expecting stern admonitions and reminders only half-veiled as jokes that he was never allowed to leave his mother's side. "You're not…worried?"

"About you? Only every second of my existence." She smiled ruefully. "But you're like my Phil was. So long as you have a good woman to love, who will love you back just as fiercely, you'll be just fine."

"But what about you?" Elliot asked.

"I've been worried about me for far too long, little man. It's the reason I was never a very good mother to you."

Elliot's jaw fluttered open. "You were – er, *are* – a wonderful mother. Honest. I don't know what I would have done if you hadn't—"

"Shh!" Libby swatted at his arm. "None of this maudlin talk! We'll scare your new girlfriend away… Just like the last one," she couldn't help but mutter under her breath.

Elliot stiffened but didn't reply. June had just walked out of the bathroom and was making her way downstairs. His eyes darted to her hand, which was thankfully clutching the banister. Nevertheless, he strode over to her, offering his arm before her foot had even touched the last step.

"Such a gentleman," June grinned as she took his hand.

"Come on over, sweets." Libby gestured toward the kitchen table. "I want you both to catch me up on everything that's happened while I make dinner." Her smile turned into a frown as she looked around the kitchen. "El, it's a mess in here! And what's this?" She flung open the refrigerator door. "Hot dogs and moldy buns? Oh no, no, this won't do!"

Elliot bit his lip as he watched her, tromping around the kitchen with more pluck and vivaciousness than he had seen in her in a very, very long time.

"How can I help?" June asked, following her into the kitchen.

"Grab the step stool and see if you can find any Pasta Roni in the cabinets," Libby grunted from inside the refrigerator. "I might be able to slice up these hotdogs and serve them with spaghetti. Does that sound okay?"

"That sounds great!" June answered brightly. "My mom used to make me Spaghetti-O's with hot dogs all the time."

"Oh yeah? That was my favorite food growing up!"

Elliot's heart leapt into his throat as he watched the two women he loved most in the world laughing and cooking and joking as though they'd known each other for years instead of moments. It brought an unexpected flare of warmth to his chest.

"El, you okay?" Libby called over to him. "You look like you've seen a ghost." She flashed him a playful wink.

"I'm…great," he replied, surprised by the fervor in his voice.

Indeed, it was true; for the first time in his life, Elliot knew, deep in his bones, that everything was going to be okay.

CHAPTER 17
LOST SOULS

Lilah hugged her body tightly, trying to warm herself against the cold.

A few feet ahead of her, Elliot was walking briskly toward the sunset, seemingly unbothered by the frigid wind that lashed at his t-shirt. He'd glanced back only once, to make sure Lilah was following, while she darted glances over her shoulder every few seconds. Though she was glad to see Jace, her father, and Sheriff Reid were not following – leaving them behind, in safety, was the sole reason she had willingly left with an undead serial killer – worry pitted in her stomach.

"Will they be okay?" she called after Elliot, more concerned, for the moment, for her loved ones than for herself. "A-Are they still frozen, or—"

"They'll be fine," Elliot replied, not bothering to look back. "They're probably already looking for you, though most likely in the wrong direction given the note I left with the receptionist."

Note? Lilah chewed on her lip. *Oh God, they must be worried sick.*

Of course, as Elliot led her away from the station, in the opposite direction from town, and the sun was setting lower and lower in the sky, she had other, more time-sensitive issues to fret about. Like why they were headed away from civilization and into the woods.

As they crossed the road – which was bereft of cars, and therefore witnesses – and made their way into the frost-covered evergreen forest, a chill slithered down Lilah's spine. Her biological mother had been murdered in a Montana forest, her bones left and forgotten for sixteen years. Was Lilah about to suffer the same fate?

She stumbled to a stop.

Elliot glanced over his shoulder, frowning. When he pulled his hands from his pockets, Lilah flinched. But he wasn't holding a weapon. With a casual flick of his wrist, he warped time around them, conjuring a warm summer breeze that melted the frost from the trees and sprouted bright green grass from the thawed soil. The residual chill, however, still clung to Lilah's skin.

"My apologies," he said. "I hadn't realized it was cold." He then continued walking as though nothing unusual had happened.

Lilah blinked in surprise. "I…wait!" she called, chasing after him. *What kind of murderer makes sure his victims are warm before killing them?* "Why are you doing this? Please – tell me!"

Elliot stole a sideways glance in her direction as she fell into step beside him. After a long moment, he said. "Tell me about your powers."

"You first," she shot back, then bit her tongue. Probably better not to antagonize a serial killer. Sighing, she unzipped her jacket, vaguely annoyed that she hadn't thought to warm the air herself. "Fine. I can control time – or rather, the age of things in my immediate surroundings. But you already knew that." She chewed on the inside of her cheek, wondering whether she would be able to use her powers against him the way he had done to Jace.

Elliot shot her a look.

Lilah gulped. Better to ask a few more questions first. "What about you? I mean, how are you doing this?" she asked, biting her lip. "Maintaining this form, that is."

"You reviving my body was the catalyst I needed. After that, it's just been a matter of concentration," he said, his tone casual. "So, do you consider yourself to be a chronomancer or a necromancer?"

"A necromancer?" Lilah gaped at him. "As in, someone who raises the dead?"

"Is that not what you did with me?"

"I…well, no. I mean…" she swallowed, then shook her head. "No, I'm not raising people from the dead! I'm just reviving their bodies – temporarily," she added hastily. "And even then, that's purely through time manipulation. The people I speak to are just carbon copies of their previous selves. Their souls have already moved on."

Elliot cast her a sideways glance.

She bit her lip. "Haven't they?"

He sighed, shoving his hands deeper in his pockets as he wove between the trees. "Perhaps. Perhaps, because you're merely rousing their bones, their souls remain undisturbed." He stopped, turning to look at her, his steel-gray eyes boring into hers. "Then again, here I stand, body, soul, and all. You did that. Not me."

Lilah gasped, taking a step backwards. *If that's true, then that means all those people I woke up...* Her eyes widened. "Willow," she whispered.

"Pardon?"

"My mother"—she glared at him, not bothering to mask the contempt creeping into her voice—"was murdered when she was just fifteen years old. It's only because I was able to talk to her after the fact that we were able to find the guy who did it. The version of her I woke up had only minutes to live." Her hands balled into fists, and it took everything she had to keep her voice from cracking. "When she asked me if she would have to go back and be killed all over again, I told her no, that it had already happened… That her soul had moved on…" She bit her lip as a squirrel emerged from the grass, bounded to the edge of the time aberration, then returned to eternal sleep beneath the snow-covered soil. "Is…" She cleared her throat roughly. "Is that not true?"

Elliot stared into the distance, his expression unreadable. "Perhaps it was," he murmured. "Perhaps you roused a mere husk of your mother, causing no further harm to her past self." He turned to look at Lilah, hardness creeping into his expression. "Or, perhaps, you sentenced her to a fate far worse than death."

"Says the murderer," Lilah shot back, blinking back tears.

"You are as much a murderer as I am."

Lilah stumbled backward as though she'd been slapped. "What?"

"I killed my adoptive mother," Elliot said, his voice scarcely louder than the wind. "When she fell down the stairs and broke her neck…that was because of me."

Lilah's eyes rounded in horror.

"I killed her dog, her fiancé…her entire family." He took a step toward Lilah, who was inching backwards. "Before them, I killed my mother and my father, the nuns who tried to rid the orphanage of me, two little girls who may have otherwise survived the fire that consumed them… All of those people you saw in the forest are dead because of me."

Lilah found her back pressed against the rough bark of a pine tree.

"I don't have proof, of course, beyond the three I watched die right in front of me. But one can infer." His eyes narrowed sharply. "How do you know Willow's soul wasn't summoned when you roused her? Do you know what happens when you revive a person's body from the moment of their death?"

Lilah slid around the tree, moving farther and farther into the woods.

"At the exact moment my mother's soul should have been ascending into a higher plane, I snatched it away from the light, artificially implanting it into a version of her that no longer existed. In doing so, I created a ghost – a soul that's missed its singular opportunity to ascend from this corporeal realm. Her spirit returned to me whenever I revived her, but the moment she reverted back to ashes, her soul was left wandering in limbo." He closed his eyes. "And now that I've lost her ashes, she's trapped in a permanent purgatory – a hell of my own creation."

Tears were rolling down Lilah's cheeks – tears she couldn't muster the energy to wipe away. "H-How do I know if I've done the same thing to my mother? If I…I…" She tried to swallow but couldn't. *What if I'm the reason she's dead?*

"That"—Elliot looked her dead in the eye—"is exactly what we're going to find out."

At that, something inside of Lilah snapped. "As if you care!" she shouted, shoving off of a tree. Her feet propelled her forward, until she was almost toe-to-toe with the monster that stood before her. From here, she could clearly see the dark circles under his eyes, the morose expression that prematurely lined every inch of his twenty-year-old face. "What is it to you if I'm a murderer or not?" she demanded, her increasingly shrill voice echoing through the trees. "What do you want with me?"

Elliot didn't reply. He merely turned his back to her and continued walking in the same direction he had been before.

"Where are you going?" Lilah shouted, jogging after him. "Answer me!"

Ignoring her, he approached a rusted chain link fence, his ashes phasing into the shadows as he walked to and through it. When he reappeared on the other side, he kept walking, not bothering to check and see if she was following.

Lilah's eyes bulged with fury and indignation. With one final, furious look behind her – she had to be at least three miles from the police station by this point – she hoisted herself over the fence. Her boots landed in snow once more, and as the sun dropped below a familiar line of willow trees, she suddenly realized where the boy had taken her: the back entrance to the Tri-Forks cemetery.

"Why are we here?" she demanded, her rib cage tightening around her lungs with every step forward. It was as though her heart suddenly understood what her mind had yet to grasp – or perhaps, had refused to grasp.

Elliot expertly slunk between the gravestones as though he'd taken this walk many times, his eyes locked directly ahead. When he finally came to a stop several minutes later, his head bowed before the well-kempt grave nestled at his feet, Lilah's heart was racing faster than it ever had. Not only had she visited this grave before, she knew exactly who it belonged to without having to look.

"How?" she tried to whisper. *How does he know?* But she couldn't bring herself to ask the question aloud.

In truth, she already knew the answer.

CHAPTER 18

NEGATIVE ENERGY

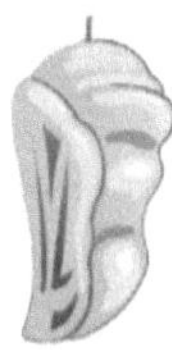

Elliot lay awake, listening to the sound of the ticking clock on the wall and the rumbling purr of June's cat, who was snoozing on his chest. His arm had fallen asleep well over thirty minutes ago, but he didn't dare shift even an inch for fear that June might wake. He brushed a strand of auburn hair from her face with his free hand, his chest tightening with emotion. It was during quiet, perfect moments like this that he struggled the most, unable to comprehend how he'd come to be with someone as precious as June. Their relationship often felt more like a dream than reality – a fragile, fleeting dream from which he might wake at any moment.

As she stirred, letting out a contented hum, the tightness in Elliot's chest turned into a familiar twinge of panic. Despite the terrible things he'd seen and lived through in his meager nineteen years of life, the most frightening thing Elliot could think of was the possibility of June leaving him – a fear further compounded by the fact that her eventual departure was more than plausible. After all, everyone Elliot had ever loved had left him, either through abandonment or premature death. Moreover, how many high school romances managed to survive graduation? And even *that* felt like a pipe dream; Elliot couldn't even see June at school, though pimple-faced weasels like Dillon Harold and Nicholas Weisse got to see her every day. How long did he have before she grew tired of dating someone she had to go all day without seeing? At least the school year was nearly over; they'd have the whole summer ahead of them.

But, come August, then what?

I could go back to school, he thought, and not for the first time in recent months. His mother only managed to wake up a couple of times a week those days, finalizing her dissertation – now a five-hundred page stack of papers that could double as a bludgeoning weapon – for an hour or two before fatigue caught up with her again. The bigger problem was that Elliot was barely making enough money to cover food and utilities, not to mention the ongoing cost of refurbishing Libby's old Saab so he could drive to and from June's house easier. Just the other day, he had to pay *fifty-five* dollars to register it, which didn't include the penalties for letting the registration lapse for the last six years. That alone nearly wiped out his and Libby's joint bank account. There was no way he could go to school and work full time and still have time to see June as often as he'd like.

I wonder how long it takes for a bank vault door to rust? The once-rhetorical question was becoming less and less hypothetical the longer he thought about it. *Is a hundred years enough? Two hundred?* He'd never pushed his powers that far into the future, but it was worth a shot. Of course, if he was caught and subsequently sent to prison, that would defeat the entire purpose of trying to rob a bank to spend more time with June. And his mother would be stuck in her dusty urn on the mantle for decades – a thought that made Elliot's stomach twist into knots.

The sound of the garage door opening made him jump, startling both June and her cat, who hopped off the bed and began scratching at her bedroom door.

"What time is it?" June whispered groggily, rubbing her eyes.

"Time for me to go," Elliot whispered, kissing her forehead. "I'll just sneak out the win—"

"Juniper!" Vivienne's shrill voice echoed through the house. "Juniper, wake up!"

"Hide!" June hissed, yanking the covers off of them.

Elliot's eyes widened as she yanked him out of the bed. "Where—"

"Juniper!" her mother called again.

June flung the closet door open, ushering him inside. "Get in!"

The closet door had just clicked shut when the door to the bedroom flew open and the ceiling light flicked on.

June whirled around in surprise. "Mom? What's—"

"Oh, Junie, the book signing went so well!" Vivienne exclaimed, stepping on the poor cat's tail as she burst inside. It let out an aggrieved yowl as it darted between her legs and into the hallway. "We had a record number of people show up, didn't we, Shaman?"

A tall, slender man followed Vivienne into the room, looking around June's bedroom with a pinched expression. "Indeed we did, Viv, thanks to your valiant efforts."

Two spots of pink appeared in Vivienne's plump, beaming cheeks.

Blanching, June snatched her terrycloth robe from the back of her desk chair and wrapped it around her body in an attempt to hide her rumpled Garfield nightgown. Why her mother was gallivanting some stranger around the house at half past midnight, she had no idea. The man was a few years older than Vivienne, perhaps in his late thirties, and wore his receding, stringy brown hair in a low ponytail that hung halfway down his back. With a paisley shirt that had been unbuttoned to his navel – displaying a caved in, hairy chest and collection of crystals that hung from leather cords around his neck – hand-dyed parachute pants, and bare feet, he looked and smelled as though he'd walked straight out of a hippie den.

"Juniper, this is Michaelangelo Z. Hastings," Vivienne all but purred, placing a hand on the man's arm. "He has graciously offered to pay us a house call after what was a *very* long and arduous day of signing books all the way out in Waterloo. Shaman Mike, this is my daughter – the one I've been telling you about."

"It's an honor to meet you, Juniper." Before she could protest, the "shaman" clasped her hand in his, flipped it over, and kissed the inside of her wrist. "Oh, Viv, you were right." He sniffed, dropping June's hand so he could inspect a stain on the rose-patterned wallpaper. "This place positively reeks."

"Excuse me?" June stammered.

"Tone!" Vivienne admonished.

The door to the closet creaked open ever so slightly, though no one over the age of thirty noticed.

"When you told me there was negative energy pooling around the house, I of course believed you. You have great instinct for that," Mike murmured, knocking on various places on the wall, then pressing his ear against it as though expecting something to knock back. He worked his way around the room, edging closer and closer to the closet, the wrinkle between his brows getting deeper and deeper.

Elliot and Juniper sucked in simultaneous breaths.

"Shaman, darling, before we start the official cleansing, could I interest you in some limeflower tea?" Vivienne batted her eyelashes at him. "I took the recipe directly from your book. I even added cardamom, like you recommended."

Mike's eyes darted between the closet door and Vivienne, who was beckoning him from the doorway. "Entirely up to you, my dear." He shrugged. "I am billing this house call on a quarter-hour basis, so it makes little difference to me how that time is spent."

Disappointment flickered across Vivienne's features, which she quickly replaced with a wide, saccharine smile. "Of course. Come downstairs. I'll brew us a pot while you tell me all about your latest book."

At that, Mike perked up. "Oh, well, that is quite the venture – one that I expect will take me all the way to Tibet this time."

"You don't say!"

June watched the two of them leave with bated breath, which she only released after her bedroom door had clicked shut.

The door to the closet flew open.

June lunged forward to catch it before it smashed into the wall.

"Who *is* that creep?" Elliot snarled, his features contorting into a scowl. "And why the hell is your mother bringing some stranger up to your bedroom in the middle of the night? Is she crazy?"

"Shh!" June was casting anxious glances at the door. "He's not a stranger. She's been hanging around him for months now—"

"I don't care if she's known him for a decade!"

The lights flickered.

"Elliot, please!" she pleaded, dropping her voice to a whisper while gesturing for him to do the same. "If my mom catches you in here she'll kill me! You have to leave – now!"

Elliot's hands balled into fists as he regarded the door. "And the way he kissed your wrist— who does he think he is? Burt Reynolds?"

"He doesn't even live around here. He lives in some cabin a few states away," June reassured him. "I'll change my clothes and head downstairs. And if there's any problem at all—"

"You'll call me?" Elliot interjected. "You swear it?"

"I swear." She held out her pinky finger, which he grasped in his. "Now please, you have to leave!"

With one last begrudging look at the door, Elliot stalked over to the window, which June was in the process of quietly opening. Before climbing through, he wrapped his arms around her, pulling her into a rib-cracking embrace. "I love you," he whispered against her lips, kissing her fiercely.

June teetered, a warm shiver racing down her spine. "I love you too – now go!"

After giving her one more kiss for good measure, Elliot climbed out the window, using the trellis to climb down to the ground. "I'm going to stick around for a few minutes," he stage-whispered up to her.

"Just don't let them see you!" June whispered back before quietly shutting the window.

Elliot stood beneath her window for a long moment, turning to go only when the bedroom light went out.

When he spun around, he found himself standing face-to-face with the shaman.

Before Elliot could stammer a word, the older man reached out and snatched him by the arm, dragging him over to the back porch with surprising force. Vivienne was waiting for Mike in the doorway to the kitchen. When she saw Elliot, the two mugs she was holding in her hands crashed to the ground.

"I have tracked down the source of the *sha chi* pooling in your home," Mike announced. He jerked Elliot's arm behind his back, eliciting a hiss of pain from the boy. "I found him sneaking out of your daughter's bedroom window just moments ago."

Vivienne gaped at Elliot for a long moment, her eyes doubling in size while the color drained from her cheeks. "JUNIPER!" she screamed, clutching the doorway for support.

The lights in the next-door neighbors' house flicked on.

"JUNIPER, GET DOWN HERE RIGHT NOW!"

Her daughter skidded into the kitchen a few seconds later, her eyes growing wide when she saw Elliot.

"What have you *done?!*" Vivienne screamed. "And *you!*" She jabbed a red-painted fingernail in Elliot's direction. "How *dare* you!"

"Mom, please—" June started.

"Did you touch her?" Vivienne demanded. "Answer me!"

Elliot swallowed tightly but said nothing.

Vivienne's hand flew up so unexpectedly, Elliot didn't even have time to flinch. The slap she laid across his face echoed through the neighborhood, where more and more bedroom lights were flickering to life.

"Mom, stop!" June cried, lunging forward to grab her mother's wrist. "It's not his fault!"

Vivienne roughly shook her daughter off, sending June tumbling to the ground. She let out a cry of pain as her bare knee smacked into the concrete.

Elliot's eyes darkened, and for the briefest moment, the warm, balmy air turned frigid.

Mike let out a gasp, jerking Elliot around so he could stand between the boy and Vivienne. "What is this foul witchcraft you employ?" he demanded, ripping one of the crystals from his neck and thrusting it in Elliot's direction. "Name yourself, demon!"

"Vivienne? June?" a woman's voice called out. Violet's mother and father, both clad in slippers and robes, let themselves in through the backyard gate. Violet was trailing behind them, her eyes doubling in size when she saw her best friend sprawled on the ground.

"Are you okay?" she cried, dropping beside June.

"Viv, what's—" Violet's mother started.

"Tammy, call the police!" Vivienne rasped.

Tammy faltered.

"Call them!" Vivienne screeched. "Tell them that this *pervert*"—she jerked a trembling finger in Elliot's direction—"broke into my daughter's room!"

"Mom, no!" June cried, scrambling to her feet with Violet's help. "It's not his fault. I invited him—"

Her mother whirled on her again, raising her hand above her head.

Elliot shoved past the shaman, knocking him aside, and grabbed Vivienne's wrist.

She let out an agonized gasp, dropping to her knees. "He's hurting me!" she screamed. "Tammy, hurry! Call the police!"

"I'm getting my rifle," Tammy's husband snarled, spinning on a slippered heel to run back toward their house. After snatching their daughter, Tammy darted after him, shouting over her shoulder, "I'm calling, Viv, I'm calling them right now!"

Elliot dropped Vivienne's wrist. "Don't touch her," he growled, stepping around her to help June to her feet. June collapsed into his arms with a sob.

Taking his cue from the younger man, Shaman Mike hastily pulled Vivienne to *her* feet, which was a more arduous task. Once she had been properly righted, Mike blew out a long breath. "I think it would be best if I didn't wait around for the authorities to arrive, given our disagreement on which herbs ought to be legal and which oughtn't." He cast Vivienne an apologetic grimace. "I'll just, uh, be waiting in the van."

With that, he too spun on his heel and ran.

Vivienne took a threatening step toward Elliot, prompting June to stand between them. "Mom," she pleaded. "Mom, listen to me, please!"

Ignoring her, Vivienne met Elliot's eyes. "Get away from my daughter," she hissed, "and never come back here again."

"Mom, you can't—"

"Because if I ever see you here again, I'll grab Hank's rifle myself—"

"MOM!" June screamed. "I'm pregnant!"

The final word echoed through the neighborhood like a death knell.

Both Elliot and Vivienne froze in their spots.

June whirled around to face Elliot, clutching his shirt in her hands and flashing him an imploring look. "I'm so sorry, El… I-I wanted to tell you."

Sirens echoed in the distance.

"You're…what?" Elliot whispered, shock – mixed with profound, inexplicable joy – rendering him otherwise speechless.

June dropped her head. "I'm so sorry I didn't tell you. I…I just didn't want you to freak out." With effort, she forced herself to meet his piercing gaze. "I only found out a few days ago. I-I've been trying to figure out how to tell you."

Pregnant? Elliot's heart leapt into his throat. His mind was all at once accosted with flashbulb images of June, her belly round and full; of their baby, her eyes wide and green just like her mother's; of him and June tucking her in, forehead to forehead above their newborn's crib.

"Are you angry with me?" June whispered, emotion tugging at her voice.

He opened his mouth to reply, but no words came.

Red and blue lights illuminated the backyard, and the distant chirps of radios filled the silence. Somewhere in the back of Elliot's mind, he vaguely registered Vivienne running around the side of the house, and Shaman Mike chasing after her. But he couldn't tear his eyes away from June's.

"El?" she whispered, her tearful gaze pleading. "Won't you say something?"

"He's in the back!" Vivienne's voice filtered over from the far side of the house. *"Hurry! The man who assaulted my daughter is standing right over there!"*

"What—no!" June let out a frightened cry, her head whipping in her mother's direction. She turned back to Elliot, frantic. "Elliot, you have to go!" When he didn't move, she shoved him as hard as she could, causing him to stumble backward. "Get out of here, now!"

He blinked rapidly, shaking his head to clear it, before his blurry gaze settled on the approaching line of shadows that stretched across the neighbor's house – menacing black silhouettes stamped against a flashing backdrop of blue and red.

When he turned back to June, she was transfixed, her unblinking eyes glued to the line of officers that had just burst through the back gate. All five of them were frozen mid-step. Vivienne stood a few paces in front of them, her immobilized arms outstretched at her sides as though conducting traffic, while Violet's father was frozen mid-step, his cocked rifle balanced between two petrified hands.

Though the leaves fluttered and distant crickets could be heard, nothing else in that backyard moved – save for the tear that rolled down June's frozen face.

Elliot gently brushed it away with his thumb, his breath catching in his chest. He could unfreeze her right now, take her away from all of this… But if he did, she would discover his secret, something he'd sworn to his mother he would never let happen. Worse, he risked frightening June – possibly irreparably so.

He took a half-step backward. He would go home, explain the whole situation to Libby. Together, the two of them would come up with a plan. This would all be fixed. He would ask June to marry him, and then he would be able to tell her everything – no more secrets, ever. Together, they would make a family – something he'd longed for his entire life – just him, her, their baby, and Elliot's mother. Libby would be so happy when she found out she was going to be a grandmother, she'd forget all about her depression. She'd happily wake up every day, helping Elliot with the baby so June could finish school.

He took a deep, steeling breath. *Everything will be okay,* he told himself. *We just need time.*

Brushing one last kiss against June's parted lips, Elliot spun around and ran, willing his feet to move faster than they ever had before. His mother's car was parked half a block away, beneath a streetlamp. The moment he slumped in the driver's seat and started the engine, the police sirens began flashing again.

But by then, Elliot was already driving in the opposite direction.

Mom will help me explain the whole situation, and the police officers will realize they made a terrible mistake. Everything will be alright. He glanced in the rearview mirror, his heart lodging in his chest at the sight of red and blue lights.

Please, God, let everything be alright.

A TREE BY ANY OTHER NAME

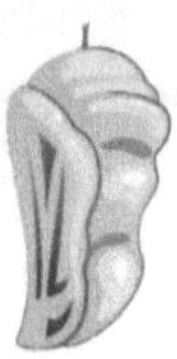

The clock above the stove blinked 2:00 a.m.

Vivienne was still pacing the length of the kitchen, as she had been for the last hour. After the boy had disappeared, her idiot daughter refused to tell the police his full name or address. Not only that, she'd refused to utter even a single word in her own defense, sealing her fate as the town harlot.

The police left shortly after that.

After she'd dragged June up to her room, Vivienne ripped the phone out of the wall and locked the bedroom door from the outside. Mike was chivalrously keeping watch outside June's window to make sure no one tried to go in or out.

What *he* must have thought of this whole debacle, Vivienne could only imagine.

Fury and humiliation heated her cheeks. Having heard her screams, the entire neighborhood had gathered in the surrounding backyards and watched, their hands cupped around their mouths as they gossiped. What exactly had they been saying, anyway? That her fifteen-year-old daughter was a loose-legged tramp? That Vivienne was a failure as a mother?

She ground her teeth together so hard, pain zinged through her jaw.

Vivienne had only been nineteen when she fell pregnant with Juniper. Of course, the biological father fled the moment he found out, leaving Vivienne to struggle on her own – at least until she started dating another man a few weeks later. He believed the baby was his, thank God, thereby saving her reputation. After June was born, Vivienne swore to herself that her daughter would be different, that she wouldn't repeat her mother's mistakes. But here she was – the laughing stock of the entire town.

She could abort it… But then they'd blame me for that too. Her pacing intensified. *We could just say it was a miscarriage, of course, but that doesn't fix the fact that she was knocked up in the first place… What if I told them the whole thing was a ruse – that she was just looking for attention?* She darted a furious look up the stairs.

But she has such a big mouth, she'll tell all her blabbermouth little friends at school. Maybe if she switches schools...

She stopped dead in her tracks. *What about the boy? What if he comes back and convinces her to raise it with him?*

"No." The word rushed from her mouth.

The sliding glass door slid open and Mike stepped inside, his jaw cracking from a wide yawn. "No sign of the young man." With a sigh, he slumped into the kitchen chair. "But just to be safe, I have placed several wards to protect the perimeter of the house. Whatever energy that boy carries with him, it's about as dark as I've ever experienced." He ran a hand through his stringy, disheveled hair. "Truth be told, I have not felt such a vile wave of *sha chi* since I made a house call in Wisconsin for an ad-hoc exorcism. You must do whatever you can to protect your daughter from such a demon."

"We have to leave," Vivienne whispered.

"I was going to suggest the very same," Mike said with a tired nod. "Of course, the girl won't go quietly, besotted as she is. She'll more than likely chain herself to her bed, kicking and screaming. We could fabricate a lie, of course – perhaps even enlist your neighbors to help."

Vivienne shook her head. "She'd never believe us. You said so yourself. She's besotted."

"Indeed." Mike looked thoughtful for a moment. "Unless… Oh, of course." He stood up abruptly, scraping his chair across the ceramic tile. "Where do you keep the phonebook?"

"There." Vivienne pointed to the cabinet beside the microwave, a dubious expression on her face.

"I have a friend – an actor – who lives a few hours from here. Perhaps if you were willing to add a few more billable hours to our ongoing tab…?"

Swallowing – she'd all but scraped her bank account dry for this man already – Vivienne mustered a weak nod.

Mike's grin was practically feral as he punched in the phone number. "Excellent."

. . .

Vivienne finally unlocked June's door at around 7:00 a.m. that morning.

June opened the door, clutching their mangy tabby cat against her chest. Her blotchy, tear-stained face brought a wave of bile-fueled contempt to Vivienne's stomach.

"Downstairs. Now." Vivienne turned on her heel, striding down the hallway. "There's a man here to see you."

With a heavy sigh, June gently set the cat down and followed her mother to the kitchen, where Shaman Mike and another middle-aged man June had never seen before were at the kitchen table, each of them clutching steaming mugs of limeflower tea. The stranger wore a brown trench coat and a wide-brimmed brown fedora that was slightly too big for his head.

"Good morning, Miss Brown," the stranger said, gesturing for June to sit. When she did, he cleared his throat. "My name is Detective Lucas Saunders, and I'm sorry to tell you I have troubling news."

June darted an anxious glance over at her mother, who had managed to compose her features into a vaguely sympathetic expression as she crossed her arms and leaned one shoulder against the wall.

"Now, before I go off rattling classified information that you have not been cleared to hear, I need to verify a few details with you." Detective Saunders glanced down at his notepad. "Your, ah, friend, Elliot – would you mind confirming his last name to make sure we're speaking about the same person?"

Mike leaned forward on the table, steepling his fingers.

"You'll send the police after him," June accused, her glare flitting between the two men. "I'm not stupid."

"June, I swear to you, that's not why he's here," Vivienne interjected. "In fact, I'm deeply sorry for losing my temper last night." She kept her voice calm and level, just as she and Mike had practiced earlier that morning. "I realize now that I overreacted, and I'm very sorry for that."

June's eyes widened.

"However, I do want to make sure your Elliot is not the same Elliot as the one Detective Sanders—"

"Saunders," Mike interjected, casting her a tight look.

"—er, yes, Detective *Saunders*, is looking for." Vivienne's smile was a saccharine one. "Please dear, just tell him. He's working on a criminal case at the moment, and as soon as we confirm it's a different man that's under investigation, the detective will be on his way. And then I'd be glad to have your Elliot come over for lunch. We can discuss this whole m—er, *situation* then." She forced a wider smile. "I won't try to keep you from him."

"Really?" June swallowed tightly. "You promise?"

Vivienne drew a solemn X over her sternum. "Cross my heart and hope to die."

June nodded to herself, absorbing her mother's words, then turned back to the detective. "My Elliot's name is Elliot Whitman—"

Mike covertly scribbled a quick note on the pad of paper in front of him, catching Vivienne's eye as he did.

"—and he's the nicest, most caring person I've ever known. So would you please tell my mother that everything's fine, and it's not the same person?"

Detective Saunders's head drooped. "Oh, Miss Brown…this is so much worse than I ever could have anticipated."

"Oh, come on." June rolled her eyes. "You can't be serious."

"I'm afraid, Miss Brown, that I have never been more serious."

At that, Vivienne came over and squeezed June's shoulders, doing her best not to throttle her daughter in the process.

"What are you talking about?" June demanded.

Detective Saunders dabbed at the perspiration forming beneath the rim of his hat. "Miss Brown, I respect you far too much to mince words, so I'll just tell you facts outright: Elliot Whitman is a stalker and a pedophile. He preys on young women with the intention of getting them pregnant – some sort of sick fetish, we believe."

"No." June shook her head firmly. "You've got the wrong guy."

"Oh no, Miss Brown, I assure you, there is no mistake." He abruptly leaned forward, making

June lean back. "Let me guess…he told you he loved you? That you were the best thing to ever happen to him?"

"Well yes, but—"

"And he insisted on seeing you whenever he could, going so far as to sneak inside your room when your mother was away?"

June flinched away from her mother's tightening grip on her shoulders. "Yes, but only because I—"

"I'm afraid it was the same with all the other girls, Miss Brown." Detective Saunders shook his head sadly. "He fed them the same lies too, stroked their poor, fragile egos the same way. And then the moment he got them pregnant, he fled. Just like he did last night. Tell me, Miss Brown, has he tried to contact you since then?"

"I…I wouldn't know." June rubbed the back of her neck to smooth the hairs that were standing on end. "My mom disconnected my phone."

"But the downstairs phone has been plugged in all night," Vivienne reassured her. "To be honest, I had hoped he would call so I could apologize to him for losing my temper. But he never did."

"Then I'll call him—" June rose from her chair, reaching for the phone on the wall.

Vivienne flashed the "detective" a sharp glare.

"You can't!" He stood, blocking June from the phone. "Because my men are already there, taking him into custody."

"What?" June gasped.

"Yes, my men raided his house just a few minutes ago. And though it pains me to tell you this, they found him in bed with another girl – one who was even younger than you, I might add."

June's eyes widened.

Detective Saunders *tsked*, shaking his head in righteous indignation. "When they burst in his room, Elliot just threw his head back and started laughing. He's already admitted everything, June, right there, lying naked in his bed. He even mentioned your name – Juniper Brown," he reiterated. "I'm more than happy to take you to the police station to see for yourself."

Vivienne shot him another glare.

"*But*," he added swiftly, "we're one hundred percent certain it's the same man, June." He pulled a small, lined notebook from his pocket, flipping to the notes Mike had scrawled for him a few minutes earlier. "Elliot Whitman – stands at around six-foot-one, about one hundred and sixty five pounds, with wild black hair and…" He squinted down at the notepad. "Well, I can't tell you what he was wearing, since he was naked as the day he was born when they found him. But he must have been wearing a long-sleeved black t-shirt the night before, because it had been tossed on the floor beside the rest of the clothing he'd removed from his *other* young victim."

"Elliot was wearing a black shirt last night." June pressed her fingers to her mouth. "But…I mean, there's no possible way…"

Detective Saunders stood up, repositioning his lopsided hat as he did. "I'll give you some time to process, but we'll need you to come down to the station to give your witness statement."

"A statement?" June repeated.

"Yes. Elliot Whitman will be charged with twelve counts of statutory rape, plus eight counts of, uh, impregnating a minor. So we'll of course need your testimony to make sure that monster is locked away for a very, very long time." His eyes darted to her stomach. "My sincere condolences to you and yours."

"I'll show you out, Detective Saunders," Mike said, rising to his feet. "Thank you very much for coming by this morning. And for getting predators like this off the street, of course…"

Their voices faded away as June stared straight ahead, unmoving and unblinking. Vivienne threw her arms around her. "Oh baby, I'm so, so sorry!" She pulled away. "There's no way I'm going to make you go to that police station and stare your attacker in the face. *No* way." She squeezed June's chin, tilting her face toward hers. "Listen to me, Juniper. I'm taking you away from this place – today. We're going to go up to Montana, where Shaman Mike has already arranged a place for us to stay. We're going to start over – you, me, and…and the baby." She forced a tight, wavering smile to her face. "I'm so sorry I haven't been around much these past few months, June. But that's all going to change now, okay? I'll never leave you again. I love you so much." She leaned over to give June another hug, this one even tighter than the last.

June couldn't find the words to speak.

Vivienne stood up. "Now, go pack up your things, my darling – just the essentials. Mike is leaving in the next hour and has just enough room in his van for us and a few boxes… Well, come on!" she prompted, ushering June to her feet. "There's not much time to waste!"

Mike returned from the foyer, putting an arm around Vivienne's shoulders.

"Don't forget Pebbles' cat food!" she called after her daughter.

As if in a trance, June made her way to her bedroom, stopping just before reaching the hallway. She turned around slowly, finally finding the words to speak. "I'd like to see for myself."

"See what?" Vivienne frowned.

"See him. To know for certain."

Vivienne opened her mouth to protest, but Mike squeezed her shoulder, silencing her. "We'll stop by his house on the way. After that, we can even go to the police station, if you'd like. We don't want you doubting this very wise decision for even a moment."

June nodded mutely, then turned to go upstairs.

Once her daughter was out of earshot, Vivienne rounded on Mike. "Why did you say that?"

"Because we know his full name now," Mike replied, pressing the notebook into her hands. "So you're going to report him to the police."

Vivienne's eyes widened, then narrowed. Nodding, she walked over to the phone and punched in the numbers.

"Nine-one-one, what's your emergency?" a voice answered.

"Yes, I'd like to report a serious crime," Vivienne murmured into the receiver, keeping her voice as low as possible. "A man named Elliot Whitman has just assaulted my daughter."

Smiling, Mike nodded his approval.

When she hung up the phone a few moments later, he gave her a tight hug. "You did the right thing," he murmured, pulling away quickly. "Now the only thing we'll have to worry about is the child."

"You mean June?" Vivienne asked, biting her lip.

"No." Mike shook his head firmly. "The one she's carrying."

An hour later, Shaman Mike drove his two passengers by Elliot's house, where they found a squadron of police cars parked outside. June watched in silence from the backseat as Elliot was escorted from his house in handcuffs by four armed police officers, who surrounded him on all sides.

As if sensing her presence, Elliot's head jerked up. "June!" he cried out when he saw her. "June!"

She quickly rolled up the window, unable to meet his gaze as their van sped away.

"Do you want to go to the police station, sweetheart?" Vivienne asked tentatively. "Make your witness statement?"

June shook her head. "No. I…I just want to leave."

Vivienne tried to conceal her smile as she nodded and turned back around.

June didn't say a word for the duration of the drive, tuning out her mother's incessant chatter as she curled into a ball in the backseat, her eyes squeezed shut.

At one point, Vivienne glanced back at her. "June?" she asked softly.

June didn't answer.

Satisfied that her daughter was sleeping, Vivienne turned back around in her seat, casually resting her hand on Mike's thigh.

He eyed her hand warily, clearing his throat. "What are you going to do about the girl's child?"

"Oh, June's not actually pregnant," Vivienne chuckled, waving her free hand. "I gave her a pregnancy test myself this morning, when you were talking on the phone."

June frowned. That had never happened. In fact, she still had her positive pregnancy test, which was buried at the bottom of the paper bag she'd hastily filled with underwear and socks.

"Turns out this was the first time he'd snuck into her room," Vivienne lied. "Who knows what he tried to do with her – or would have, if he hadn't been caught – but I can assure you she isn't pregnant. Can you imagine? A pregnant fifteen-year-old?" She cleared her throat roughly. "What kind of mother would I be if I had allowed that to happen?"

"I am glad to hear it," Mike admitted. "That boy is marked by profound evil, no doubt about it. I'd have been very concerned for June's wellbeing – and yours as well – if he had managed to infect her with his seed."

June squeezed her eyes shut even tighter, fighting back a fresh deluge of stinging tears.

"Er, hypothetically…" Vivienne hedged, keeping her voice carefully blasé, "what kind of cleansing herbs would you have suggested for something like that? If she *had* been pregnant, that is?"

"Oh, why, I have an entire stockroom of home-brewed, energy-cleansing salves and unguents that I sell in my shop! I'll send you a brochure, if you're curious. Ten percent off, of course!" He took that opportunity to shift gears, strategically knocking her hand off his leg.

Vivienne's face fell. "Oh. Well. I'd love to look…just for curiosity's sake, of course."

That prompted an animated discussion on the various types of medicinal plants and minerals that could "hypothetically" ward off evil spirits and energy. It wasn't until they had crossed the border into South Dakota several hours later that Vivienne turned around in her seat to check on June.

"Honey?" she asked. "Have you put more thought into what you'd like your new name to be?"

Still curled up in the fetal position, June shook her head, her eyes red-rimmed and faraway. "No."

"Well, Mike and I were talking, and we thought that it would be really lovely to keep to the arboreal theme of your old name. What do you think about that?"

Her daughter hugged her body tighter, blinking back tears. "Fine," she whispered.

"Wonderful." Mike smiled at her in the rearview mirror. "How about Olive?"

Vivienne crinkled her nose at him. "Ugh, no. That's dreadful. Jasmine, maybe?"

"A bit too exotic, if you ask me… Hazel, perhaps?"

"Definitely not." Vivienne winced. "I'm allergic to hazelnuts!"

Despite her best efforts, June's thoughts drifted right back to the first time she'd laid her eyes on Elliot, half a year ago. He had been sitting alone on a park bench, feeding a flock of geese beside a grove of willow trees when she'd sat down beside him.

"What about Holly?" Mike offered.

"Willow," June whispered.

"Did you say 'Willow'?" Vivienne repeated, frowning.

She nodded.

The older woman let out a harrumph. "A little hippie-ish, but I suppose that could work."

"That settles it, then," Mike chimed in. "Willow, named after the graceful, slender tree, and Celeste, for the bright light that burns in your mother's heart like a shining star."

"It's perfect." Celeste beamed at her daughter in the mirror. "Once we get to Montana and leave this nightmare behind us, we can start from scratch – be anyone we want to be, you know?" She reached behind her to pat the top of Willow's head. "It's going to be the start of a wonderful new life. You'll see. From now on, everything is going to be perfect – I promise."

CHAPTER 20
THE APPLE DOESN'T FALL FAR FROM THE TREE

Lilah stared at the name etched in the gravestone, her racing heartbeat roaring in her ears. She had chosen that quote shortly before laying her mother's remains to rest. And while she had often fantasized about speaking to her biological mother once more, Lilah hadn't returned to Willow's grave since her burial.

"You…" Swallowing hard, Lilah licked her lips and tried again. "You…knew my mother." It wasn't a question.

"I loved your mother."

Tears filled Lilah's eyes.

Elliot knelt in front of the gravestone, resting his hand atop it. "Her name wasn't Willow. It was June. And she was the kindest soul I'd ever known."

The tears that had gathered in Lilah's eyes spilled over, pouring down her face. She knelt beside Elliot, unable to find the words to speak. And so, she listened.

"I didn't have any friends growing up," Elliot murmured, his eyes focused on memories that had happened far away and long ago. "I was strange, and often unwelcome. After all, everywhere I went, people seemed to die. My biological parents. The nuns who cared for me at the orphanage. My adoptive mother, whom I loved with all my heart… She, too, had lost so many people in her life." He blinked rapidly, unwilling to free the tears from his eyes. "I couldn't stand the idea of anyone else leaving me, so I kept them close, even after their deaths – some of which I had a direct hand in."

"You killed them…on purpose?" Lilah managed to whisper.

"No." Elliot shook his head. "Never on purpose. When I was ten years old, my mother

tripped and fell down the stairs because she
blacked out at the top of them. But the reason she
blacked out – the reason she fell – is my fault.
When I found her body at the bottom of the stairs
moments later, I panicked, reverting her body
back to its last living iteration. At that point,
instead of her soul moving on, I redirected it into
a lifeless vessel, permanently untethering it from
both this world and the next. Of course, I had no
idea that would happen. Neither did she. But she
was lonely, and so was I. And so, together, we
brought back the family she had lost, surrounding
ourselves with the ghosts of the past in order to
create some semblance of family." His head hung
in shame. "But every time I called their souls
back, I put their previous selves in grave danger."

Lilah brought her hand to her mouth. "That's
why they died?"

"My adoptive mother, yes. My caregivers at
the orphanage, almost certainly – had Sister
Constance not blacked out, she wouldn't have
crashed into that tree, killing her and the other nun
instantly. As for the others, what difference does
it make? I brought their ashes back to life so
frequently, I eventually caught all of them at their
exact times of death, damning their souls to
purgatory."

"So…that's the difference?" Lilah asked.
"It's not that reviving them alone displaces their
souls? It's jerking their soul from the past and into

the future, at the exact time of death, that creates these…ghosts?"

"Yes."

"How could you have known?" she asked, shaking her head slowly. "I mean, you were just a boy…a boy afraid of losing the people he loved most in the world."

At that, the corner of Elliot's mouth quirked up. "Your mother often looked at me the same way – with bright green eyes so full of kindness and compassion."

"Tell me about her?" Lilah asked. "Please?"

Elliot was quiet for a long moment. When he finally spoke, his voice was low and hoarse. "When I met your mother, I was only a year or two younger than you. By then, I was mostly on my own. I didn't intend to become her friend," he explained, sorrow creeping into his words. "In truth, I had every intention of keeping my distance from her, to protect her from the cloud of death that followed me everywhere I went. But, like you, June had a way of tearing down others' defenses without even trying, drawing me out from my self-imposed prison. We became friends, she and I. In time – a very short amount of time, in hindsight – she became my everything."

Lilah listened intently as Elliot recounted the first time he and June had met; the many nights thereafter they spent talking well into the night, sometimes until sunrise; the way June made him feel safe, in a way no one else ever could or had. He tried to express the depth of his love for Lilah's mother. That, in his mind at least, he had wished to spend the rest of his life with her – if she would have him.

"Until the day she told me she was pregnant," he eventually finished, not quite meeting Lilah's eyes. "That was the day everything fell apart."

Lilah's breath caught and held in her throat. "The baby…was yours?"

He nodded.

She sat back on her haunches, hugging her knees to her chest. "You're…my dad." The word came out as a hushed whisper. Elliot didn't need to provide an answer for her to know it was the truth. "Then why… I mean… Where *were* you?" she demanded. "When she was giving birth? When she was trying to raise me? When she…" The word lodged in her throat.

"Died?"

Lilah could barely muster a nod.

"When her mother found out about me – what I'd 'done' to June – she called the police. Told them I had assaulted her daughter."

Lilah's eyes widened. "Celeste did that?"

"Her name was Vivienne at the time, but yes."

"And the police…they just…*believed* her? Without any evidence?"

"The neighbors corroborated the story. It was my word against theirs."

"What about June? What did she have to say about it?"

Elliot's eyes settled on her gravestone. "I never found out. I ran home to ask my mother for help, to see if she would help explain things to the police officers and June's mother. I told her…" He swallowed hard. "I told my mother I intended to marry June right away. She supported it wholeheartedly, telling me she would explain everything to the police. But when the police kicked in the door a few hours later, with a warrant in-hand, I was too afraid something would happen to my mother – to her ashes," he clarified. "And so I left her urn on the mantle with the others and went with them willingly. But when they took me outside, I saw her."

"Who?"

"Your mother."

Lilah's eyebrows rose in surprise.

"She was in a van with her mother. I…I called to her. I know she heard me. But she didn't answer. She just…rolled up the window and drove away. I couldn't bear to watch her leave. To not be able to speak to her or know where she was going. I couldn't let myself be locked up – not without talking to her first. And so I escaped the same way I did before, freezing the officers' bodies long enough to steal the keys to the handcuffs, fill a cardboard box with my belongings and my family, and then I got in the car and drove. When I got to June's house, she and her mother were gone – no lights, no van. A note had been taped to the front door. It read, 'Violet, I'm so sorry I couldn't say goodbye. Please forgive me. June.' That was your mother's best friend at the time. But there was no note addressed to me." Elliot closed his eyes, slowly clenching and unclenching his fist as though reliving the story caused him physical pain. "I knew I couldn't stay there; the police were probably already on their way. And I knew I couldn't go home. So I lived out of my car. I drove all over Iowa looking for her until someone recognized me at a gas station and I was forced to leave the state. From there, I went to Nebraska, South Dakota, Wyoming. I searched for June's name everywhere I went, showing people her picture every chance I found. No one had seen her. Eventually, it occurred to me to track down the shaman that her mother had become obsessed with—"

"A shaman?" Lilah asked, her eyes rounding.

"Yes. He was a friend of Vivienne's. When I finally tracked him down, he was living in a cabin in the middle of nowhere in Montana—"

"Mike Hastings," Lilah whispered in disbelief.

Elliot's eyes narrowed. "You knew him?"

"More than knew him." She was quiet for a long moment before lifting her eyes to meet his. "I accidentally killed him."

CHAPTER 21

LOST AND FOUND

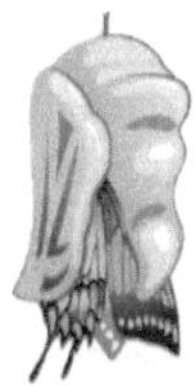

Elliot pounded on the door to the cabin, breathless and trembling from the cold. "Mike!" he shouted, banging on the wood with his palm. "Mike, open up!"

The door swung open a few moments later, revealing none other than Michaelangelo Z. Hastings, looking as strung out and disheveled as ever. When his bloodshot eyes honed in on Elliot, they narrowed, then widened in alarm. But before he could slam the door in his face, Elliot stuck out his foot, blocking it with his boot, and shoved past him. A half-dozen different smells lambasted his sinuses all at once, with the most pungent odors – molasses, patchouli oil, pine needles, onion, peppermint, and bacon – emanating from the various pots simmering on the stovetop. It was a combination of smells that Elliot had never smelled before and never wanted to smell again.

He rounded on Mike, his eyes watering. "Where are they?" he demanded.

"Where are who?" Mike sniffed. "You can't expect me to—"

"Where are they?" Elliot snarled, grabbing the collar of Mike's laced linen shirt in two fists and shoving him against the door. "Tell me!"

To Elliot's surprise, Mike started laughing. "You can't possibly mean to tell me you don't know? The man who walks around with a legion of ghosts at his back?"

Elliot's glare narrowed. "I'll ask you one more time, *shaman*, before turning you into a ghost myself. Where is June?"

"June?" Mike tapped his chin. "I don't know a June… Oh!" He smiled wickedly. "You must mean *Willow*."

"Willow?"

"Mm-hmm. That's the name June chose for herself after fleeing Iowa – to get away from you, that is," he added blithely.

"Why?" Elliot demanded. "What did you tell her?"

Mike tried to shrug, but Elliot's grip on his shirt was too tight. "We merely told her the truth. That you're a predator and a degenerate."

"What?" Elliot took a step backward, allowing Mike to wriggle free. "But I would never—"

"Hurt her?" Mike spat. "Convenient you say that, since it's your fault she's dead."

Elliot staggered backward as though he'd been slapped. "What?"

Chuckling, Mike side-stepped around him, snatching up a newspaper clipping from the kitchen table, which was concealed by a layer of open books, mushroom stems, ground-up herbs, glass beads, and what appeared to be a store-bought Ouija board. He shoved the article into Elliot's hand without preamble. "Willow disappeared without a trace shortly after she was forced to carry your demon spawn to term. I had no idea she'd been suffering – or was even pregnant – until I received a hysterical call from Celeste several weeks after the child was born, telling me the baby had killed their cat."

Elliot couldn't be sure whether it was a smirk or a scowl that was tugging at the corner of Mike's mouth as he recounted all of this.

"I told her to dispose of it, of course – the baby, that is, not the cat. The last she told me, they were on their way to do just that. And then – *poof* – I never heard from them again."

Elliot dropped his eyes to the newspaper clipping Mike had given him, struggling to read the blurred words clenched in his trembling hands.

January 29th, 1984

This morning, at approximately 5:15 a.m., authorities discovered an abandoned vehicle on the side of I-90. Records indicate that the van, whose engine was still running at the time of discovery, is registered to Celeste Mayweather, aged thirty-four, also known as Vivienne Brown. A search is currently underway for the woman, as well as her 15-year-old daughter, Willow…

He scanned the rest of the article, which only mentioned Willow's name once, and made no mention of a baby. "This only says they disappeared. Not what happened to them."

"Oh, you can be sure the baby – or whatever it was you put in that poor girl – is to blame. Since that hysterical call, I have tried on several occasions to reach Celeste. When corporeal methods proved fruitless, I attempted to contact their spirits using every method possible. Pentagrams, planchettes, selenite crystals, Ouija boards…" He gestured to the kitchen table blithely. "Nothing worked. It's as though they are neither in this plane nor the next. But of one thing I am sure: *you* did this to them."

"No." Elliot staggered backward. "You're wrong."

Mike shrugged. "I suppose it's possible. It has happened before, once or twice. If there's nothing else you need from me," he slunk behind Elliot and flung open the door, "I suggest you be on your way." His eyes narrowed. "Now."

Crumpled newspaper clipping still clenched in hand, Elliot turned to go, his feet dragging across the floor as though they weighed fifty pounds each. He stopped at the threshold, using his last ounce of strength to lift his head. "Do you know?"

"Know what?"

"Whether it was a boy or a girl?"

"They called *it* Lilah." Taking advantage of the young man's shock, the shaman shoved him out the doorway with surprising force, causing Elliot to stumble and fall headfirst in the snow. "Come here again, and I will make you and your army of specters regret this life *and* the next. *Ah Kha Sama Ranza Shanda Rasa Maraya Phet!*" With that, he spat at Elliot's feet and slammed the cabin door shut.

. . .

After spending months fruitlessly searching for June – or rather, "Willow" – Elliot spent the next two years holed up in his own remote cabin in the woods, with only ashes to comfort him. He seldom left, save for monthly trips for food and supplies. And when he did, he spoke to no one, dutifully keeping his head down. Libby did her best to appear and comfort him whenever she could, though her skin had long lost its vibrance and her cheeks were the color of ash. Most days, Elliot didn't bother waking her. Most days, he couldn't be bothered to wake himself.

But dreams of his daughter haunted him.

Eventually, he mustered the strength to pull himself out of bed, his mind clear and focused for the first time in months. After jumpstarting his and Libby's long-neglected car, he made the long trek into town, snuck into the public library, and started skimming through old birth records, starting from December 1983 – the month his daughter had allegedly been born. When he found nothing there, he moved onto old newspapers, poring over every page from the last two years. It took many weeks, and many long trips into town, but eventually he stumbled across a seemingly random obituary dated October 22nd, 1984. He skimmed through it once, and then a second and third time, his eyes widening with every pass.

It is with heavy hearts we announce the passing of a beloved daughter, wife, and mother, Marie Quinn. Marie passed on October 20th at the age of twenty-eight in her hometown of Tri-Forks, MT after a year-long battle with cancer. Her death was peaceful and painless, with her devoted *husband, Stanley, lying beside her, and her adopted infant daughter, Lilah, cradled in her arms.*

Elliot stared at the obituary for a long moment, blinking rapidly, before shoving his chair out from under him so fast it toppled over. "Ma'am!" Elliot jumped up, shouting. "Ma'am!"

The librarian glared at him over her computer. "Shh!" She jabbed her thumb at a nearby sign that said QUIET PLEASE!

Elliot all but lunged at her. "I need the white pages from Tri-Forks, Montana—"

"Residential records are based on county, not town—"

"Just show them to me! Please!"

"Shout at me one more time," the librarian said, casually cleaning the lenses of her glasses with a delicate lace handkerchief, "and the only thing I'll be showing you is the exit."

Elliot gritted his teeth, mustering a forced "Yes, ma'am," between gritted teeth.

The next day, he pulled up to the residence of Tri-Forks Fire Chief, Stanley Quinn. His mother's urn was strapped in the backseat, its lid taped shut. She was sitting beside him in the passenger seat, two spots of color painting her normally pallid cheeks. "Is she home?" Libby asked excitedly. "Do you see her? Why don't you go ring the doorbell?"

"I'm not going anywhere near her," Elliot snapped. "I just…" He tried to swallow. "I just want to see her."

They parked across the cul-de-sac, where they waited for over an hour, until Libby's eyes started drooping and her pale skin began to flake. "Sorry, El. I think I need to—"

"Look!" he pointed, ducking beneath the steering wheel. Libby followed his lead, sinking in her seat until only her eyes could be seen above the dashboard.

The front door to the Quinn residence burst open, and a tiny little girl dressed in bunny footie pajamas – complete with a puffy tail and two bunny ears flopping atop her pink hood – ran out the door. As she jumped into a tall pile of dried leaves, her hood fell away, displaying soft curls of auburn hair.

Elliot's heart leapt into his throat, where it stuck.

"Daddy!" the little girl shouted at the open front door. "Hoowy up!"

A few moments later, a tired-looking young man came outside and sat on the front step, balancing his chin on his fists. Even from this distance, his hair looked unkempt and his face unshaved. Elliot had done his research before staking out the man's house; his name was Stanley Quinn – a local hero. At thirty-one years old, Quinn was the youngest Fire Chief Tri-Forks had ever seen and had already saved more lives than his predecessor. But he looked twenty years older than Elliot, not ten – the toll of grief, perhaps. Elliot certainly knew something about that.

Libby rolled down the window, tilting her ear toward the crack to hear what they were saying.

"Daddy, wook at the weaves!" the little girl was exclaiming, throwing handfuls of them in the air.

"I see them, honey."

"Daddy, you wanna frow the weaves?"

"Not now. You go ahead."

"She's beautiful," Libby whispered. "I can't believe it… I have a granddaughter, and she's absolutely precious!" She turned toward Elliot, her eyes full of tears. "Oh, El, we have to—"

The rest of her sentence was drowned out by the engine revving and the car peeling away.

"El!" she cried, craning her neck to look behind her. "What are you doing?! We've gotta turn around, go back and get her—"

"No."

She gaped at Elliot. "What do you mean, no? That's your daughter! Your own flesh and blood!"

He was gripping the steering wheel so hard, his knuckles had gone white. "It's for her own good. You of all people should understand that."

"El, we've talked about this!" Libby implored. "I was wrong, and I've apologized for it a hundred times since. Those little girls' deaths weren't your fault. They couldn't have been. Neither were my parents' or Peggy's or Phil's, I'm all but sure of it. You didn't kill them and it's high time you stop beating yourself up for what happened to me. You were just a little boy. You couldn't have known!"

Elliot didn't reply as he reached over and rolled up her window.

"You can't just abandon her, El!" Libby's voice was rising in shrillness and intensity. "For God's sake, the girl looks just like J—" Her sentence cut off as her body promptly dissolved, her ashes returning to the urn from whence they had come.

"I'm sorry, Ma." Elliot glanced at his mother's urn in the rearview mirror. "But I won't let myself hurt her like I hurt you."

Chapter 22
Memories

"I watched you from afar for many years," Elliot confessed once he'd told Lilah the truth – all of it. By then, the sun had fallen well below the line of trees, heralding nightfall. Cold wind lashed at the surrounding trees, though it didn't touch the warm pocket of summer air that encapsulated the perimeter of Willow's gravestone, where Elliot and Lilah were sitting toe-to-toe. "But I just couldn't let myself go near you. Not after what I did to my mother... And to your mother."

"That's not fair," Lilah argued, rubbing her temples. "My mother's death wasn't your fault. She was murdered. You had nothing to do with that."

"I should have been there – protected her," Elliot rasped, tracing his pale fingers over the etched letters of Willow's grave. "If it hadn't been for me, she wouldn't have come to Montana."

"Again, Mike and Celeste did that, not you."

Elliot didn't reply.

Lilah sighed, shifting her weight on the soft tuft of grass beside her mother's grave. "How did you know where to find her gravestone, anyway?" she asked. "We didn't find Willow—er, *June's* body until almost a decade after you had, um…" She cleared her throat, fighting the question she so desperately wanted to ask. "Um, after you'd died. And then we had to wait until after the trial had ended to give her a proper burial."

Elliot was quiet for a long moment. "It's…not an easy story to tell – or to hear," he murmured, his eyes focusing on something far away and long ago. "Are you sure you want to hear it?"

After a second's hesitation, Lilah nodded.

CHAPTER 23

THE TENTH HOLE

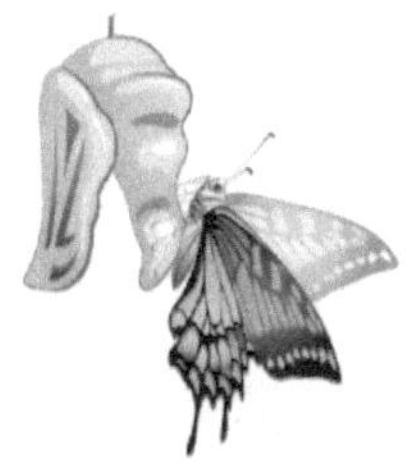

After driving for nearly fifteen hours straight, Elliot trudged through the trees that hid his cabin from the rest of the world, balancing a large, heavy box in his arms. He pushed open the door of the cabin forty minutes later, surprised to find his mother waiting for him in the rocking chair beside the wood burning stove. Before that, she hadn't woken up in months.

"Did you get them all?" she asked, eyeing the box in his hands.

He nodded wordlessly as he gently set the box on the ground.

"I'm glad you're back safe." Libby smiled tightly. "It's been a long time since you made that drive."

Indeed, since coming to Montana nearly seven years ago, this had been Elliot's one and only one trip back to Iowa – and an extremely risky one at that. After strategically arriving in his town of birth in the middle of the night, he'd managed to retrieve his biological mother and father's remains from the cemetery where they'd been buried twenty-two years ago, careful to put the dirt and sod back exactly how it had been once he was finished. During the day, he slept inside his car, out of sight, beneath a bridge. When night fell once more, he made his way to the next town over, where the St. Nicholas of Myra Orphanage for Wayward Youth now functioned as a private Catholic School. In the back of the school, partially hidden by the overgrown weeds and dense foliage that had crept in from the bordering forest, was a small graveyard where many of the children who had died in the 1953 fire – including Kimmy and Mari – had been buried beside former stewards of the orphanage. There, Elliot spent the remainder of the night unearthing Sister Margaret and Sister Constance's remains, along with the two girls. If he had, in fact, been responsible for their deaths, it was his job – his life's mission – to try and make it right. And in order to do that, he needed to keep their remains close at hand.

Just as the sky was beginning to lighten with the first rays of dawn, Elliot arrived at the crematory with his morbid and ill-gotten possessions. Using all but the very last of his money, he'd paid off Craig – the "morally-flexible" mortician that had dutifully cremated his family's remains for the last decade.

"I'll need double what you paid me last time," Craig had informed Elliot, raising an eyebrow at the half-dozen garbage bags he'd carted inside the funeral home. *"And this is the last time, dude. This is getting weird even for me."*

Libby followed Elliot around the back of the cabin, where ten shallow, circular holes had been dug inside a small clearing of the surrounding evergreen forest. She watched in silence as he carefully, painstakingly mixed the ashes from each urn into the soil, then buried a single acorn inside each of the holes. When he withdrew his biological mother's remains from the box, Libby's heart skipped a beat, wondering if he'd try to speak with her. But Elliot didn't attempt to rouse her or his father. In fact, he buried them faster than anyone else, his shoulders slumping even deeper as he did. Burying the rest of their family members took the better part of the morning, with the heat of summer baking the back of his neck. But he didn't stop, not even for water.

Somewhere around the eighth hole, Libby crouched beside him and asked, "Have you seen Lilah lately?"

Elliot grunted in affirmation.

"How old is she now?"

"Six."

"Already?" Libby's frail shoulders rose and fell in a heavy sigh. "Is she…like you?" she ventured.

"She's a normal child, from what I can tell."

Libby's shoulders relaxed. "And does she seem happy, you think?"

"Yes." Elliot sat up straight, rolling his shoulders forward and back to loosen the knots from them. "Her father's taking good care of her."

Libby opened her mouth with her usual retort – that *he* was Lilah's father, not Stanley Quinn – then closed it again. By then, Elliot had started working on the ninth hole, carefully placing the broken pieces of Peggy's pink urn atop her mother's ashes, which had already been mixed in with the fresh soil. He gingerly placed a green acorn in the center, then topped it with several inches of damp soil, patting it down firmly.

"Something strange happened today, El."

He glanced at her over his shoulder as he worked, his eyebrow arched quizzically.

"No, not today," she corrected herself, knuckling the ache in her forehead. "Yesterday – early in the morning, I think, when it was still dark

– I watched you standing outside our old house in Scarville. It was pouring rain, but you weren't wearing a jacket."

Elliot stiffened. It *had* been raining when he'd stopped there to see their old home, its windows illuminated by another family that was just waking up to start their day. But Libby couldn't have possibly known that.

"What?" He set his trowel aside and rose to his feet. "What are you saying?"

"I watched you," Libby repeated, gazing up at him. "Phil was there too. And my mom and dad. Even Peggy. She waved at me."

At that, Elliot's shoulders slumped. "You must have been dreaming."

"I don't dream."

Elliot ran his fingers through his long, shaggy hair in frustration. "Phil and Peggy are gone, remember? I couldn't bring them back even if I tried. We lost their ashes."

Libby shook her head. "I *saw* them, El. They were all standing around you, in the front yard."

A muscle in Elliot's jaw clenched as he knelt back to the ground and continued filling the holes he had dug earlier that week. "One day I'll bring you all back, Ma. I just have to get stronger. Figure out how to put your souls back in your bodies. And when that happens, we can be a family again. Like before – but for real this time. Lilah too. We'll all be together."

Grief twisted in his stomach. *All of us…except June.*

Forcefully pushing her from his mind, he reached for Libby's urn and went to fill the last hole, his thoughts trailing back to Peggy and Phil, both lost forever to the wind. "I just have to keep you safe until then."

"Wait." Libby knelt beside him, putting a cool hand on his arm. "If you bury me here like the others, I won't be able to go anywhere with you anymore."

Elliot looked over at her, a knot forming in his throat. Her hair, once blonde, was so pale the garish light of the afternoon sun made it look white. Her eyes, which used to be vividly blue, were now as colorless and gray as early morning clouds. And though her face bore no wrinkles, she appeared weathered and weary – far older than the three decades and five years her body had been allowed to age.

He sucked down a deep breath, trying to free his lungs from his tightening rib cage, but it didn't budge. "I can't do this to you anymore, Mom. I have to find a way to bring you back…or let you go for good." He hung his head. "I have to find a way to make this right."

"Oh, El." Libby flashed him a sad smile. "Being your mother is the greatest gift I could have been given. Sure, our relationship hasn't exactly been conventional. And my life…" She bit her lip. "Well, it hasn't gone the way I had once imagined it would. But I am proud of my life's work." She tilted her head toward the cabin, where her dissertation was safely hidden beneath the floorboards. "*Our* life's work. As soon as we figure out how to wrap up that last section, that dissertation is going to change how the world looks at life, death, and the human soul. You"—she tapped his sternum—"are going to publish that paper, turn your life around, and make me proud. You'll make *her* proud, too."

Elliot pressed his lips into a tight line, not wanting to tarnish his mother's uncharacteristically good spirits.

"Now, before you leave me out in the backyard, there's just one thing I want."

"And what's that?"

Libby grinned. "Take me out for a beer."

Elliot straightened. "Huh?"

"You heard me. I want to taste one last ice-cold beer before you bury me in the ground for good."

"Don't talk like that, Ma." Elliot winced. "It's not forever. It's just until I can figure out how to bring you back."

"Yes, and that could take a long time," Libby pointed out, grunting as she stood up. "So at the very least, you owe me a beer."

Elliot wordlessly regarded the ad hoc graves of his long line of victims: not counting Phil and

Peggy, there was his biological mother and father, Libby's parents, Woofers, Mari, Kimmy, Sister Margaret, and Sister Constance. And, of course, Libby – though her hole, for now at least, remained unfilled.

He sighed, stifling a yawn. He hadn't slept in two nights. But his mother was right; the least he could do was take her out for one last hurrah before he bound and rooted her to the ground.

"Okay." He smiled, though it didn't quite meet his eyes. "Let's go get you that beer."

• • •

Nearly two hours later, Elliot and Libby stepped inside The Waterhole, a dingy dive bar located just outside of Butte, Montana. It was so full of smoke, Elliot immediately began coughing as the door swung shut behind them. Some heavy metal song was playing over the speakers, and a few clusters of rough-looking patrons were scattered around an assortment of scuffed-up pool tables, yelling and guffawing at one another. To add to the cacophony, icy sleet pattered against the roof while thunder shook the small, grimy windows.

Elliot cast Libby an incredulous look. "Are you sure about this?"

"One hundred percent." She grinned, displaying a glimpse of the vibrant woman she had once been – rosy-cheeked and full of life.

"Fine," he relented. He tightened his grip on the strap of his backpack, where Libby's empty urn was safely tucked, and trudged over to the bar.

A grizzled man was wiping the counter with a dirty rag as the two of them set down. "IDs?" he barked.

Elliot raised an eyebrow at the man. "I'm twenty-six years old."

"I don't care if you're eighty-six. We've had some undercover cops busting my chops for serving liquor to minors. No ID, no service."

"Yeah, Elliot." Libby snickered as she pulled a faded wallet from her back pocket. "No ID, no service."

"Yours is at least ten years expired," he muttered to her under his breath.

"Shut up," she muttered back.

Elliot sighed. "I'm just gonna wait for you over there, okay?" He pointed to a ratty booth in the far corner. "Don't wander off."

Rolling her eyes, Libby swatted him away, then strategically unzipped the grimy yellow rain jacket she'd borrowed from Elliot's closet for the occasion, displaying just enough of her bosom to keep the barkeeper distracted. "So," she purred, quickly flashing him her ID, "crazy ice storm we're having, huh?"

He expertly snatched the card from her hand and brought it up to his nose, squinting. "You know this ID's expired, right?"

"Ugh, I know." Her plastered smile wavered only slightly. "I lost my Montana license a few nights ago, so I grabbed my old one from Iowa. But at least you can see I'm definitely old enough to drink." She tapped her birthday on the front of the card.

The groove between the bartender's eyebrows deepened. "Am I reading this right? That you were born in—" He squinted so hard his eyelids were nothing but narrow slits, then let out a loud laugh. "1939?! There ain't no way you're fifty years old!"

"But I am!" Libby protested. "Really. I just have, uh…good genes."

"Oh yeah?" The bartender cast her an incredulous look. "Without looking at your ID, what's your name?"

"Libby Shermann."

"Aha!" he barked. "Nice try."

"No, wait!" Libby stammered. "Sorry, I forgot! Elizabeth Simmons, right?"

"Whaddya mean, 'right?'" His bushy eyebrow arched even higher. "Don't you know your own name?"

"Of course I do." She blew out an exasperated sigh. "Libby is short for Elizabeth. And Simmons is my maiden name. I, well…I

unofficially took my fiancé's name after he died."
Her eyes dropped to the counter, filling with tears.
"It was so long ago, I sometimes forget I never
legally changed it."

"Alright, alright." The bartender's expression
softened as he handed her back her ID. "Sorry to
have hassled you about it. What can I get you?"

At that, she perked up a bit. "Whatever
you've got on tap, please."

"I've got four beers on tap."

"Then I'll have one of each!"

An hour and a half later, Libby was nursing
her fifth beer over by the jukebox, having the time
of her afterlife flirting and dancing while Elliot
dozed in the booth, using his backpack as a pillow.

A rough-looking, heavily muscled man was
leaning on the juke box beside her, laughing at
some off-color joke Libby had just told him.
"Looks like you'll be needing a refill," he said,
pointing at her nearly empty glass. "What'll you
have?"

"Whatever you're buying me!" Libby
playfully poked him in the arm. "I gotta use the
ladies' room. Be back in just a minute."

"For you, doll, I'll wait all night." He winked.

"El, I'm just running to the bathroom," she
called over to him, though her voice was drowned
out by the Nine Inch Nails song that was blaring
through the speakers. "El!" she tried again, then

waved it off as she stumbled over to what she thought was the restroom door.

As she shoved it open, an icy gust of wind and water blasted her face, startling her. Head spinning, she took an unsteady step forward, and then another, holding out her hands to catch the slushy clumps of snow in her palms and on her cheeks. Above, a lightning bolt forked across the sky.

Lightning and *snow?* Libby marveled. She spun in a slow circle, feeling the earth spin with her as the edges of her vision began to feather to black. She steadied herself on a streetlamp, her gaze landing on an elderly couple across the street. They were standing under an open umbrella, watching her with obvious concern. The woman took a step forward as though she might call out to her.

"Hey!" another voice yelled, startling her. "Hey lady! You doin' alright?"

Libby's head jerked up as a white Miata pulled up beside her, its window rolled down. A young man was leaning toward her, concern etched across his features.

"Hey lady – you need a ride or somethin'?" he called again.

She shook her head, disoriented and confused. "No, I...I just need to get back inside..." she mumbled, turning back toward the bar. "Have to...get...back..."

"Suit yourself." The man shrugged, rolling up his car window.

Libby held her hand out in front of her, groping for the door handle of The Waterhole. Instead of grasping it, her fingers passed right through it.

They had already turned to ash.

The driver in the white Miata – a troubled young man named Anthony DeWitt – peeled off without casting another glance behind him, while the rest of Libby's body crumbled to dust. As her ashes floated up to the sky, the yellow jacket she'd borrowed from Elliot fluttered to the ground.

• • •

It didn't take long for Elliot to realize Libby had gone missing. He burst out of the bar not three minutes later, head swiveling and eyes bulging. When his gaze fell on the yellow jacket resting in a muddy puddle, he sank to the ground beside it, letting out a howl of grief that was swallowed by a deafening clap of thunder.

Twenty minutes later, his clothes soaked through and his throat hoarse from repeatedly calling out his mother's name, Elliot got back in the car. He sat in the driver's seat for a long moment, cold water dripping into his eyes while his hands gripped the steering wheel so hard, pain throbbed in his knuckles. A million thoughts and emotions pelted his mind, pulling him in a million different directions; but in the end, only one stuck.

He flipped over the car engine and drove without thought. Without restraint. Without a plan. Relentless curtains of sleet pounded the vehicle, freezing the wipers to the waterlogged windshield, while an angry, flaying wind tugged at the steering wheel. Despite the dangerous conditions, Elliot shoved his foot against the accelerator, spurred by grief and self-hatred. The dilapidated Saab careened across the deserted highway, its bald tires spinning against the sheet of ice that was quickly forming atop the asphalt. By the time he fishtailed to a stop at the first major intersection of Whitehall, Montana some twenty minutes later, his fingers were gripping the steering wheel so hard, the veins in his hand were bulging. The swinging traffic light had turned green, but his addled mind didn't register the color. An angry driver blared their horn as they whizzed past, sending a torrent of slush across the hood of the Saab. With a startled jolt, Elliot reflexively slammed his foot on the accelerator, swerving wildly into the first parking lot on the right.

Its sign read: *First Presbyterian Church – All Are Welcome.*

Elliot staggered out of the car, not bothering to shut the door behind him. Ice and snow lashed at his face as he stumbled across the parking lot, an assault that continued until he lurched through the double front doors, panting for breath. The modestly sized church was completely empty, its rows of wooden pews vacant. In the far back corner of the church, behind the altar, a door was cracked open, sending a stripe of pale light across the otherwise unlit chapel. Unable to continue standing, Elliot sank to his knees in the middle of the aisle, letting out an anguished wail that echoed against the walls of the church. When he had no more breath to feed his sorrow, he pitched forward and pressed his face to the ground to blot out the rest of the world.

Soft, swift footsteps padded across the floor, growing louder, until Elliot felt a warm hand pressing against his back. "What has happened, my son?" A man asked, his voice soft and full of compassion.

Elliot didn't answer. Couldn't answer. A fresh wave of deep, uncontrollable sobs had gripped his entire body as he pressed his face into the worn carpet of the church, trying to smother his grief.

"Come, I've got you." Surprisingly powerful arms wrapped around Elliot, hoisting him up to his knees, and enfolded him in a tight embrace that only made his sobs grow louder. "There is no obstacle too great for the Lord to help you overcome," the stranger murmured, patting Elliot's back. "No sin too wicked."

Elliot pulled away, scrambling to his feet.

The stranger – an old man wearing black robes and a red shawl with two embroidered crosses on the ends – made a grunt of effort as he pushed himself back into a standing position. "My son," he implored, his slender arms outstretched in a soothing gesture, "what has happened to you?"

"Get away from me – please!" Elliot rasped, stumbling backward.

The pastor took a cautious step towards him. "You may turn your face away from Him, but the Lord's love for you is undiminishable. And as a humble servant of the Lord, I would not abandon you in your time of need, my child, even if you wished it. Now please"—he rested a gentle hand on Elliot's shoulder, guiding him to the nearest pew—"come sit with me."

Broken and exhausted, Elliot collapsed on the bench with a fresh sob, burying his face in his palms.

The pastor sat beside him, resting a comforting hand on Elliot's knee as he began to pray. "Oh Lord, please bestow your cleansing power upon this child, so that he may feel relief from the afflictions that ail him. But if it is not your will at this time, I ask that you help him endure his suffering joyfully, patiently, and full of faith. In the precious name of Jesus, I pray – amen." He turned to Elliot, his crinkled eyes alight with warmth and kindness. "I am here to listen without judgment or condemnation, my son, if it would soothe your soul to ease your burden."

"I've lost every person I've ever loved," Elliot choked out. "I'm alone. And it's no one's fault but my own."

"No." The pastor shook his head firmly. "The Lord is the maker of plans, and we his humble servants. Whatever has happened to you, young man, it is not your fault, but the Lord's will."

"They're dead," Elliot whispered. "Every single one of them."

The man slicked his tongue in sympathy. "Then their souls are being cradled in the loving arms of the Lord, my child. You mustn't—"

"No!" Elliot jerked his head toward the pastor. "Don't you get it? Their souls are lost forever." He jumped up, his legs and voice trembling. "I killed them. All of them. And now – because of *me* – their souls will never find their way back to God or anywhere else. I damned them all!"

The old man slowly rose to his feet, doing his best to keep his voice level and his expression calm. "I don't think you mean what you're saying, son. I think you've suffered some great tragedy and—"

"I murdered them." Shoulders hunched, Elliot raked his fingers through his hair and squeezed his eyes shut. Tears glittered in his dark lashes. He was clenching his hair so tightly, his knuckles were white and his fists were shaking. "Twelve people – all dead because of me."

Swallowing, the pastor took a step backward, toward the aisle.

"I'm a monster." Elliot's eyes burst open, tears pouring down his face as he tilted his head back, gazing at the ceiling with tear-filled, unfocused eyes. "And I don't deserve to live."

"It's okay, my son," the pastor murmured, taking another step backward. "Truly, everything will be alright." His eyes darted toward the open door of his office. "Let me just make a phone call, and then I'll do everything in my power to help you. Okay? Just wait right here."

Elliot nodded wordlessly as the old man all but sprinted down the aisle, no doubt to call the police. "I don't deserve to live," he whispered again, every syllable imbued with truth that permeated every fiber of his being. He spun around toward the exit, above which a clock had been nailed to the wall, marking the hour as midnight. "But death would be a mercy."

He closed his eyes, accepting what he must do – what he deserved. "Forgive me," he murmured, knowing full well that there would be no forgiveness for a monster such as himself.

The pastor emerged from his office a moment later, just as Elliot collapsed to the ground.

"What in the…" He blinked, rubbing his eyes furiously. The young man's hair, which had been black moments before, had gone stark white. And from that distance, his cheeks seemed to be etched in deep wrinkles, as though he'd aged sixty years in the span of a breath. But when the pastor knelt beside the boy and rolled him over on his back, his features had returned to normal – save for his lifeless, unblinking eyes.

"Help!" the old man cried out. "Someone please help!"

Elliot watched dispassionately as the pastor furiously tried to revive his body, knowing there was nothing to be done; for once a soul has been wrenched from the natural confines of its mortal coil, it cannot be returned.

The days following were a blur of police officers and sirens and the glaringly bright lights of the Whitehall Hospital morgue. Elliot found himself dragged alongside the furor, aimless and adrift, like a shipwreck lost to the sea. Two weeks later, at the pastor's request, his body was buried in the graveyard behind the church. As the lone attendant at Elliot's funeral, the clergyman uttered a brief prayer for the young man and his victims, then turned, head bowed, and walked away. For the next twelve years, Elliot sat alone in that graveyard, his soul permanently attached to his own lifeless vessel, yet wholly untethered from both this world and the next…

Until a strange young woman named Lilah Quinn pulled him from the shadows.

Chapter 24
Family Reunion

By the time Elliot had finished his story, the sun had long ago set behind the line of willow trees on the western edge of the cemetery. Darkness had settled on the surrounding forest, the chill of mid-autumn dusting the dried leaves and grass with creeping frost. Lilah sat beside him from the safety of their warm summer bubble, where the air was balmy and still, and the grass sprouting from June's grave was lush and green. Neither of them spoke for a long time, though the second hand of Lilah's watch was ticking softly, marking the silence.

Lilah's shoulders rose and fell in a slow, deep breath. "I never truly knew the pain of losing a mother, because I'd never known my own – either of them, really." She turned to Elliot, her heart swelling with sympathy. "But you did. You lost not one, but two mothers."

Elliot averted his eyes from her prying gaze.

"I can't begin to imagine what that pain must have been like," she said softly. "And then, on top of all that loss, to feel as though you had a direct hand in it. But you didn't. You have to know that." Elliot opened his mouth to interject, but Lilah steamrolled past him. "*Especially* my mom's. You loved her. And from the little I know about Mike Hastings, I'm all but certain he and Celeste wove some BS tale to trick her into leaving. For all we know, they kidnapped her against her will."

"I highly doubt that," Elliot muttered. "I saw her expression when she saw me – pure fear and contempt."

"Look, if you're my father, you're probably at least as stubborn as I am. So instead of arguing, let's just go straight to the source." She rose to her feet, dusting the grass from her jeans, then extended a hand to Elliot to help him up.

He regarded her hand warily. He looked younger now, no more than seventeen or so, and could have passed for Lilah's dark-haired younger brother.

"You asked me for my help," Lilah pressed. "Well, I'm here. And I'm not going anywhere."

The Adam's apple in Elliot's throat bobbed as he wordlessly gripped her hand.

Lilah helped pull him to his feet, surprised at how light he was – as though he were more ash than flesh.

Elliot stood beside her, regarding June's grave with tear-filled eyes. "I'm terrified to see her."

"Me too," Lilah admitted. "But Dad – Stan, that is – always told me that the best thing to do when you're scared is just tear off the bandage." She gave Elliot a small, knowing smile. "He took *really* good care of me, you know. So, if you feel any guilt about that, don't. You left me in good hands."

"And Jace?" Elliot asked softly. "He treats you well?"

"Incredibly well." Lilah smiled, the corners of her mouth wavering slightly as she shifted her attention to June's grave. "Would you like to wake her, or shall I?"

"You do it," he answered quickly. "But be careful. Don't do it too close to…" He swallowed hard. "To that night."

Lilah nodded, then set her watch atop the gravestone. The dials immediately began spinning backward as time flickered around them, a blur of seasons that passed them by like one watercolor painting bleeding into the next.

"When should I stop?" she murmured, careful not to break her concentration. Age vacillations or no, she couldn't help but marvel over Elliot's mastery of time, as though he controlled it as a reflex, not a thought.

He hesitated for the span of several short, shallow breaths. "…Now."

The dials of the watch abruptly stopped on February 19th, 1983 – the day June first told Elliot she loved him – and in a swirl of ashes and snow, she appeared.

Beside Lilah, Elliot stiffened.

Lilah, too, was frozen with trepidation, her mind returning to the first and only other time she had roused her mother from her eternal sleep. But unlike the frightened girl from before, who had sallow cheeks, limp hair, and wide, frightened eyes, this version of Willow – or rather, Juniper – was smiling and fresh-faced, with lustrous auburn hair that tumbled in waves around her full, flushed cheeks. And, a far cry from the bewildered, unfamiliar gaze that had taken in Lilah the first time, this girl's eyes were full of joyful recognition from the moment they opened.

"Lilah," she whispered, abruptly reaching forward to pull her daughter into a tight embrace. "Oh, I've missed you so much – I was starting to worry we would never talk again."

"Y-You remember me?" Lilah gasped.

"Of course I do – I've been with you every day for the past three years!" June smiled, tears glinting in her round, green eyes. When her gaze fell on Elliot, however, a whimper lodged in her throat, and the tears that she'd previously been blinking back spilled down her cheeks.

"June," he started, his voice shaking. "June, I'm so—"

She let out a loud sob, throwing herself into his arms. Elliot stiffened, his wide eyes darting from June to Lilah, as though he were a deer caught in the headlights.

"I heard every word," June wept against his chest. "Oh, El…I had no idea!"

Still frozen, Elliot's eyebrows pulled together in bewilderment, as though he were trying to make sense of her words. But his arms, two steps ahead of his mind, moved of their own volition, wrapping her in a warm embrace. "I've missed you so much," he whispered against the top of her head.

"I've missed you, too." June sniffled against his shoulder. Without warning, she reached out and snatched Lilah by the jacket sleeve, pulling her into their embrace. "Both of you."

Lilah stiffened as she found herself sandwiched between her two dead parents – both of them slightly younger than her in appearance and smelling vaguely of sulfur – but soon relaxed. "This is the weirdest family reunion ever," she half-laughed, half-sobbed.

"I've been waiting for you for so long," June whispered into her daughter's hair. "I was worried this day wouldn't come."

Lilah pulled away, guilt chipping away at joy. "Did… Did I do this to you?"

June's smile was a sad one as Elliot wrapped his arm around her, pulling her against his side.

"Oh, God," Lilah whispered, pressing her hand to her chest. "I swore that you wouldn't have to go back and die all over again… Not only did I send you right back to that moment, but I—" A quiet sob caught in her throat. "I trapped you here."

"No." June caught Lilah's trembling hand in hers. "After I spoke with you, I did return to my previous body – sort of." She glanced up at Elliot, whose face was contorted with fresh grief. "I must have blacked out at the exact moment I died. Because of that, when I returned, it had already happened." She scrunched up her face in consternation, struggling to find the proper words. "I don't know how to explain it – it's like I was standing in two places at once. When I looked to my left, I was standing in the forest and my murderer was getting away. When I looked to the right, my grown daughter was reuniting with the man who had raised her for the past sixteen years. But there was no pain. No terror," she quickly reassured Elliot and Lilah. "A light appeared above me, like it was calling to me… But I said no." She squeezed Lilah's hand tightly. "I didn't want to go to a place of strangers. I wanted to see my baby again. And in that moment, I was sitting right beside you in the forest. You were talking to Jace, telling him that you had spoken to me, but that I was just a husk – a photocopy of my former self that would never remember you. I wanted so badly to tell you that I'd remembered everything that had happened. That I was right there with you."

"I'm so sorry," Lilah said, wiping the tears from her cheeks.

"Don't be." June's smile was wide and genuine. "Had I died that night, and my soul left this plane, I never would have been able to get to know the daughter I abandoned. And I never would have had the chance to see your father again." She turned to Elliot, taking both of his hands in hers. "I want you to know I loved you until my very last breath, and long after," she told him, brushing a stray tear from his cheek. "I'm only sorry I couldn't tell you that sooner."

"June." Elliot's voice was barely a whisper.

"Now we can finally have the family we never had," June said, squeezing his hands. "You, me, and Lilah."

Elliot's eyes tightened, and Lilah understood why.

"I can't tell you how much I would love that," Lilah said, the truth of her own words tightening around her chest like a vice. "But...I have to get you both back to where you belong. You're not supposed to be here – either of you."

June looked between her daughter and Elliot, who was gazing down at her, sorrow etched into his features.

"She's right," he said. "We don't belong here. But…" He ran a hand through his hair, exhaling sharply. "I don't know how to fix what we've done. What *I've* done."

"I—Wait." June frowned, cocking her head away from him as though she were listening for something. She squeezed her eyes shut, muttering something under her breath.

"Mom?" Lilah took a step forward. "Are you—"

June held up a finger, silencing her, before her eyes flew open with a gasp. "It's him."

"Who?" Lilah asked.

Letting go of Elliot's hand, June spun in a slow circle, searching for a voice neither Elliot nor Lilah could hear. "I've heard him from time to time over the years," she muttered. "He follows you around, just like I do."

Lilah's eyes rounded in horror while Elliot inched closer to her. "Someone *else* has been following Lilah around? Who?"

"One second," June replied absentmindedly. "Oh, wow!" Her eyebrows arched in surprise. "I've never heard him yell like this before. He seems extra agitated today."

"What's he saying?" Elliot pressed, at the same time Lilah asked, "Who seems agitated?"

"It's hard to make out the words, especially now that I'm back in my body." She tilted her head again, frowning. "I wonder if he's trying to get you to wake him up too? …Oh, yeah, I definitely think that's what he wants."

"Who?" Lilah demanded.

June didn't answer.

"June!" Elliot took her hand, drawing her attention away from the mysterious specter. "Who's been following Lilah around for years?"

"Oh." She blinked. "I didn't say? Sorry, I'm still getting used to having to speak out loud. Bodies are weird after you've been out of one for so long, you know?" June shrugged one shoulder. "Anyway, the other ghost that's been following Lilah around is Shaman Mike. And he definitely wants to talk to you – right now."

CHAPTER 25

GHOSTS OF THE PAST

Michaelangelo Z. Hastings' grave wasn't far from June's – a mere ten minutes' walk to the other side of the cemetery. With Elliot's guidance, Lilah was able to lead June away from her gravestone without losing control of her remains – something that strayed a little too far into the realm of necromancy for Lilah's comfort. Still, it was certainly convenient. By then, the moon was high in the sky, illuminating the frozen, overgrown path ahead as the three of them tiptoed around the gravestones, careful not to wake anyone. When they arrived at the shaman's gravestone, which was covered in what appeared to be Sanskrit, Elliot wasted no time rousing the man from sleep.

Mike's body appeared in an instant, letting out a long, wheezing gasp, as though he'd been holding his breath for the past three years. "Finally!" he barked, directing his annoyance at Lilah. "Do you *know* how long I've been shouting at you?!"

Lilah gaped at him in shock. "Huh?"

"Ever since you skewered me on that evergreen tree like a pork kebab!" he blustered, flailing his arms wildly. "I *knew* when you and that boy arrived at my front door that you were the malignant spirit I'd foreseen! I even asked you, 'Are you the malignant visitors or the benign ones?' *Clearly*," he steamrolled ahead before Lilah or anyone else could interject, "I should not have bothered asking and should have instead thrown you out on your rump the moment you opened your mouth! And *you!*" He rounded on June, who took a timid step behind Elliot. "I've been shouting at you for the last *three years!* How did you not hear me?"

She recoiled even further. "I mean, I heard you...I just didn't really want to talk to you."

He threw his hands up in exasperation.

"Why should she have paid you any mind, anyway?" Lilah snapped at him. "You ruined her life!"

"*I* ruined *her* life?" Mike repeated, affronted. "*She's* the one who chose to copulate with a lich!"

"I wasn't even dead at the time," Elliot scoffed.

"No, but you certainly had a lot to do with the dead, didn't you? And besides, it was her deranged mother who dragged me into all this nonsense, and her *daughter* who killed me!" Mike jabbed an accusatory finger in Lilah's direction.

"I didn't mean to!" she protested. "And besides, the coroner said you had enough toxic mushroom compounds in your system to kill a steer! I just…uh…hastened the inevitable," she added with a contrite grimace. "I really am sorry about that though."

"Oh please." Mike rolled his eyes. "Those mushrooms aren't poisonous, they're how I used to communicate with the—*oh, would you shut up!*" he snarled, whirling on Elliot. "I can't even hear myself *think* with all the constant chatter!"

"I didn't say anything!" Elliot protested.

"Not you! Them!" He jabbed a finger over Elliot's shoulder.

Lilah frowned. The four of them were standing at the northern edge of the graveyard, which bordered a wide swathe of plains known as Buffalo Ridge Monument. Moonlight illuminated the wooden fence and the rolling expanse of wild grass that stretched far into the distance. But apart from an owl that had swooped overhead, carrying its squirming dinner in one talon, no one else was there.

"Who are you talking about?" Lilah asked, eyeing Mike warily. Shirtless, barefoot, and wearing nothing but purple parachute pants, he looked no more or less deranged than he had before death. If anything, he seemed sharp-eyed and lucid, rather than half-baked and slurring as he'd been during their last visit.

"The parade of people that follow this man wherever he goes," Mike answered impatiently. "When I was alive, I sensed them. As a ghost, I saw them. And now, as a—well, whatever it is I am," he muttered, examining his hands in front of his face, "I can still hear them. Can't you?" He arched an eyebrow at Elliot, who was shaking his head slowly from side to side.

June let out a soft gasp.

Lilah, too, was beginning to catch on. She narrowed her eyes at Mike. "If you can talk to other ghosts, why have you been following *me* around all this time? We're nothing to each other."

He shrugged. "I felt drawn to you, somehow. Probably because you talk to dead people on a regular basis, which makes you vaguely more interesting than the general populace."

"You and my mother are the only ones who regularly followed me though? There weren't any other ghosts?"

"Indeed – just our modest party of two." He cast her a dubious squint. "Why?"

"What happened when you died?" Lilah demanded, ignoring his question. "What did you see?"

"I saw my young body dangling from a tree, my present body lying on the floor of my cabin, and a white light I was unable to reach no matter how far I stretched," he answered, a touch of sullenness tingeing his words.

"I turned your soul into a ghost," Lilah whispered, her eyes growing wide. "Just like I did to my mother." She turned to Elliot. "Just like *you* did with your family members." Before Elliot could stammer out a response, she rounded on Mike again. "Who are the ghosts that follow him around?" she asked, jerking a finger toward her father. "Can you describe them?"

"Of course I can." Mike sucked his teeth. "His line of victims is a long and sundried one, though I distinctly remember their faces. There are three young girls, a pair of nuns, an older couple I can only imagine were married in their prior lives, since they often stand right beside one another without even knowing it…"

Elliot's eyes were growing wider and wider as Mike ticked the ghosts off on his fingers.

"…a dog, if you can believe it, and a man who looks to be in his thirties…Phil, he says his name is…" His eyes darted just past Elliot's shoulder. "I'm getting there!" he snapped at the air. "And a woman who is insisting, quite obnoxiously, that I tell you her name is Libby. There!" he barked at the ghosts. "Are you happy?"

Elliot staggered backward, leaning on a gravestone for support, while June's hands flew to her mouth.

"They're all there?" Lilah whispered, too stunned to find her voice.

"I will do no such thing!" Mike was rubbing his temples. "All of you are giving me a splitting headache! Either learn how to speak one at a time, or find another medium to harass!"

"What won't you do?" Lilah demanded. "What are they saying?"

"Among the cacophony of blather, the one called 'Libby' is insisting I hug her son for her and regale him with how much she's missed him – which, for reasons that need no explication, I have no intention of doing!"

"They're all here?" Elliot whispered. "My mother? Peggy… Phil…? All of them?"

"Yes." Mike sighed, slumping down on the headstone beside him. "And they've apparently been standing around for a very long time, waiting for you to notice them. They—what? Oh. Yes. *That* I can certainly do." Without warning, he swatted Elliot upside the head – roughly. "That's from your mother. She says you'll know why."

Rubbing the back of his head, Elliot gaped at the man in shock.

"She's okay, El," June cried, throwing her arms around him. "They're all okay!"

"'Okay' is a bit of a stretch." Mike sniffed. "They, like you and I, are permanently bound to this world, forbidden from entering the next phase of the afterlife, and can neither see nor interact with one another."

"But I heard you!" June protested. "Why can't they—"

"What part of 'shaman' don't you understand?" he sniped. "I have been endowed with extrasensory powers of perspicacity and insight that mere mortals such as yourselves lack."

"Holy crap," Lilah muttered. "And all this time, I thought you were a crackpot."

He cast her a dirty look.

"So, how do we fix this?" she muttered to herself, pacing back and forth amongst the graves. "We have the spirits, but we don't have the bodies to return them to."

"And even if you did, it would only be a temporary fix, as your poor father learned the hard way," June pointed out.

"Right. So, we…what? Try to help them move into the next, uh, realm?" Lilah asked, darting a questioning glance at Elliot, who was slowly shaking his head as though he still couldn't believe it.

"The blonde woman is still yammering at me, explaining in no small amount of detail that this only happened because their souls were pulled out of their prior selves at their respective times of death." Mike was knuckling his forehead as he spoke. "If that's the case, why not just put us all back in our previous bodies?"

"You think I didn't try that?" Elliot croaked, his first utterance in several minutes. "Once a soul has been pulled from its body, it can't be put back."

"*You* couldn't put them back," Mike said mildly. "Your daughter, however, is significantly more powerful than you are."

"*Me?*" Lilah squeaked. "No way. I'm nowhere near as p—"

"She *is* far stronger than me," Elliot agreed, eliciting a startled noise from his daughter. "But she's untrained, not to mention entirely unfamiliar with the necromantic side of chronomancy—"

"And who better to teach her than her father, a gifted lich?"

Lilah was gaping between the two men in disbelief. "What exactly is a lich?"

"An undead spellcaster – one who seeks to defy death by supernatural means," Mike supplied. "Combined, I don't see why father and daughter could not put our souls back in our prior bodies."

"The timeline, for one!" Lilah protested. "I mean, we can't just go around messing with the past. That's why—" Her eyes suddenly darted to the far side of the graveyard, where blue and red lights had appeared behind the distant backdrop of trees. "Crap. That's gotta be Sheriff Reid and my dad." Turning back to the others, she chewed on her lip, struggling to find the words. "Look, the whole reason my 'powers' are safe is because I'm not traveling *through* time. I'm just manipulating time around me. There's no way to, you know, do actual damage—"

"Apart from skewering people on trees and damning their souls to purgatory for all eternity," Mike griped.

"Purgatory is better than hell," Elliot shot back, "which, I'm told, is where leeches and conmen go."

"Conman?" Mike made a wide, sweeping gesture toward his invisible crowd of ghosts. "As you can see, I am perfectly legitimate!"

"A broken clock can still be right twice a day," Elliot muttered, earning a filthy look from the shaman.

"Guys, while I fully understand the irony of what I'm about to say, we are *running out of time.*" Lilah again regarded the blue and red lights parked at the entrance of the cemetery, from which the distant shouts of her name could be heard echoing across the graveyard. "Now, anyone who's seen *Back to the Future* knows how time paradoxes work—"

"What's *Back to the Future*?" June asked.

"Oh, right." Lilah sighed. "Um, it's a famous time travel movie from the eighties. Basically, whatever we do in the past affects the future, so if we mess with the past, this future – this very conversation – doesn't happen. Hence the paradox."

Mike cleared his throat. "The older, pompous man—fine, *George*—wants me to tell you that, quote, 'because we will all retain our memories of our prior lives, you wouldn't be altering the past. You'd be allowing us a second chance at life.'"

Lilah faltered. "I don't see the diff—"

"He's right," Elliot said, rising to his feet.

"He is?" She cast him a confused look.

"Yes. And I think I know what to do." Elliot's eyes darted to Lilah's. "But I can't do it without you."

"*Lilah!*" Stan's booming voice echoed through the cemetery, while the faint beams of flashlights shone in the distance. *"Lilah, where are you?!"*

She chewed on her lip.

"I know we haven't known each other for long," Elliot whispered, taking Lilah's hand in both of his. "But I think, with our combined powers, I might be able to fix the sins of my past."

His eyes bore into hers, pleading. "Please, Lilah…will you help me?"

"Lilah!" Jace shouted. *"Are you out there?"*

A million questions, as well as a million different fears of what could go wrong, swirled in Lilah's mind.

When she turned to her mother for support, June nodded her head in encouragement. "Your father is the kindest, brightest, most trustworthy soul I've ever known. If he says it can be done, I believe him."

"If the sheriff finds you rubbing elbows with a serial killer, you may not have this unique opportunity again." Mike said, inspecting his fingernails. "In my experience, I find that law enforcement officials act first and ask questions later."

June shot him a look. "Indeed."

Lilah stood there for a long moment, her eyes locked on the roving flashlights in the distance. If her father was right, the two of them could repair the past, potentially saving a dozen souls from an eternity of grief and solitude.

But if he was wrong… She forced herself to push the terrifying thought from her mind.

Sucking down a deep breath, she turned to Elliot. "Show me what to do."

A wide, grateful smile broke across his face, like the moon emerging from behind a veil of dark clouds. "Thank you – truly," he whispered fervently, then quickly cleared his throat. "First things first… Mike, I need you to help me organize everyone. We have to synchronize this perfectly – down to the exact second."

"Shh!" Mike snapped at the empty air. "One at a time!" He listened for a moment, nodding, then said, "I'm supposed to remind the blonde woman's mother that smoking exacerbates, uh, 'hyper-tro-phic cardio-myo-pathy,'" he sounded out, "and something about L-arginine for the sister… Of course, if you're looking to lower blood pressure, I highly recommend eating several spoonsful of concentrated garlic paste a day," he added with a prim sniff. "That's what I do, anyway."

"We can smell," June muttered.

"So everyone gets one chance at a do-over?" Lilah asked her father, frowning incredulously. "How will we know if any of this works?"

"You'll know." Elliot smiled tightly. "Are you ready?"

She hesitated.

June stepped forward, taking Lilah's free hand in hers. "You can do this," she whispered. "I believe in you."

Squeezing both her parents' hands in hers, Lilah took a deep breath and nodded. "I'm ready."

CHAPTER 26

PICKING UP THE PIECES

Mariela woke with a start, sitting bolt upright in bed. Below her, her big sister, Kimberly, was already scrambling out of the bottom bunk, shouting at the other girls in the dormitory. Mari rubbed her eyes, trying to clear the blurriness from her vision. Outside her window, the sun hadn't woken up yet, and for the briefest moment, she considered going back to sleep – until the smell of smoke reminded her of the very special job Elliot and Lilah had given her.

Wake the others, she whispered to herself as she hopped off the final rung of the ladder. "Gotta wake the others!"

Fortunately, Kimmy was already on it. Nine years old and the self-appointed "mother" of the dormitory, she darted from bed to bed, shaking their sleeping occupants awake. "Go through the window, not the door!" she shouted to the growing gaggle of sleepy-eyed children. "There's fire in the hallway!"

Taking her big sister's cue, Mari pushed the wooden play table under the single window in their dormitory, then climbed atop the table to unlatch it. "Come on!" she cried, her eyes darting to the flames licking at the smoking gap underneath the door. Reaching out a hand, she helped pull the smaller girls onto the table.

Kimmy rushed past them, snatching up their smallest roommate – a sound-asleep three year old girl – in her slender arms. With Mari's help, they helped push the yawning toddler up to the open window, where several sets of hands pulled her up and out. Kimmy waited until all the other kids were outside the window, then gestured to her sister. "Come on, Mari! It's your turn!"

By then, the smoke had grown so thick, Mari's eyes were stinging and her lungs were burning. "I can't do it!" she whimpered, which devolved into a series of violent coughs.

She started to lay her head down on the table, but her big sister's hand was around her wrist, dragging her to her feet. With Kimmy's repeated shouts of encouragement, Mari managed to scramble on top of her shoulders and crawl through the window to join the others.

"Come on, Kimmy!" she grunted, reaching for her sister while two other girls held onto her bare feet. "Take my hand!"

With one last look to make sure every bed was empty, Kimmy grabbed a smoldering chair, stacked it on the table, and climbed atop it to grab Mari's outstretched hand. As soon as she clambered out, Mari threw her arms around her big sister in a tight hug.

Kimmy hugged her back for the span of a single, gasping breath, then shoved her forward. "Go!" she shouted hoarsely, pushing Mari toward the large cluster of students and nuns that had gathered on the playground.

As they approached the others, coughing and wheezing, the nearest nun reached out and snatched them, pulling the girls into her open arms. "God bless you, my darlings," she wept, hugging them close.

Mari and Kimmy watched tearfully as the upper floor of the orphanage caved into their dormitory with an explosion that sent smoldering shrapnel and embers flying through the smoke-filled air, just as it had before. This time, however, not one single child was left inside the burning building.

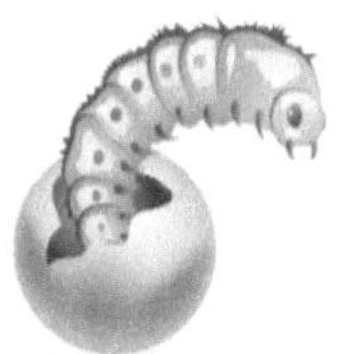

Elliot's eyes burst open to find Sister Maggie standing over him, finger pressed against her lips to silence him.

"Did it work?" he whispered. "Did she do it?"

"Hurry," Maggie said, grabbing him by the wrist. "Don't wake the others."

Without bothering to put on his shoes, he followed her outside, his small heart thrumming inside his chest. Constance was waiting for them outside the front doors of the orphanage, clutching the keys to Father Isaac's Ford station wagon in one hand while fingering her rosary with the other. "Get in," she urged Elliot, quietly opening and closing the car door for him.

Maggie hurried over to the passenger side, holding her breath as she shut the door behind her as gently as possible. "They were gone," she muttered to Constance. "Both of them."

The older woman nodded once before turning over the engine. All three of them winced at the noise, but the orphanage windows remained dark; miraculously, no one else had awoken. After slowly backing out of the long dirt drive, which was surrounded by shadowy evergreens, Constance turned the car onto the main road, steadily picking up speed. The dark silhouettes of soybean fields, silos, and cattle fencing went whizzing by like a hastening blur, while the street lights that illuminated them became fewer and farther between. When the car turned onto the highway twenty minutes later, following the signs for White Pine Hollow National Forest, Maggie darted an anxious look over her shoulder, sighing in relief when she saw no one was following them.

"Are you sure you want to do this?" she asked Elliot, turning around in her seat. "You don't want to stay with us?"

"None of this works without me." He smiled – an oddly adult smile on a little boy's face. "And besides, my mother would kill me if I didn't show."

"Which one?"

"The only mother who loved and raised me, even after death. My biological parents weren't part of the assembly of ghosts that hung around me, so I can only assume they moved on." He swallowed tightly. "I can only hope, that is."

Constance flashed him a reassuring smile in the rearview mirror. "You will see them again. Just hopefully not for a very, very long time." She turned to Maggie. "And you? If we make it back to the orphanage safely, what will you do now?"

When Maggie didn't answer, she reached over and patted the young woman's hand. "Twenty-five years old seems a little young to be devoting your life to the convent, doesn't it? Especially when you've got a lovely young gentleman back home who's been sending you titillating love letters and poetry, hmm?"

Maggie cast her a startled look, but Constance only chuckled. "Your whole life awaits you, Maggie. Best not spend it collecting dust as I have."

"Thank you, Sister Constance," Maggie whispered, squeezing her hand.

Constance nodded as she turned onto the unmarked, seldom-used service road that led deep into miles and miles of untouched forest. When they approached the correct mile marker, she pulled over on the side of the road, opened the back door, and extended a hand to Elliot.

"I'm so very sorry," she whispered as she knelt on one creaking knee to pull him into a tight hug. "Truly, I am."

Maggie did the same, wrapping him in a warm blanket. "May this life grant you the love and tenderness you did not know before."

"Amen," Constance whispered.

"And to you both as well," Elliot said, casting each of them one last grateful smile before making the long, cold trek toward the hospital.

It didn't take long for the same good Samaritan to find Elliot standing on the side of the road, shivering from the cold. "Son, are you alright?" the man asked, crouching in front of him. "Where are your parents?"

"At the hospital," Elliot answered, praying they would be.

The man muttered a sharp word, then carefully scooped the little boy into his arms. "Let's get you back where you belong," he said, placing Elliot in the front passenger-side seat. After making sure Elliot was safely strapped in and wrapped in his blanket, he sank into the driver's seat, wrenched the transmission to "D," then hit the gas so hard the tires squealed in protest.

It was hard for Elliot to keep his eyes open after everything that had happened, and as the movements of the car lulled him back into a heavy sleep, the man, the road, and the forest feathered in and out of existence. In their place, Libby's broad smile, June's loving arms, and his daughter's beautiful hazel eyes appeared as flashbulb memories, each one brighter and more wonderful than the last.

His eyes briefly fluttered open when the nice man scooped him out of the car and laid him atop a rolling stretcher, where a man in a white uniform and a black leather belt, and a blonde doctor in a white physician's jacket were waiting for him. With a small sob, the doctor reached out and pulled him into her arms, squeezing him so tightly he could scarcely breathe.

"Mom," he sobbed, burying his face against her shoulder. "Dad!"

Phil wrapped his arms around them both, kissing the top of Elliot's head, and then Libby's.

"I take it you're the boy's parents?" the good Samaritan asked.

"Yes," Libby wept, pressing her face against the top of Elliot's head, "we are."

"Thank you for everything," Phil said, extending a hand to the man.

A male doctor, dressed in a tie and white jacket, strode outside. "What seems to be the trouble here?"

"I've got it, Dr. Jacobs," Libby said, scrubbing the tears from her cheeks as she straightened.

"I beg your pardon, *Miss* Simmons, but you don't get to make that—"

"I believe the *doctor* said she's got it under control," Phil said, stepping between them. "By the way, it looks like you left the lights on in your Lincoln – might want to check that before the battery dies."

Letting out a curse, the doctor raced toward the parking lot.

Phil turned back to Elliot. "Thank you," he murmured. "While my accident was never your fault, this time around, I remembered to set out the flares. You saved not one but three lives that day, El. Mine, the driver, and the driver of the truck that safely drove by us."

Elliot's vision blurred with tears.

"We postponed the wedding until next month, by the way." Libby smiled at Elliot. "We had to wait for the guest of honor to arrive, after all."

When Phil, Libby, and Elliot returned from their family honeymoon a week after the wedding, Libby's family was already inside the house, waiting for them.

"Welcome home!" Jean cried, lavishing the three of them with kisses. "How was everything?"

"It was gorgeous," Libby enthused, setting down her traveling bag.

"I've never been to the beach before," Elliot admitted.

"Never?" Jean gasped. "In either life?"

"Neither had I!" Phil grunted as he set down the four bags he'd been carting up the driveway.

"Maybe we need to arrange a trip to the beach," George mused, wrapping an arm around his wife's shoulders.

Upstairs, the bathroom door slammed. "Libs!" Peggy cried, running down the steps.

"Banister!" Libby, Phil, and Elliot called out in unison.

"Oops." Peggy grinned, reaching out to grab the handrail. "Sorry." Hopping down the final two stairs, she rushed forward to give Libby a hug, followed by Elliot. "I've missed you, nephew!" she laughed, ruffling his wild black hair.

"I missed you too." Elliot returned her hug with gusto. "Are you staying for dinner?"

"Depends on what you're cooking!"

Libby laughed. "Could you imagine if someone else were standing here, watching my nineteen year old sister ask the six year old what he's cooking for all of us?"

"I like to cook." Elliot shrugged. "Besides, if you count the total number of years I've been – well, not alive, exactly, but sentient – I'm closer to forty-six!"

"Ah, but trapped inside an underdeveloped six-year-old brain." George laughed, lightly slugging Elliot in the shoulder.

He grimaced. "I do crave a lot more chocolate milk and naps these days."

"Oh, the neurological studies we'll publish, my boy – once you go to college, that is."

Elliot's smile faltered. "I wonder if your and mom's paper still exists, trapped underneath some wooden floorboards in the future?"

"Who knows?" Libby said with a rueful smile. "I guess that means we'll just have to write another paper." She reached out and wrapped an arm around Peggy's shoulders. "At least some of the knowledge we acquired the first time around survived – like treating congenital hypertrophic cardiomyopathy with high doses of L-arginine, since beta blockers didn't exist in nineteen-fifty."

"And the fact that my constant smoking made Peggy's underlying issues so much worse." Jean sighed. "None of us knew back then."

Libby turned to Elliot, winking. "See, little man? You didn't kill most of us. Big tobacco and antiquated medical practices did."

"Stress and alcohol for me," George chimed in.

"Forgetting to set out flares was my Achilles tendon." Phil grinned. "See, El? Not a serial killer after all. Just a regular killer!"

"Phil!" Libby exclaimed, swatting at him. "That's not funny! He's saved more lives than you and me combined. Think of all those children who would have otherwise died in that fire!"

"Hopefully none of *them* grow up to be killers," George muttered to his wife, who nodded thoughtfully.

"Dad, we've been through this." Libby sighed. "With all the time bending that went on in El's previous life, who's to say which timeline is the correct one? As far as I'm concerned, we've righted the mistakes of the past. Case in point: none of us have had any blackouts this time around."

"That is true," George conceded.

"Do you ever have, I don't know…" Peggy started, rubbing the back of her neck. "Like, survivor's guilt? That we all got second chances when so many other people didn't?"

"Yes," Libby answered. "It's one of the reasons I'm changing my specialty to pediatric care." She squeezed Peggy's hand. "And why I know you'd make an amazing doctor too."

Elliot's eyes settled on the single urn resting on the mantle, which had a paw stamped on the front. "What about Woofers?" he asked softly.

"George and I snatched him out of the road just in time," Jean reassured him. "And he lived to the ripe old age of sixteen before passing peacefully in his sleep."

"I wish I'd been there to say goodbye," Libby said with a sad smile. "But I'd argue I came back at just the right time – wouldn't you, Phil?"

"Indeed," he said, kissing her cheek. "It seems all of us did – thanks to Elliot."

"No." Elliot shook his head. "The thanks goes entirely to Lilah."

"I wonder if we'll be lucky enough to meet her?" George murmured, glancing at the clock.

Jean laid her head on his shoulder. "Only time will tell."

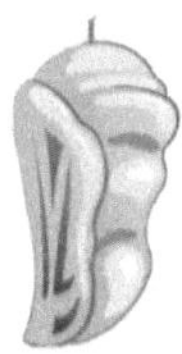

"Elliot!" Libby hollered from the kitchen. "Breakfast is ready!"

"Coming!" Elliot took one final look in the mirror to tame the dark waves of hair that spilled across his forehead before shutting the bathroom door behind him. He jogged down the stairs two at a time, clutching the banister for safety, then skidded to a stop at the bottom. "How do I look?"

Phil glanced over the top of the newspaper he was reading, smiling. "You look like a million bucks, my guy! Are you nervous?"

"Nope." Elliot grinned. "After nearly five decades, I think I'm ready for high school. And this time, without the crippling headaches and meal planning and constant financial worries."

"At least we know you'll pass Home Economics with flying colors." Phil winked. "Just try not to show up the teacher, wouldja? That would make for an awkward parent-teacher conference."

Elliot laughed. "I can't remember a thing I learned in high school the first time around, to be honest. I'm excited to be able to go back."

"Not to mention all the cute high school girls." Phil nudged him with a wink.

"Phil!" Libby thwacked him on the back of the head with a spatula. "That's terrible! He might have the body of a high schooler – and okay, maybe the brain of one too – but deep down, he's got the soul of—"

"—an old fart." Phil chuckled. "Just like us. And anyway, I was only pulling his leg. We all know he's only got eyes for one gal in this world." His expression grew uncharacteristically serious. "What's the countdown now, son?"

"One-thousand two-hundred and fourteen days," Elliot replied automatically, the lump in his throat bobbing at the thought of it."

"Well, then, you'd better make sure you keep your grades up," Libby said, placing a stack of pancakes in front of Elliot. "June's a smart girl. She won't have patience for a lummox."

"She did the first time around," Elliot pointed out, shoving a huge bite of pancakes in his mouth before guzzling it down with a swig of milk. "But…"

"But?" Libby prompted.

"But I do worry… What if she doesn't like me this time? What if I've changed too much since we last knew one another?"

Libby put an arm around his shoulder and kissed the top of his head. "You have the biggest heart of anyone I've ever known, Elliot

Shermann. It doesn't matter how many lifetimes you live, that will never change. Now hurry up, or you're going to be late for school."

Elliot quickly wolfed down the rest of his breakfast, gave each of his parents a quick hug, then jogged over to the door.

"El!" Libby called as he stepped outside.

"Yeah?"

"You'll be grown soon enough, with all of life's responsibilities weighing you down." She smiled tightly. "For now, just go out there and be a regular kid…okay?"

The corner of Elliot's mouth quirked up. "Yes, ma'am."

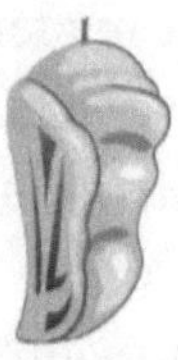

One-thousand two-hundred and fourteen days passed in the blink of an eye, while also being the longest three years of Elliot's life. That day, in particular, felt as though it were passing slower than every other day he'd ever lived combined. He paced back and forth in front of the park bench, reciting the words over and over again, making sure he remembered them exactly as he'd said them the first time. The only difference between now and then was that his heart felt like it might leap out of his chest, and his palms were so sweaty, he could barely hold the bag of breadcrumbs without it slipping through his trembling fingers.

Unlike the rest of his family, who had all been there waiting for him this second time around, Elliot and June had agreed that the events surrounding Lilah's conception, birth, and upbringing had to happen exactly as they had before – that altering them even in the slightest posed too great a risk to their daughter. Because of that, Elliot was preparing to meet June for the second time, while this iteration of June had yet to meet *him*.

The sound of a releasing air brake made his head shoot up.

There, across the lake, was the bus that would drop June off from school for the last time before winter break. Unless something had gone wrong, of course. Who knew what sort of butterfly effects their future actions may have caused? After all, the passage of time is meant to be linear, and unbroken, with no second chances offered. But like his mother often said, Elliot had to believe that *this* iteration of their lives was as it was originally meant to be – a reparation of his past mistakes.

When a beautiful young woman with striking auburn hair and a cherry-red jacket stepped off the bus, Elliot felt as though he might faint at the sight of her. He hadn't allowed himself even a glimpse of June before this moment, too frightened it might ruin everything if they'd met even a single moment earlier than they were meant to.

"Hey June – think fast!"

June let out a loud shriek as a snowball went whizzing past her ear, exploding on the sidewalk in a shower of white powder.

"Oh yeah?" she shouted, bending down to pack a grapefruit-sized ball of snow between her red mittens. As she straightened, poised to hurl the icy missile at her pimple-faced aggressor, a second snowball hit her square in the rump, eliciting an even shriller scream. "Dillon Harold, I'll kill you for that!" she screeched, chucking the snowball in his direction. It went careening through the air, exploding on impact in the center of Dillon's upturned pug nose.

"You may have won the battle, but the war shall be ours!" Dillon crowed as he and his equally idiotic friend retreated to the transient safety of their crumbling snow fort.

"Yeah, you'd better run!" June shouted after them, waving her mittened fist in the air.

The knot in Elliot's chest tightened. He'd waited so long for this moment. What if she turned left instead of right? What if she went straight home instead of stopping by the bench? What if she walked right by him without even noticing he was there? He started to rise to his feet, then forced himself back down, shoving his hand in the bag of bread crumbs he'd brought from home. Everything had to go exactly as it had; Lilah's future depended on it. The one and only difference he'd conceded to was limiting his feeding to living geese as opposed to those resting at the bottom of the lake. He could feel their bones there now, the potential for life that he alone had the power to reanimate. But the old urge – and the crippling fear that it had originally stemmed from – had been quelled long ago.

Let the dead sleep, he reminded himself as June and her friend slowly walked closer and closer. He pulled up his hood and leaned back on the bench, telling himself not to look at her.

He may as well have ordered himself not to breathe.

"I am so *sick* of high school boys, Vi," June was lamenting, making the corners of Elliot's mouth curl into a secret smile. "Do they ever grow up?"

"According to my mother, no." Violet snorted. "Speaking of which, she wanted me to ask if you and your mom are coming over for charades tonight?"

It took every ounce of self-control Elliot possessed to keep his eyes on the gaggle of geese that had gathered in front of him. From the corner of his eye, he could see the bright spot of red that was June's jacket recede into the distance, making his heart skip a beat. But then, as though reconsidering, June shoved her hands in her jacket pockets and hurried past her house, which Elliot knew would be empty, to take another lap around the lake. As she slowed, her attention drawn to the geese that were honking for more crumbs, Elliot momentarily forgot how to breathe.

A few moments later, she swept aside the bare branches of willow trees that formed a curtain around the park bench, brushing the falling snow from her knitted hat as she sat beside him. On the outside, Elliot was as still as a statue. On the inside, he was crumbling at the mere sight of her.

"Hi," she said shyly.

He started at the sound of her voice, high and clear and more beautiful than he had remembered, then quickly turned back to the geese, who were eating crumbs directly from his hand.

June watched, transfixed. "That's so neat," she breathed. "Can I try?"

Elliot glanced at her from under the shadow of his hood, shifting uncomfortably. *Do* not *screw this up,* he warned himself, reciting his words, exactly as he had remembered them, in his head one final time. "Um…sure," he finally answered, handing her the heel of bread from the bottom of the bag. "Just don't make any sudden movements. They startle easily."

She nodded, breaking off tiny bits of bread to feed to the flock that had gathered.

Sucking down a deep, steadying breath, Elliot leaned back against the bench with a heavy sigh, letting his hood fall away. His love for June had only grown since the last time he saw her, decades ago, in the graveyard where they'd said their goodbyes.

His thoughts trailed to Lilah then, their daughter that didn't yet exist, and the warmth in his heart spread, hardening his resolve and feeding his determination. These next six months wouldn't be easy. And even harder would be the months after that, when he would have to say goodbye all over again. But if everything went to plan – and he had tremendous faith in his daughter that it would – everything would turn out all right.

As he darted a quick glance at the girl he loved out of the corner of his eye, he whispered a silent prayer for the first time in many, many years.

Please, God – this time around, please help me make this right.

Willow picked at a hangnail on her thumb, tugging at it until it bled. The pain barely registered. There hadn't been a single day in the last year when her cuticles hadn't been torn and bleeding. She glanced over at her mother, who was gripping the steering wheel with two white-knuckled fists as they sped along the highway, well above the posted speed limit. Yellow light from the overhead freeway lamps streaked across Celeste's face every so often, highlighting the harsh wrinkles permanently etched between her brows. She hadn't said a word since the two of them left – or rather, fled – the fire station. Though they both checked the rearview mirror every few minutes, it appeared that no one had followed them. The highway was all but deserted and the lights from the town were far behind them now, just a faint orange glow on the dark horizon.

As the light from the last streetlamp streaked past, Celeste peered behind them one final time. The rearview mirror was completely dark now. No one was following them. No one would know that they had driven through there. She finally released the breath she had been holding for what felt like the last hour and eased up on the accelerator. She had done it; the child – or whatever it was – would be someone else's problem now. And she would sleep soundly, knowing there was no blood on her hands. It might not have been Shaman Mike's first choice, Celeste reasoned, but he'll be so proud when he hears. *And with it gone, I'll finally be able to invite him over for dinner. Maybe even "dessert!"* The thought sent a happy shiver down her spine. She had to compose herself before speaking again, lest Willow hear the giddiness in her voice.

"When we get back, I'm going to enroll you at the high school in town."

"Really?" Willow gasped. "You mean it?"

Her mother nodded tersely. "You are to tell them that I've been homeschooling you for the past year. And under no circumstance are you to mention anything about the… well, you know. To anyone. Am I clear?"

Willow nodded, feeling the lump in her throat begin to shrink. "Mama…what do you think is going to happen to her? Will she be—"

"I don't know. I don't want to know. And after we get home, I never want to hear the subject raised again. I knew that boy in Scarville was no good, putting all sorts of strange ideas in your head so he could take advantage of you. And look at what he did to you! What he put in you! There will be no consorting with boys at this new school, Willow – do you understand me? The universe saw fit to punish you for your idiocy but I'll be damned if I continue to be punished by proxy!"

"I'm sorry, Mama," Willow whispered. "I promise I'll never make that mistake again. Thank you for helping me fix everything. And thank you for letting me go back to school. I promise I'll be good this time. And I won't tell anyone about…anything."

"Good," Celeste replied, gritting her teeth. A hot soaking bath with lavender salts had been calling her name for some time. "Now, you're sure you threw everything in the dumpster back there? The crib, the bottles, everything? We can't have anyone back home asking questions."

"All of it's in there."

"The clothes and toys too?"

A small knot formed in Willow's stomach. She'd thrown everything in the fire station dumpster, just like her mother instructed – everything, save for a small, wooden rattle that had the name "Lilah" hand-painted on the side. For some reason, she couldn't bear to part with that. Her hand went to her back pocket, where it was safely hidden.

"All of it's gone, Mama. I–I promise."

Celeste smiled to herself. Soon enough, she and her daughter would be home, and everything would be back to normal. The universe had seen fit to send her its greatest challenge yet, and she knew she had passed with flying colors. Life would be easier from here on out, she just knew it. Heck, she might even stop at the Corner Market on the way home and buy a lottery ticket – after all, good things were coming her way. She could feel it.

"What's that?" Willow asked, pointing.

"What's what?"

"That red thing by the road. Is that a… person?" she asked, squinting to make out the moving shape in the fog.

Celeste took her foot off the gas. A woman in a bright red rain jacket was walking alongside the road, just ahead. She didn't appear to notice their van as Celeste slowed down to pull onto the shoulder in front of her.

"What are you doing?" Willow asked, chewing on her thumbnail.

"It's the middle of the night and it's freezing outside. Shaman Mike says the only way to earn karma for this life and the next is through acts of kindness. So, we'll take her to the nearest gas station. I wanted to make a quick stop there, anyway."

Willow bit her lip, doing her best not to think about the other little person they had left out in the cold that night.

"Roll down the window," her mother instructed as she shifted into Park.

The woman continued walking along the dark shoulder, her hooded silhouette barely visible in the faint glow of the nearly full moon.

"Excuse me, ma'am?" Celeste shouted, leaning over her daughter. "Are you stranded? Do you need a lift?"

She didn't look up.

"Hello?" Celeste waved.

The woman was only a handful of yards away from the van now. From the red light of the van's brake lights, Willow could see the holes in her jeans, the blackened toes that stuck out from her tattered sandals.

"Mom—" she started to say.

"Hello, ma'am?" Celeste called again. "Do you speak English? Do you need help?"

The woman stopped a few feet from the open window, slowly turning her head to look at them. Willow let out a gasp. Though she was young, perhaps only a few years older than Willow, her copper skin was haggard, and she had angry sores blossoming across her chapped lips. She gazed at them with the saddest, deadest eyes Willow had ever seen.

"Run," the young woman whispered into the fog. A cold shiver ran down Willow's spine.

"What did you say?" Celeste called, leaning on her daughter's leg for support.

Just then, a knock sounded on the driver's side window. As the door to the van tore open, Celeste and her daughter barely had time to scream.

"Get out," a man growled, his black hood casting the sharp angles of his face in shadows.

"What—"

"I said get out!" he snarled, reaching forward to snatch the keys from the ignition.

Recoiling from his penetrating gaze, Celeste awkwardly stumbled backwards and over the console, shoving Willow out the passenger door. "Run!" she screeched, pushing her daughter forward. But Willow stumbled to a stop on the side of the road, paralyzed with shock as the man stalked closer and closer.

"Please!" Celeste choked out, shoving her daughter in front of her like a shield. "I can explain! Just don't hurt me!"

The man pulled back his hood, exposing a darkened expression and a contemptuous sneer.

Willow gazed up at him with wide, terrified eyes – eyes that momentarily glazed over as her future soul once more entered her body, then quickly filled with glimmering tears of disbelief.

"It worked?" she whispered, taking in her surroundings for the second time.

"Do you know what you did to your daughter in your previous life?" the man growled, taking a menacing step toward Celeste. "Is there any part of your festering soul that remembers the sins of your past?"

"Get away from me!" Celeste screamed, stumbling backward.

"You abandoned her right here in this forest. While she cried out for you again and again, you fled, saving your own life while leaving your only daughter to die."

"What?!" Celeste sputtered. "I would never—"

"But you did." The man's voice had become as icy as the biting winter wind, sending a fresh chill down Celeste's spine. "And you'd do it all over again if it meant having the freedom to live your life, unburdened by the child you never wanted. Isn't that right?" As he reached for her throat, the skin melted straight off his bones, leaving nothing but sinew and bone.

"Get away from me!" Celeste screamed, turning on her heel to flee in the opposite direction.

"Mom!" her daughter shouted after her. *"Mama!"*

Without sparing even a fleeting glance over her shoulder, Celeste disappeared into the forest, once again leaving her only daughter to the cold, indiscriminating whims of fate.

June turned back to the man, trembling.

Without wasting another moment, he reached forward and snatched her by the front of her jacket, crushing his lips against hers.

A sob caught in June's throat as she kissed him back – ardently, and full of passion. "You saved my life," she whispered against Elliot's parted lips.

"Just as you saved mine," he whispered back, kissing her once more.

She sank into the kiss, into his arms, where she sobbed freely, grieving the loss of both her mother and her daughter in the span of one evening.

"I've got you," Elliot said, stroking the back of her head softly. "You're safe now."

She gave a small start, jerking her head over her shoulder. "But what about the other man – the one who killed me?" she whispered, wild-eyed and full of panic. "Is he—"

"No." Elliot shook his head firmly. "Your murderer won't be hurting you, or anyone else, ever again. The police will be here shortly, where they'll find his body tied to a tree and a note to run his fingerprints."

June's shoulders relaxed slightly. "And the girl?"

"She ran off as soon as she realized her kidnapper was incapacitated. We can go look for her, if you'd like – drop her off at a soup kitchen, or somewhere else she'll be safe."

"Thank you," June whispered, cupping his cheek in her hand. "But…" She swallowed, reaching into her back pocket to finger a small wooden rattle with hand-painted letters on the side. "But what about Lilah? Isn't there some way we could…?"

Elliot shook his head. "Not if we want her to grow up to be the same brilliant, beautiful woman she's meant to become."

June regarded the darkened road leading back to the Tri-Forks Fire Station, as well as the van her mother had abandoned in her frantic haste to escape, then turned back to Elliot. "If Lilah doesn't find my body in these woods, how will she know…?" She licked her lips, trying to put moisture back in her mouth. "I mean, won't that change her future?"

"It's the one thing I'm not sure about," Elliot admitted. "But something tells me that time is not a linear, singular thread. It exists everywhere and all at once, multiple, converging threads that all weave into the same tapestry. Elliot, the broken and lost orphan, still exists. So does the Willow that died in this forest. I don't know how or why – all I know is that you and I will be there to greet our daughter in nineteen years, just as we promised her. We just have to be strong enough to let her grow up first."

June chewed on her lip, darting one last look in Lilah's direction. "I miss her already."

"Me too. But speaking of growing up…" He pressed his lips against her questioning eyebrows, murmuring, "Since we have quite a bit of time to kill until we can see our daughter again, how do you feel about going back to high school?"

June made a noise somewhere between a laugh and a sob. "After everything we've been through?"

Elliot shrugged one shoulder, the corner of his mouth quirking into a wry smile. "We've lived through more hardship and grief than most people will ever experience in a single lifetime. So I figure, maybe this time around, we should just…live. Happily, if possible."

She nodded, the smallest hint of a smile showing through her tears. "Okay," June agreed, sucking down a deep breath. "Let's live the best lives we possibly can. For us…and for her."

"The years will fly by in the blink of an eye," Elliot said softly, gently cupping her face in his hands. "I promise."

CHAPTER 27
FREE SPIRITS

"They'll be here within minutes," Mike remarked, referencing the long line of flashlights that were creeping closer and closer. "Let's hope all is going as planned on the back end of this convoluted plan of yours."

Gulping, Lilah turned back to her mother and father's bodies, which had been gazing straight ahead with glassy, unfocused expressions for an increasingly discomforting amount of time. "Guys?" she called, waving a hand in front of their unblinking eyes. "Are you okay?" Chewing on a hangnail, she turned back to Mike. "What if I did it wrong? What if we messed up and somehow made things worse?"

"His and June's souls are no longer with us," Mike interjected, plopping down on his own headstone. "None of their spirits are. Whatever you did, they are no longer trapped here."

"What about you?" Lilah asked, the sinking realization suddenly dawning on her. "How will we fix what's happened to you?"

"You only now are beginning to understand the conundrum?" Mike smirked, coolly inspecting his fingernails. "Well, allow me to further elucidate it for you: Had you not skewered my body on an evergreen tree, and then hysterically jerked me back the moment my soul was attempting to flee my dying body, I would not be puttering around this graveyard as an aimless spirit; nor would I have been able to speak to Elliot's army of ghostly victims on his behalf. Furthermore, as you have no doubt come to realize, had you 'replanted' my spirit into a prior version of myself alongside the others, I never would have become a ghost, which means I would have not been able to avail myself as your spiritual mediator earlier tonight." The smugness he exuded made it profoundly difficult for Lilah to feel pity for the man. "You've created quite the paradox, it would seem."

"But Elliot told me that time isn't a linear path – 'that it exists everywhere and all at once.'" She argued. "So maybe—"

"Would you take such a risk – prioritizing the tarnished soul of a man you loathe while simultaneously endangering the spirits of your father and mother?" Mike tapped the side of his hooked nose. "If they do not meet in the past, if everything following does not go perfectly, who's to say you would even exist? Even without the added risk of saving my soul, so to speak, you could disappear at any moment."

"I know," Lilah muttered, suppressing a shudder. "But—"

"I have accepted my fate as a spiritual envoy." Mike sighed dramatically. "Embraced it, even."

Lilah arched a dubious eyebrow.

He leaned back on his gravestone, crossing his arms. "You might even say I've begrudgingly embraced it. After all, I was not, in my past life, the most…noble…of people." He feigned a cavalier shrug, though Lilah could see the shame etched between his brows. "After several years of self-reflection, I see now that my actions caused irreparable harm – both for your parents, and, as a consequence, for you. Truly, the ripples of my misdeeds have been felt across the very fabric of time itself. I can only assume this is my sentence for that. My…penance." His shoulders rose and fell in a resigned sigh. "It is not *all* bad, however. Unlike most wandering spirits, *I* can interact with the other ghosts in this realm. I can even tap into the vast fungal networks of the forest – which function much like the neurons of our own brain – and see miraculous, wondrous things that even my most potently-brewed mushroom tea did not grant to my corporeal vision. I am finally one with nature, as I have always longed to be but could never attain. And when summoned back to my body, I can speak to the living as well." He flashed Lilah a surprisingly self-deprecating smile. "If the living can tolerate me, that is."

"I don't accept that," Lilah said, shaking her head. "Maybe if we could just—"

"*LILAH!*" Stan's booming voice sounded from what had to be less than a hundred feet away. *"Can you hear us?"*

Lilah swore under her breath, casting an anxious glance at her parents' unmoving bodies – just in time to see them abruptly crumble into dust. "No!" she gasped, stretching out her fingers as Elliot and June's ashes swirled just out of reach. Mouth hanging open in horror, she watched helplessly as they floated up and away into the starry night sky.

"I wouldn't fret." Mike smiled wryly. "It would seem your rendezvous is occurring right on time." He pointed just past her shoulder.

Lilah spun on her heel. "What—Oh!" Her hands flew to her mouth in shock as two figures emerged from the shadows of the graveyard: a slender blonde woman in her early sixties, who was holding out a steaming thermos, and a tall, lanky man with gray hair, thick spectacles, and a wide, infectious grin.

"Well, hello there!" the man beamed at her, his eyes twinkling. "You must be my granddaughter!"

Before Lilah could answer, the woman rushed forward, exclaiming, "I feel like I have been waiting to meet you for an eternity!" She pulled Lilah in for a tight one-armed hug, then gently pushed her away, taking her in from head to toe. "Oh wow, Elliot was right – you really are the spitting image of your mother!"

"Could be sisters," the man agreed, sticking his hand out to shake Lilah's hand. "I'm your Grandpa Phil, for all intents and purposes. Thanks a lot for helping me avoid that truck the second time around! Being flattened into a human pancake is not fun."

"Phil!" Libby nudged him in the side. "Ignore him – old age has made him looney."

"I've always been a loon!" he argued.

Rolling her eyes, she handed Lilah the thermos, which was full of hot chocolate and dissolved marshmallows. "Here, dear – we were worried you'd be cold, so we brought you this."

Lilah opened her mouth to reply, then snapped it shut as three more figures stepped into the clearing: a stooped, elderly woman who was clutching the arm of a sprightly, middle-aged blonde woman, as well as a dark-haired nun who also appeared to be in her fifties.

"Lilah," Libby smiled, gesturing to the two women standing closest to her. "This is my mother, Jean, and my little sister, Peggy."

"At fifty-six years old, I'm nobody's 'little' anything!" Peggy grinned as she scooped Lilah into a tight hug. "Hello, my darling! It's a pleasure to finally meet the woman who saved my life."

"H-Hi," Lilah stammered, setting the hot chocolate on a nearby grave.

"You really are the spitting image of your mother!" Jean smiled at her, eyes twinkling. "But you've got your father's smile."

"But not his beard, thank goodness." Phil grinned.

Libby elbowed him in the ribs. "Oh, would you shush!"

The nun squeezed past them, clasping Lilah's free hand in hers. "Hello, dear. My name is Mariela. And thanks to you, I – along with my sister and ten other children – escaped that fire with our lives. Two of those children went on to become doctors, and several more went into the helping fields. So many lives saved, thanks to you, and so many more touched – like ripples in a pond." She wiped a stray tear from her eye. "My sister, Kimberly, passed into the Lord's arms two years ago, but before she died, she asked me to give you this." Mariela pressed an envelope into

Lilah's trembling palm. "It's a list of all the children she and I have fostered over the years – all of whom were raised in a caring, safe home environment instead of a cold, unfeeling orphanage. And every one of those children has you to thank."

Lilah tucked the envelope safely away in her pocket, eyes brimming with tears as a handsome, smiling man appeared from the shadows, his dark, untamed hair graying at the temples. Behind him was a beautiful woman with long, auburn hair – the spitting image of Lilah, save for a few strands of gray hair and the crow's feet on the outer edges of her tear-filled eyes.

"Mom…Dad!" Lilah's feet moved of their own accord as she ran toward her parents, flinging herself into their open arms with a strangled sob.

"It's okay," June whispered into her hair. "We're all okay."

"You did everything perfectly," Elliot said, hugging his daughter tightly. "We couldn't be prouder of you – or more grateful."

"I-I can't believe it," Lilah stammered, gazing up at him. "Are you…?"

"Alive?" He chuckled. "Oh yes. Very much so."

"Here, my love," June said, reaching into her back pocket, where she retrieved a small wooden rattle. "I've always wanted to give you this in person."

Lilah gazed down at the rattle, awestruck. Her fingers ran over the familiar hand-painted letters of her own name, though the paint was far less faded than the rattle she'd unearthed just beside her mother's bones. "But…how?"

"LILAH!" a voice shouted from behind her.

She whirled around, shielding her eyes from the half-dozen flashlights that were trained directly on her, just as Stan and Jace burst through the trees with Sheriff Reid and a squadron of breathless police officers in tow.

"Li!" Jace rushed forward, pulling Lilah into a spine-cracking hug. "Are you okay?" he demanded, inspecting her face for any sign of injury.

"I'm fine," she reassured him. "More than fine, really."

"What the…?" Stan stepped forward, his eyes bulging in bewilderment as he looked from Lilah, to June, then back again.

"What is the meaning of this?" Sheriff Reid demanded, training his flashlight on the crowd of people that had gathered around Lilah. "Quinn, who are all of these people?"

"Uh, guys…" Lilah gently pulled away from Jace, rubbing the back of her neck. "I'd like you to meet Elliot and June, my biological parents. And this," she turned to the sheriff, gesturing her open hand in Libby's direction, "is Elizabeth

Simmons…our missing woman in the yellow jacket.”

Sheriff Reid’s jaw dropped.

Libby gave him a shy finger wave.

“Okay, now I’m *really* confused,” Stanley muttered, his eyes flitting from Elliot to June to Shaman Mike, who was casually lounging beside his grave.

Elliot took an abrupt step in Stanley’s direction, spurring several officers to cock their guns at him. Ignoring them, Elliot reached forward and gripped Stanley’s hand, pulling him in for a tight hug. “Thank you for taking care of our daughter,” he whispered fervently.

Stiffening, Stan cast a bewildered glance in Lilah’s direction. “Huh?”

“What?” Jace parroted, also jerking his head in Lilah’s direction.

She took Jace’s hand in hers, casting him and her father a sheepish grin. “It’s a really, *really* long story.”

“One we have plenty of time to tell,” June said, reaching down to clasp Lilah’s other hand.

Elliot let out a mirthful laugh. “All the time in the world,” he agreed, clapping a hand on Stanley’s shoulder.

CHAPTER 28

NO BONE UNTURNED

Lilah's eyes were blurry and her head was aching from staring at her computer screen for the last three hours, but as soon as she clicked that bright green "Submit" button, a wave of relief washed over her. One and a half years of online college, plus two semesters of accelerated summer courses – all while concurrently working thirty hours a week for Sheriff Reid – had culminated in this, her final Criminal Justice exam.

And now, *finally*, it was done.

Leaning back in her chair, she took a moment to reflect on everything she'd accomplished, from writing essays on forensic studies to unearthing the bones of the victims themselves. While she might not have graduated at the top of her class – her habit of forgetting to turn in assignments had been primarily to blame for that – she'd solved more cold cases over the years than anyone else. Not that anyone outside of the sheriff and her immediate circle knew that. But Lilah had done it for justice, not glory, and the closure she'd brought to the victims' families made the work far from thankless. Still, that didn't make the job easier or any less heartbreaking. In fact, there were days she'd seriously considered swapping out her badge for a Baskin Robbins apron.

But Sheriff Reid had always managed to convince her to come back, even on the hard days – especially on the hard days. *"If not for us, there'd be no one else to keep the bad guys in line,"* he'd say, giving her shoulder a reassuring squeeze. *"Besides, Quinn, if there's one thing in this world I know, it's that you were born to do this."*

Lilah couldn't help but smile. Though Reid had often hounded her for getting the order of operations backward, he'd put his own career on the line more than once both for the sake of justice and for her – something Lilah would forever be grateful for. Her eyes flickered to the honorary TFPD badge he'd commissioned specially for her, which sat beside two hand-painted rattles that still boggled her mind six weeks later.

Two rattles. Two Willows. Two lifetimes, both experienced by the same soul.

Lilah stood up from her desk, stretching her hands over her head while the growing sounds of company milling about the living room filtered in from downstairs. After shutting down the trusty iMac G3 her father had gifted her last Christmas, she threw on her favorite red sweater, flung open her bedroom door, and made her way toward the commotion.

"Banister!" Elliot and Phil called out when they heard her thumping down the steps two at a time..

"Sorry!" She slowed down, melodramatically clutching the handrail for dear life until she'd made it safely to the bottom.

Elliot nodded his approval from the couch, while Phil turned back to the crossword puzzle he'd been filling out beside him. "What's an eight-letter word for the study of time?" he asked, absentmindedly tapping his pen on the arm of the sofa.

"Chronology?" Libby offered as she swept past him and into the kitchen.

"That's too many letters!" Phil protested.

"I believe it's 'horology,'" Lilah supplied, squeezing between her father and grandfather –

yet another thing that felt utterly surreal, yet completely right.

"How did it go?" Elliot asked while scooting over to make room for her.

"It—"

"Did you finish your exam?!" June shouted from the kitchen.

"Yes!" Lilah shouted back.

"Already?" June stuck her head out the doorway, her auburn hair slightly frazzled from running around the kitchen all afternoon. "How'd it go?"

As Lilah opened her mouth to reply, the front door swung open and Stanley and Jace clambered inside, lugging a massive snow-dusted pine tree in tow. "Oh hey, Li," Stanley grunted while he and Jace awkwardly angled the towering tree through the not-so-towering doorway. "How'd your exam go?"

"Fi—"

"Here, let me help you with that," Elliot interjected, rising from the couch to help.

Stanley made a grateful huff. "Thanks, pal."

Together, heaving and wheezing and grunting, the three men managed to unceremoniously hoist the tree upright in the corner, knocking off bits of plaster from the ceiling as they did.

"It's a little big, don't you think?" Lilah asked, regarding the stooped-over tree, the top ten inches of which had been crammed at a ninety-degree angle beneath the low ceiling.

"Did you guys get the oranges?" Libby shouted from the kitchen. *"I can't make my famous cranberry sauce without orange zest!"*

"We got 'em!" Stan yelled, holding a bag of oranges over his head like football as he made his way through the crowded living room, arm outstretched as though he were attempting to cross an imaginary goal line. "Oh, hey, Lilah – tell us about your exam!" he called over his shoulder just before disappearing into the kitchen.

"I bet you aced it." Jace grinned, wrapping an arm around her waist.

"She totally aced it," Elliot agreed.

"What's a seven-letter phrase that means both uncertainty and assault?" Phil asked, chewing on his pen cap.

"Beats me," Jace answered.

Phil frowned. "I guess I'll just have to leave that one blank for now."

Lilah and Jace exchanged amused glances.

"Dinner will be ready in ten minutes!" June called. *"Are Dave and Annie here yet?"*

"We'll go check!" Lilah yelled back, a well-timed excuse to snatch Jace's hand and dart outside, away from the clamor and bedlam that was Christmas Eve dinner.

Shutting the front door behind them, Lilah sucked down a deep breath, filling her lungs with cold, crisp winter air for the first time that day. The snow had been falling, softly but steadily, all day long, covering the neighborhood in a tranquil blanket of white, while colorful strings of Christmas lights softly glowed from underneath.

"Have I ever told you how much I love this color on you?" Jace murmured, fingering the hem of Lilah's sweater.

"Only once or twice." She smiled up at him, brushing a strand of hair from his striking blue eyes. "Have I ever told you how much I love you?"

"Only once or twice." He leaned down to brush a soft kiss against her lips, which Lilah returned with fervor.

When Jace pulled away a moment later, he had that tell-tale nervous crease etched between his eyebrows. "So, um," he started, running an anxious hand through his hair, "I've been meaning to ask you, and I completely understand if the answer is no, but uh…" He sucked down a deep breath, then blurted out, "What do you think about you and me getting an apartment together in Helena?"

Lilah's eyebrows arched in surprise, but before she could reply, he barreled on, "I know I still have a year and a half of college left, but I've been thinking of taking time off from school anyway. Breaking into the Major Leagues was always something everyone *else* pressured me to do, you know? And the more my coach goes on about it, the more daunting it feels. So, if you're heading to Helena for the Police Academy, I was thinking I could maybe come with you and work and take care of rent so you can go to school and not have to worry about any of that stuff. And once you've graduated, I could go back to school and finish up my business degree, which is what I've always wanted to do but never really had a say in the matter – not 'til now, at least." He rubbed the back of his neck, not quite meeting Lilah's eyes. "So…what do you think?"

It was becoming harder and harder for Lilah to contain her smile. "And here I was going to ask you if I could come to Washington with you."

Jace's jaw dropped. "Really?"

Lilah shrugged, grinning widely. "I've lived in Montana my whole life, you know? I figured it's time I spread my wings a bit. And anyway, I've decided I'm not going to the police academy – in Helena or anywhere else."

Wide, rounded eyes now accompanied Jace's dangling jaw. "Really?"

The crunching sound of tires rolling over snow drew their attention to the driveway, where Sheriff Reid's truck had just pulled in. "Howdy, Detective Quinn!" he called, dutifully helping his wife, Annie, and their dog, Bandit, out of the truck.

"I'll tell you before dinner," Lilah muttered to Jace through a gritted smile, flashing their guests a polite wave. "But the short version is, yes, I would love to move in together."

She let out a small yelp as Jace lifted her up into his arms and spun her around in an exuberant circle. "This is the best news, ever!" he whooped.

"What's going on over here?" Sheriff Reid asked, flashing the two of them a wink. "Did someone just propose or something?"

"Nah." Jace grinned as he gently set Lilah back down. "That'll be next Christmas."

Lilah glanced up at him to see if he was joking or not, a small thrill fluttering through her stomach when she saw the earnestness shining in his eyes.

. . .

Not long afterward, Lilah found herself admiring the massive spread of food that was weighing down their cramped kitchen table, the leaves of which had been completely extended for the first time in the table's twenty-five-year history. Never before had so many people been crammed into their tiny kitchen, and yet, somehow, it didn't feel crowded. It felt exactly right.

While everyone else dug in, Lilah looked around the table with a growing smile. Her two fathers were seated beside each other, with Elliot barking out a tear-filled laugh at Stanley's terrible Clint Eastwood impression. Sheriff Reid sat on Stanley's opposite side, reassuring Annie that *her* stuffing was still his favorite despite the fact that he'd just carelessly blurted out that Libby's was "the best damn stuffing" he'd ever eaten. Lilah's mother, June, was seated between her daughter and Elliot, and was having an animated conversation with Libby about the scientific study she was preparing to publish on death and consciousness. Meanwhile, Jace, who was seated on Lilah's left side, was busy talking to Phil about their shared experience of playing college baseball.

"Here's the thing with the big leagues"—Phil was leaning forward on his elbows as though sharing a wild conspiracy theory—"everyone wants in, but once you're in, you're *in*. You want a life outside of baseball? Too bad. You wanna travel the world? Nope, not with primary season, post-training, and then more training. You wanna start a family? Oh sure – if you count the one month out of the year you can stay home to help your wife with the new baby."

Jace's eyes darted to Lilah, who suddenly felt a warm flush creeping up her cheeks.

"There is a reason I chose a career in healthcare over the big league, and I tell you what – I have never once looked back," Phil declared, his tone uncharacteristically serious. "Turning down that talent scout was the greatest decision I ever made. As an EMT, I got to be home with the love of my life and our little boy. What more could a man ask for?" He squeezed Libby's hand tightly, prompting her to blow him a kiss.

Lilah again met Jace's eyes, flashing him a shy smile, before turning her attention to the conversation June and Libby were having.

"Whatever happened to that dissertation you wrote in your first life?" June was asking. "I think you told me at one point that it was something like five-hundred pages."

"Five-hundred and forty-six pages." Libby exhaled through her nose. "The culmination of my entire afterlife's work."

"I remember you and El found it underneath the floorboards of his old cabin," June said, tapping her bottom lip thoughtfully. "But what did you do with it after that?"

"Oh, I still have it. It's locked in a safe deposit box back in Iowa."

"Do you think you'll ever publish it?" Lilah asked, her stomach knotting. After all, that five-hundred-and-forty-six-page paper had discussed her and her father's death-defying chronomantic abilities in exhaustive detail.

Libby shook her head. "Oh, no, dear. That paper is yours and your father's to do with as you wish. It's not my place to publish it on your behalf. And besides, I get enough flak from the medical community for my 'wild conjectures' on consciousness existing as a separate entity from the random electrical firings of our brains. Could you imagine if I tried to tell them that my son and granddaughter can unravel the very workings of time itself?"

"That…might cause a bit of backlash," Lilah agreed.

"Not to mention the end of your normal lives as you know them," Libby said, gesturing pointedly with a green-bean-speared fork.

"I definitely don't want that." Lilah shuddered. "I'm perfectly happy with only the people in this room knowing."

"A wise decision!" a loud voice barked out, making her jump.

Annie let out a sharp yelp, shooting a dirty look at the empty chair sitting between her and Libby, where a handheld police radio was resting on a stack of phone books. "I will *never* get used to that," she muttered, furiously rubbing at the fresh goosebumps on her arms.

"Coming from a life of fame and glory," Mike Hastings continued from the walkie-talkie, which had been set to the one frequency Lilah had accidentally discovered his voice could be heard, *"I can tell you first-hand that the constant recognition, the relentless badgering for*

signatures and photographs becomes old very quickly!"

"Didn't he sell like sixty books in total?" Jace muttered under his breath.

"Nonsense!" Mike shot back. *"I sold at least...er...well, far more than that! Vivienne alone must have bought at least fifty of my books!"*

A hush fell over the table.

"I...er..." Mike's radio crackled contritely, emphasizing the awkward silence.

Lilah darted a look at her mother, who gave her hand a grateful squeeze.

"I'm fine," June reassured her. "Really."

Setting down his fork for the first time since the ham had been carved up twenty minutes ago, Sheriff Reid shifted uncomfortably in his seat. "Well, I suppose now is as good a time as ever to tell you...um..." His eyes flickered over to Stanley's.

"Tell us what?" Lilah asked, raising an eyebrow.

Stanley sighed. "Dave found June's mother."

"What?!" several voices exclaimed at once.

"Where?" June asked, leaning forward.

"A small town in Saskatchewan, if you can believe it."

Elliot and Lilah met one another's eyes, no doubt wondering the same thing.

"She's alive," Reid answered their unspoken question, drawing out another series of gasps from people and ghosts alike. "She currently goes by the name 'Vivienne Mayweather' – a bastardization of her two previous aliases." He took that opportunity to take a long swig of beer, then used his flannel sleeve to wipe it from his mustache, earning a reproachful look from his wife. "If you can believe it, Vivienne's joined some sort of cult up there—"

"Joined?" Stanley interjected dryly. "She's married to the cult leader and has four kids with the guy."

June and Lilah's mouths simultaneously dropped open, while Elliot instinctively reached over and took June's hand in his, casting her a worried expression.

"Is *that* where she's been this whole time?" Lilah asked, anger rising in her chest.

"Near as I can tell," Sheriff Reid said, scratching the top of his head, "she appeared up there in April of 1984, four months after June's death-slash-disappearance. The woman didn't dilly-dally either – made herself right at home, as though she were familiar with the cult and had planned it in advance."

"It's not, perchance, called 'The Brotherhood of the Goat,' is it?" Mike asked.

Sheriff Reid arched a suspicious eyebrow. "And how exactly would you know that?"

Mike's sigh crackled with static. *"Because the leader of the cult is my older brother, Donatello."*

Jace snorted so hard he choked on his apple cider. "Michaelangelo and *Donatello?*" he sputtered, doing everything he could to contain his laughter. "Do you also happen to have two younger brothers named Raphael and Leonardo?"

If walkie-talkies could cast filthy looks, this one would be doing exactly that. *"If you think I'm eccentric, you should see him! Vivienne was aware of his existence and often asked me about his beliefs, any openings in his commune, and so on. I warned her that Don was a bit 'extreme,' but that only seemed to arouse her interest further. Perhaps, in her haste to flee her crimes and her shame, she sought Donatello out. He does look quite a bit like me – but markedly less handsome, of course."*

"Of course," Jace snorted under his breath.

"It would make sense," Mike continued, ignoring him, *"for her to have pursued comfort in the arms of my older, slightly less charismatic brother, after I repeatedly spurned her advances."*

"Now tell them the part about how these people worship goats." Stanley coughed. "Though I'd wager they do more than 'worship' them…"

Lilah shot him a horrified look before swiveling back to her mother. "Are you okay? Do you wanna…I don't know…go up there and track her down?"

"No." June was already shaking her head before Lilah had even finished the question. "I have all the family I need right here."

"Hear hear!" Stanley said, lifting a glass. "To family – especially the chosen kind."

"To family," everyone else agreed, raising their glasses. Well, everyone except the armless walkie-talkie.

"Mike." Lilah frowned in his direction.

"Hmm?"

"Everyone else has been back for a long time. I'm pretty sure we can do something about…" She gestured blithely at his plastic form. "Well, you know. Getting you back in your body."

"Nonsense!" he chirped. *"I've become something of a celebrity among my non-corporeal brethren! That is to say, I've always been a brilliant medicine man and shaman, but now we can add 'medium' and 'spiritual mushroom guide' to my already impressive resumé."* He chuckled wryly. *"Go back to my body? It would seem, my dear, that my body was the one thing that had been holding me back!"*

"Erm…" Lilah blinked. "Okay."

Stanley rolled his eyes at Jace while winding his finger in a twisting motion around his ear: the universal sign for "What a complete and utter crackpot."

"So, Lilah," Sheriff Reid started, pausing first to take a robust bite of a buttered roll, "how did your exam go?"

She grinned. "Like I've been trying to tell you guys, I totally aced it."

"Of course you did!" He beamed. "Best damn detective I ever had, I tell you what."

"Language," Annie muttered, nudging her husband in the side.

He flashed his wife a contrite grimace, then turned his attention back to Lilah. "So now what? You need me to send that recommendation letter over to MLEA?" Before she could answer, his shoulders abruptly slumped in a heavy sigh. "Oh man. How the hell am I ever gonna replace you, kid? Those big shots in Helena don't know what a treasure they're stealing."

Stanley reached over and squeezed Reid's shoulder. "Tell me about it."

"I can't believe we just got you back and already have to say goodbye," June said, the forced smile on her face perfectly matching Elliot's. "Not that it matters, of course. You have to follow your dreams."

"Well..." Lilah started, darting a glance at Jace. "About that..."

Stanley cleared his throat roughly. "Let me guess – you want to go to the police academy in

Washington, right?" Before Lilah could answer, he barreled on, "Don't worry, kid, I get it. You two are hopelessly in love. And you've got your whole life ahead of you." His voice cracked with emotion. "I mean, all babies gotta leave the nest one day, right?"

Elliot reached over and squeezed Stanley's hand, which gripped his right back.

"I knew this day was coming." Stanley quickly scrubbed the tears from his eyes with the sleeve of his free hand. "I mean, what with Jace going to play in the big leagues, and you running off to become a brilliant detective. You obviously couldn't stick around forever." The smile he tried to force on his face ended up looking more like a crumpled grimace. "I just didn't realize it would be so hard to say goodbye to not just one, but both of my kids."

Jace's eyes widened, then became glassy. "Aw, Stan…" he said, his lip quivering. "You're like the dad I never had."

Stanley pressed his fist to his mouth, seemingly intent on not letting himself cry.

Lilah rolled her eyes. "Guys—"

"They really do grow up so fast," Phil lamented, blowing his nose loudly into a handkerchief.

Sniffling, Libby dabbed at her red-rimmed eyes. "One minute they're a sweet little boy bringing dead dogs back to life, and the next thing you know they're off having babies of their own."

"Well, to be fair, June and I were kids ourselves when she got pregnant." Elliot couldn't help but chuckle. But when his eyes fell on Lilah's, he took a deep breath, working to button up his emotions. "I know we just got you back, which means it'll be that much harder to say goodbye…but we've got the rest of our lives to catch up. In the meantime, you've got to go out and chase your dreams, even if it's hard for us parents to watch you go." He regarded Jace with a smile. "Fortunately, you've got a wonderful young man to accompany you out there in that great, big world."

Lilah pressed her lips together, working to suppress a laugh. "Are you guys done with the waterworks yet?" She cocked her head at the walkie-talkie. "Mike – anything else to add?"

"Just that afterlife will be far less interesting without you." Mike sniffed. *"It'll take a hearty plethora of mushrooms to fill the gaping void you'll be leaving in your stead…Except"*—he let out a pained gasp–*"how am I to eat mushrooms without you to put me back in my body?"*

Sighing, Lilah turned to Jace, taking his hand in hers. "Now that all of you are finally done talking, Jace and I have something to tell you."

"What?" Elliot and Stan demanded at the same time.

"Oh, God," June gasped, leaning forward. "You're not pregnant, are you?"

"What? No!" Lilah yelped, matching flushes creeping into her and Jace's cheeks.

"Thank God," Libby muttered, rubbing the bridge of her nose.

"As I've said before," Lilah hastily continued, "it makes no sense for me to spend years training to be a police officer, and then working as a cop, followed by even *more* training, only to end up doing what I'm already doing."

"But you can't just—" Sheriff Reid started.

"Which is why," Lilah interjected, "I've decided I'm going to get my PI license instead."

"I—" Reid opened his mouth, then closed it again, rubbing his chin thoughtfully. "Actually…becoming a private investigator isn't a half-bad idea."

"And Jace," Lilah continued, "has always been most passionate about business, not baseball. So he's going to help me open and run the firm, since I'm terrible at paperwork."

"The worst," Jace agreed, earning an emphatic nod from Sheriff Reid.

Lilah rolled her eyes as she pulled a piece of her paper from her pocket. "Listen to this: 'You must possess at least three years of education *or* experience before you can apply for a private detective license in Montana. At which point, you may qualify for licensure through a combination of experience, education, and training.' In other words, between my degree and all the experience I've racked up while working for Dave—er, Sheriff Reid," she quickly amended, "I can basically have a business up and running by next year."

Stanley narrowed his eyes. "With whose money, exactly?"

Lilah faltered. "Uh…"

"Finally, something we can help with!" Elliot grinned, wrapping an arm around June's shoulders. "Your mother and I have been setting aside money for the past nineteen years. Whatever you need to make this PI firm a reality, we've got you covered." He turned to Stan. "We'd also like to help repay some of Lilah's college loans."

"It's a Christmas miracle!" Stanley exclaimed, reaching forward and pulling Elliot into a tight hug.

"Oh, wow." Lilah swallowed. "I…thank you. Truly."

"It's the least we can do," June replied, smiling widely. "So, what will your PI business be called? Have you thought of a name yet?"

Lilah and Jace exchanged glances. "You tell them," she urged. "It was your idea, after all."

Jace cleared his throat, not bothering to suppress a wry grin. "No Bone Unturned."

NO BONE UNTURNED
SOLVING CRIMES IN THE NICK OF TIME

(Another) Note from the Author

. . .

Dear Reader,

You made it!!! I could not be prouder of you for sticking it out 😊 And see? What'd I tell you? All's well that ends well!

By the way, did you figure out the secret of the chapter headings?

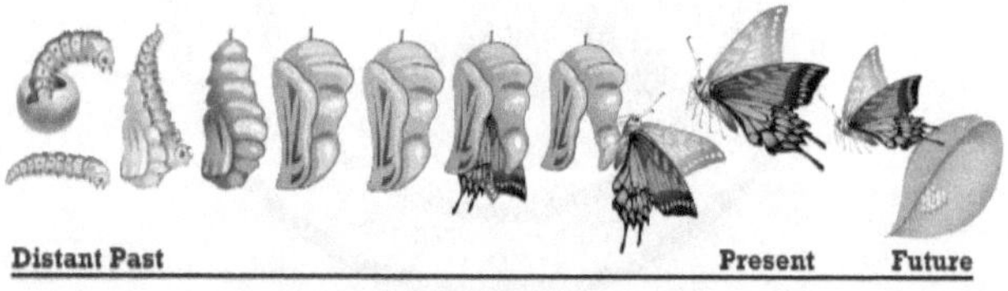

Now, before any fanatical time-travel buffs reach out to correct me on the *actual* laws of chrono-mechanics, as well as the numerous instances in which I got it wrong, I'm already way ahead of you. With the help of several well-known quantum physicists, I have generated a highly complex and data-driven graphic to explain the nuanced and multifarious webbing that comprises this unique system of time travel. (The fact that the focus of this book is about love, loss, and redemption – and *not* the theoretics of time travel – is, of course, beside the point.)

While those with but a rudimentary understanding of quantum mechanics may not possess the requisite in-depth knowledge to properly grasp the convoluted and labyrinthine intricacies of the aforementioned amalgam of chronofusion, I hope the below scientific graphic will offer some insight into the irrefutable temporal mechanics that brought *The Boy Who Lurks in Shadows* to its (hopefully satisfying) conclusion: May this bring my most zealous time-travel buffs some solace and deeper understanding of my air-tight, unassailable logic.

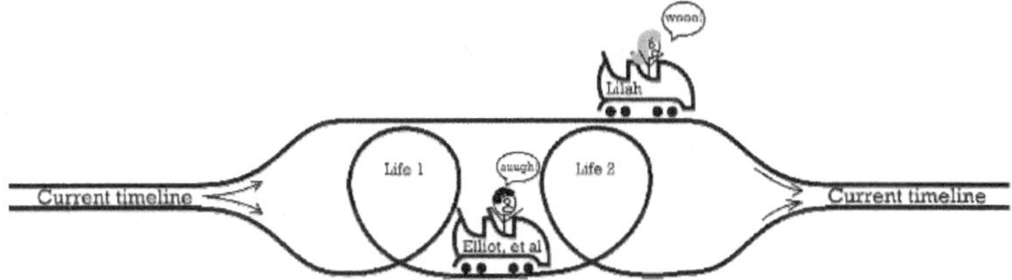

By the way, if you enjoyed reading *The Boy Who Lurks in Shadows*, please consider leaving a review! It helps reassure me that I should, in fact, keep writing stories (and not make a massive career pivot into quantum mechanics), while also alerting other readers to the awesomeness they could be adding to their own TBRs!

Rachel ♡

More books and stories are always coming, so be sure to follow me online for exciting news, updates, & giveaways!

www.RachelRener.com
(You can order signed books here!)
www.facebook.com/AuthorRachelRener
www.twitter.com/RachelRener
@AuthorRachelRener
@AuthorRachelRener

THE GILDED BLOOD SERIES

• • •

When Zayn, your smoking hot boss, tells you never to touch the cache of deluxe tattoo ink locked away in his office, you listen to him... until the day you run out of your own ink, your squirming client is on the verge of peeing his pants, and your boss is nowhere to be found. Desperate times call for desperate measures, right?

I fully expected Zayn to yell at me when he returned to the shop. What I didn't expect was the fresh cobra tattoo on my client's butt magically springing to life. Or the interdimensional filing cabinet hiding in the back of Zayn's office. And, oh, did I mention that my gorgeous, magic-ink-hoarding boss is actually an incubus?

Now – through (mostly) no fault of my own – we have to venture into a strange and distant land where a never-ending list of lethal flora, fauna, and fae await us. When you add in my Jewish mother's string of poorly-timed, hysterical phone calls, there is one thing I'm grateful for: there's no cell service in the fae realm.

THE LIGHTNING CONJURER SERIES

· · ·

Three years ago, I woke up in an abandoned cabin without a single memory – not even my own name. Since then, I've been doing my best to stay off the grid. But this week? Well, that's proving to be a problem.

From freak tornados to exploding fireplaces, strange things are happening all around me. Aiden, my new (and irritatingly attractive) college professor, says he knows "what" I am. A strange car is following me everywhere I go. And now an organization of people claiming to be "like me" are entreating me to join them. But the deeper I venture into this world, the more I wonder – is this organization a safe haven or a cult?

Whatever it may be, I can't turn back now. Because the only way to unearth my past, my name, and this growing power deep within me is to brave the lion's den...

Even if that means disclosing the one secret about me that will shake the very world to its core.

AMETHYSTS & ALCHEMY

• • •

I used to eat rocks as a child. The family doctor diagnosed me with pica, dooming me to years of intensive therapy and extensive dentistry work. It wouldn't be until much later that I would understand the all-consuming, insatiable craving that spurred me to eat a variety of rocks and minerals wasn't a mental disorder, but an innate gift that allows me to extract the magic contained inside them.

Twenty years later, I've hidden my abilities beneath a white lab coat, working as a small-town pharmacist who creates proprietary "naturopathic" tonics that treat everything from memory loss to erectile dysfunction. Those tonics, in turn, fund my expensive lifestyle of solo flying around the world to search for more rocks. What more could an airplane-loving, mineral-munching, magical alchemist want?

Unfortunately, my arch nemesis, Heath Spencer, has recently taken it upon himself to single-handedly ruin my life. No longer content with annoying me from afar with his overpriced, tacky rock shop, Heath has decided to further antagonize me by dangling the opportunity of a lifetime right in front of my face: traveling to an ancient copper mine in China, which is home to some of the rarest and most stunning minerals on Earth.

It's not until after I'm trapped halfway across the world with my least favorite person on the planet that I'm forced to come face-to-face with a terrible realizations: I'm not the only one who's been keeping secrets.

THE LITTLE MORSEL

. . .

Feral, a retired war hero with ancient bones and thinning scales, has been living in a dragon retirement home for several centuries. There, his daily routine is always the same: wake up with creaky joints, force down the stale protein bars from Bites of Knights, avoid the caterwauling old females on the shuffleboard court, and then return to bed to dream of flying.

But when a tiny stray human shows up at his front boulder, Feral's ho-hum world is turned upside down. Once a tentative agreement not to eat this strange little "morsel" is forged, the two of them embark on a journey for applesauce that ends with each of them saving the other's life – in more ways than one.

THE LITTLE MORSEL is a warm, lighthearted adventure that shines a delicate light on loneliness, neglect, found family, and purpose. Multifaceted and relatable, it is a story that can be enjoyed by children and adults alike.

THE PILFERED QUILL

. . .

From the minds that brought you the <u>Gilded Blood</u> and <u>Hell In</u> <u>Haven</u> series, comes a contemporary fantasy satire like no other...

Chet Williams, a fantasy-writer extraordinaire in his own mind, has been rejected one too many times. For too long, his genius has gone unnoticed. But when Chet stumbles upon a secret that would shake the publishing world to its core, his ambitions are finally realized...for better or for worse.

Come experience the greatest romance of all time: the love which self-absorbed author Chet Williams has for himself.

ACKNOWLEDGEMENTS

· · ·

Aaron – you are my rock. I love you. Thank you.

I also have to offer my profound thanks to my alpha readers: Ryan, David, Travis, Aaron, Vinnie, and my mom, who helped talk me through the most complex plot imaginable, which also gave me more headaches than I ever thought possible. Thanks for your insights and encouragement!

To Joey, my brother and expert on all things time-related, thank you for listening to me go on and on about chronomancy even when it didn't always adhere to fifth-dimension laws of time. Hooray for rubber-ducking!

Dad, I appreciate your insights on rotary phones. Thanks for being part of Lilah's journey!

Ashlynn, you are invaluable to me, not only as a typomancer, but as a set of eagle eyes I trust more than most!

Sarah, I'm glad to have you as an editor, and appreciate your thoughtfulness and kindness so much. Thank you for helping me polish this story into what it is today! (Adverbs be damned!)

To my friends and family who tolerate my "eccentricity" and listen to me prattle about the voices in my head, I thank you sincerely for your patience and support ;)

My ARC team is the BEST – hands down. I appreciate you all so, so much for helping me spread word of my new releases with such fervor and optimism!

Finally, to my readers, I love you more than words can say. Thank you for allowing my dream job to be a reality. I owe you everything!

ABOUT THE AUTHOR

· · ·

Rachel Rener is a #1 international bestselling contemporary fantasy author who loves blurring the line between science and magic.

She graduated from the University of Colorado after focusing on Psychology and Neuroscience. Since then, she has lived on three continents and has traveled to more than 40 countries.

When she's not engrossed in writing or hanging out at Indie Fantasy Addicts, Rachel enjoys art of all kinds, riding her motorcycle, reading fantasy books, going to rock shows (both musical and mineralogical), Vulcanology (the lava kind as well as the pointy-eared variety), and voicing Tana the Tiefling on the coolest DnD podcast around, Of Dice and Friends. She lives in Colorado along with her husband, the world's best bonus kiddos, Josh and Leah, and a feisty umbrella cockatoo named Terrance (a.k.a. "Jungle Chicken") that hangs out on her shoulder as she writes – whether invited or not.